# THE GOLD FRAME

Other Books by the Author

**THE GOLD SOLUTION**
**THE GOLD DEADLINE**

# THE GOLD FRAME

## A WHODUNIT

*Herbert Resnicow*

A
Joan Kahn
BOOK

St. Martin's Press
New York

Design by Andy Carpenter

Library of Congress Cataloging in Publication Data

Resnicow, Herbert.
    The gold frame.

    "A Joan Kahn book."

    I. Title.
PS3568.E69G59   1984         813'.54        84-11788
ISBN 0-312-33687-X

First Edition

10 9 8 7 6 5 4 3 2 1

*To my severest critic
and most wonderful agent,
Judith Weber*

# I

**"I** have to get a gun," I told Burton. "Right away."

Burton calmly furnished his *Sachertorte mit Schlag* before replying, assuming his rich, round, falsely polite barrister's tone. "Why do you want a gun, Norma?"

"Because," I said. "Twice in the last three months, when my husband caught a murderer, the murderer tried to kill my husband. And once, when the murderer stupidly missed Alexander, guess who went to the hospital with two bullets in her belly? Norma Gold, that's who. Mrs. Nice Guy." Pearl raised her eyebrows at this; I would get her for that later. "So this time, Burton, I'm going to shoot back. Maybe even shoot first."

"Being shot at doesn't help," Burton said, eyeing the rest of the *Sachertorte*. "It still takes six to nine months to get a permit."

"I know that, Burton; I was a research librarian once, remember, before I got mixed up with your rotten clients. And the reason I'm feeding you my terrific *Sachertorte mit Schlag, mit* double *Schlag* in case you hadn't noticed, is to encourage you to put your fine lawyer's brain in gear figuring out how to speed up the bureaucracy. And although it's no big inducement to someone who's been married to that blond retard for twenty-five years, the next time around the killer might shoot at Pearl.''

Pearl had already given me a look when I served her husband the rich chocolate cake, and a double-whammy look when I heaped on the whipped cream; she had put Burton on a strict low-ecstasy diet right after Alexander got his heart attack, and sweated every time Burton gained an ounce. But I was more concerned with *my* husband's life.

Burton pointedly held out his plate for a second bribe. He got a thin slice and a single helping of *Schlag*; no sense having a beautiful brown-eyed blond widow right next door, the shortage of husbands being what it is. Alexander held out his plate too. From me he got what he deserved: ''When you break two hundred, darling.'' But I carefully didn't say what he'd get when he did; Alexander's memory is very good on chocolate in spite of his certainty that he had lost brain cells when he was in cardiac arrest. What I had in mind for him was three, maybe four, tops, chocolate bits.

Burton finished his seconds, looked longingly at the *Sachertorte*, and wisely decided to stop. Pearl may be a size 5 but her vocabulary is almost as big as mine, and she picked up some interesting Anglo-Saxon when she was doing her dissertation on ''Grendel as a Father Figure.'' ''There is a way to speed up the process a bit,'' Burton said, ''and it meshes exactly with a new case I have for Alexander.''

''Forget it,'' I said. ''No more murder cases. Or any cases. Even after I get my gun. I mean, thanks for the first two, you saved Alexander's sanity, sort of, but it's too dangerous. We're rich now, so we don't need the money.''

Alexander, brooding over his *Sachertorte* deficiency, spoke up. ''I want another case, Burton. I'm bored.''

''You had two clients last week,'' I pointed out.

''Engineering consultations,'' Alexander sneered. ''Big deal. They call it engineering, but it all boils down to money. Find out how much the owner is willing to spend, then provide a solution to fit the budget.''

2

"What about that book of retrograde chess puzzles I got you yesterday?" I asked.

"Finished," he said curtly. "Elementary logic." Husbands who are used to eating all they want can get very ugly when they're losing weight. And the fact that he hadn't used a nitro pill for angina in three weeks was making him forget how badly damaged his heart was.

I tried to change the subject. "This whole gun license thing is silly. All I want is a tiny little automatic for my purse. Why, I could take the Broadway bus downtown and in one hour come back with a sub-machine gun in my tote bag."

"A real criminal could," Burton smiled. "You couldn't. You would be recognized at once by the suppliers as an untrustworthy person."

"There are no female criminals who buy guns?"

"Very few who are six-foot-one without shoes and weigh two hundred pounds. They'd figure you for a cop in disguise."

"One eighty-eight," I corrected, "stripped. I don't look like a woman to you, Burton?" and took a deep breath.

"Very much," he said admiringly (Pearl has a very terrific build, 34D on ninety-eight pounds; proportionately big but next to me, flat-chested), "but those can be strapped on."

Alexander was impatient. "What case, Burton? And how does it mesh with this?"

"It involves a very costly painting, Alec. One which, by all rights, should have been a forgery, but isn't."

"That's bad?"

"When my client explains it to you, you'll understand. Meanwhile we have another problem. You have been breaking the law. Norma too. Even Pearl."

Pearl turned blue. Even though she talks like a liberated woman, she's really very square. "You're not going to tell on your own wife, are you?" she asked. "Isn't that illegal or something, to testify against your own wife? What did I do? I didn't do anything. If I did, I didn't know it was illegal."

"You, all three of you—and ignorance is no excuse—" Burton said, taking a card out of his pocket, "have been, and I quote: 'engaging in the business of private investigator dash-dash-dash without having first obtained from the Department of State a license to do so,' et cetera."

"Nonsense," Alexander said. "Alexander Magnus Gold Associates, Consultants, is a consulting firm. Not private investigators; consultants. About anything. I just solve puzzles, period. That's all. I don't call myself a detective."

"You don't have to," said Burton, and he read, "quote—'notwithstanding the name or title used in describing such agency or notwithstanding the fact that other functions and services may also be performed for fee, hire, or reward, dash-dash-dash private investigator shall mean dash-dash-dash the making for hire, reward, or any consideration whatever, of any investigation or investigations for the purpose of obtaining information with reference to dash-dash-dash the location or recovery of lost or stolen property dash-dash-dash the causes and origin of, or responsibility for, fires, or libels, or losses, or accidents, or damage or injuries to real or personal property dash-dash-dash or the securing of evidence to be used before any authorized investigating committee, board of award, board of arbitration, or in the trial of civil or criminal cases'—unquote. That's you, Alec, any way you slice it."

"Suppose I work just by betting I can solve the puzzle," Alexander said, "the way I did in the Boguslav case."

"The law says 'for any consideration whatsoever.'"

"What happens if I keep working without a license?"

"As a first offender, probably a fine. But you'd certainly be forced to dissolve Gold Associates. And if you repeated the crime, you'd be in real trouble."

"I could live with a fine if I got caught, and then get the license."

"Could you live with a client refusing to pay you and getting away with it legally?"

"I am overwhelmed by your logic, Burt. Where do I sign?"

"Not so fast," Burton held his hand up. "You have to fill out a formal application, submit photos and five sets of fingerprints of both hands, and pay a fee. That's the easy part. Here's where the difficulty comes in. You must get five reputable citizens to swear that you are competent, honest, and of good character. How are you going to get that, Alec? And don't look to me; as an officer of the court, I cannot lie under oath." Burton was getting even for Alexander's standard introduction to strangers: "This is Burton Hanslik, world's richest criminal [long pause] lawyer. I apologize for the redundancy."

Burton, stuffed with one of my terrific meals, a portion-and-a-half of *Sachertorte*, and three portions of whipped cream, did not realize how close to the brink of madness Alexander was, nor how really strong my powerlifter husband is. Excluding what he had to be sneaking on his walks, the poor boy hadn't had a drop of chocolate anything for three weeks; it was no time to tease or annoy the animals. "I didn't wash the icing bowl, Alexander," I said. "Purposely. Go into the kitchen and scrape." He went, all thoughts of strangling Burton overwhelmed by the primal urge.

While Alexander was *fressing*, I asked, "Any real problems, Burton?"

"Any applicant for a license as a private eye has to have three years' experience on the job."

"That's out, Burton. Alexander will never work as an employee again. You must have a workable solution, Burton, or you wouldn't have brought the whole thing up."

"Of course I do." He smiled evilly. "Cross my plate with a sliver of cake and I'll tell you."

"Get written permission from Pearl," I said, moving the cake out of his reach. Anticipation, I had learned by sixteen, is better than the real thing; ask any wife. "Talk, Burton."

He knew when he was beaten. "One, you don't need a

license to work as a detective for a licensed private investigator. Two, a corporation can be a licensed PI provided at least one member is licensed."

"And we're going to form a corporation with a private eye?"

"Better than that. One of the detective agencies my firm uses is already incorporated: Arthur I. Kaplan, Incorporated, Discreet Observations our Specialty. It's a one-man firm, and Al wants to retire to Florida."

"He doesn't do anything dangerous, does he?"

"Just quiet checking out of people, shadowing them. He's very good at it; you could learn from him."

"Fat chance. Can you see me melting into a crowd? And Alexander? Ha! Five-foot-six tall and six-foot-five wide at the shoulders; even in custom-made suits he looks like a bald gorilla with glasses. Pearl? You may not have noticed lately, but your wife is the second most striking woman on the West Side of New York. No, Burton, we'll leave the shadowing to Mr. Kaplan."

"As you wish. But as long as you're employees of the agency, it won't hurt you to watch Kaplan operate."

"Why should he take us on as employees?" Pearl asked.

"I have it all worked out," Burton said. "He's already agreed. The three of you will buy ninety percent of the stock from Kaplan—the licensed PI has to have ten percent minimum—for one dollar and other considerations. You'll invest enough to pay yourselves minimum wages and benefits, plus half the fixed expenses, for the next three years. Kaplan keeps all the fees he makes from his own efforts plus ten percent of the net from what Alec brings in. When one of you gets a license, Kaplan retires and you buy his stock for one dollar. And if Alec keeps solving cases at the same rate as up till now, Kaplan retires a rich man."

"Sounds good to me," I said. "How about you, Pearl?"

Alexander came back, relaxed after his fix. "I heard everything," he said, "and I'm not going to do it. Pearl and Norma can be detectives, I don't care, but I won't. I'm a consultant; I solve puzzles. Problems too. There is no reason I have to be part of Kaplan Inc.; Pearl and Norma can consult me when there's an interesting case. Give Kaplan a flat hundred thousand when he retires; we can afford it and you certainly can. I'll keep working the same way as before: a big fee if I solve the problem; nothing if I don't, and I pay all the expenses. Only difference, Norma and Pearl take the case and they consult with me. Can you work that out, Burt?"

"A guaranteed one hundred thousand? I'm sure I can. Is that okay with you two?"

I nodded; Pearl had a question. "If we'll be getting business from your firm, won't it be a conflict of interest if I'm a part owner of the agency?"

"Not really. I'll inform my partners of the deal and I'm sure they won't have any objections. Don't forget, you won't be sharing in the business that we'll be giving Kaplan, and he won't be sharing in the business I give you. Can I go ahead with the final papers?"

"Sure," I said. "Now when can I get my gun permit?"

"The police are very good in pushing through permits for private detectives. If a man's livelihood depends on it, they really try to help. This should cut at least a month off the waiting, possibly even two."

"Four or five months?" I complained. "No wonder there is so much crime. Burton, are you sure that there is no killing in the new case? Because if there is, we're not taking it."

"Absolutely not," Burton said. "It's just as I told you; a matter of whether a painting is a forgery or not."

"I'm not an expert on painting," Alexander said. "What am I supposed to do?"

"Four experts have already authenticated the painting, Alec. What my client wants— It's very complicated. I'd prefer that he explain it to you firsthand."

7

"If we're not detectives yet," Pearl said, clearly still fearful of being sent up the river, "shouldn't we wait before we talk to him?"

"It's okay," Burton said. "I'll have the papers ready before you're really started on the case."

"Who is this mysterious client?" I asked.

"Daniel Pereira Belmont," Burton said respectfully.

"Never heard of him."

"I have," said Alexander. "Very big in charities, isn't he?"

"Very," Burton said. "One of the richest men in New York. His family owns almost as much property as Columbia University. Eighty years old, and very sharp. We'll be having lunch with him tomorrow at noon at his house. He's old school, so be on your best behavior."

"East Side?" I asked.

"Fifth Avenue, just across the street from the Fine Arts Museum of New York."

"My favorite museum," I said. The FAMONY is right in the heart of what I call Museum Row: Fifth Avenue, between the Frick on 70th Street and the Jewish on 92nd Street, has seven museums, the greatest concentration of museums in the world. One short block away, on Madison, is the Whitney. A few blocks north, at 103rd, is the Museum of the City of New York. A few blocks south, on 53rd Street, are the Museum of Broadcasting and the MOMA, the Museum of Modern Art. Pearl and I once tried to see every new exhibit in the Row in one day. And if we, experienced shoppers at sales in Bloomingdale's, Fortunoff's, and Loehmann's, couldn't do it, it can't be done.

"I take it," I said, "Mr. Belmont and the painting are connected with the Fine Arts?"

"He owns the FAMONY," Burton said.

"No one owns a museum that big," I said. "Not in New York."

"He'll tell you about it tomorrow," was all Burton would say. "Be patient."

I'd be patient. But I was absolutely sure that Burton was not telling us everything. Well, at least there was no murder involved.

# II

Inside was Dickens: the dining room panelled in dark walnut, the ceiling of carved plaster. The heavy oak table was covered with a hand-sewn raw linen tablecloth on which the delicate crystal, the bone china, and the heavy silverware were organized in perfect balance. The glow of the fireplace haloed the head of our white-haired host, slim and erect in his port-colored velvet smoking jacket.

In front of the big bay window, Currier and Ives had spread out Central Park, snow just beginning to fall on a horse-drawn carriage filled with a Kean-eyed out-of-town family.

Over the buffet was a landscape, a flat stretch of sand, water, and windmill overhung with dark rolling clouds, that just had to be a van Ruisdael. A real one, I mean. On the far wall, opposite the windows, was a tiny portrait of a girl, laughing, definitely a Frans Hals. On either side of the Hals, but far enough away so as to balance rather than detract, were a pair of drawings by Rembrandt; him I was sure of.

Daniel Pereira Belmont, looking much younger than his eighty years, graciously sat at the foot of the table, his back to the windows, so that we, Pearl, Burton, Alexander, and I, could see outside and attend our host at the same time. He was clearly determined not to discuss business while dining. "In Austria," he said, "we were Schoenberg, and in Italy, Montebello. In France it was Beaumont, and when we went to England it became Belmont. In the beginning, when the family left Spain and settled in The Netherlands, we kept Belmonte, even though there already was a distinguished family there of the same name and another, possibly related, called van Schoonenberg. We are, of course, related by marriage to the Pereiras."

"Your family sounds like the Rothschilds," I said, "interests in all European countries."

"Oh no," Mr. Belmont said. "No resemblance at all. The Rothschilds were a unified group, working together, who deliberately went to other countries in the early nineteenth century to form a business empire. My family was unwillingly, even violently, dispersed by religious prejudice in every century. We have a general feeling of relationship, loyalty even, to each other and, on occasion, provide small courtesies to each other, but we have very little contact. Of course, if any close relation were to visit the United States, I or one of my sons would make him welcome."

"I didn't know you were Jewish," Alexander said.

"I've never hidden my religion," Mr. Belmont said, "but I've carefully avoided publicity."

"And your interest in these paintings," Alexander waved at the three Dutch masters, "stemmed from your family's residence in Holland?"

"The Belmonte family has lived continuously in The Netherlands since the sixteenth century, and we all have a strong affinity for that wonderful country. I, myself, have an additional good reason to love it. But I have always been interested in Dutch art of the seventeenth century. From the time of Hals to Vermeer's death, in this little country there were more great artists per capita or per hectare than at any other time or place in history. From 1600 to 1675, in this tiny flat spot of land, there were more than twice as many master painters as there were in all the rest of Europe combined. And I have a theory why this was so."

"The Inquisition?" Alexander asked. Alexander has the widest, wildest range of information and interests, and sometimes puts apparently random facts together in patterns which, when examined afterwards, make perfect sense. "It comes from reading detective stories," Alexander always says when I ask how he knows some obscure fact. I find this hard to believe.

"Yes, Mr. Gold, the Inquisition," Mr. Belmont said. "The cruelties of Philip II of Spain, the eighty-years war of independence from Spain, the courage of William of Orange, the growth of mercantilism, the spread of Calvinism, the rise of the bourgeoisie, the beginnings of capitalism and the freedoms associated with, and required by, free trade, all these came together in Holland, all contributed to this sudden flowering, this explosion of art."

Coffee was being served, hot and strong, and the tall old man settled back in his chair. "Yes," he said, "it all came together in the first seventy-five years of the seventeenth century. And it all leads back to the Inquisition which, in addition to killing large numbers of Jews, drove even larger numbers to countries where there was relative religious tolerance, such as the Lowlands, England, and the New World."

"So it is your idea," Burton said, "that wherever Jews were driven out, the country declined, and wherever Jews were welcomed, the country flourished."

"Precisely," the old man said. "Spain, in spite of the wealth coming from the New World, became a second-rate nation. England, and The Netherlands, and what was to become the United States, all grew and prospered. Read your history."

"Hasn't art and science flourished wherever there was religious freedom and political freedom, the primacy of individual rights over the rights of rulers or states?" Burton asked.

"Yes," said Mr. Belmont, "but that isn't all there is to it. Art flourished under despotic rulers and absolute monarchs too. And wherever there were comparatively free conditions of life, we had to go there. Don't forget, the Jews who fled to the Lowlands, to England, to America, were not going to lands where there was no king.''

''I love Holland too,'' I said. ''What was the other good reason you mentioned?''

''My wife was born in Amsterdam. She introduced me to the history of that period as well as many other wonderful things. We met in The Hague, in the Mauritshuis. She was standing in front of the *Girl with a Pearl Earring.*'' He paused and looked into the past. ''I had admired Vermeer tremendously before, but after that. . . .'' He paused again, then stood up. ''The servants must clean up. We will have our liqueurs in the living room. There is something there you must see to understand my problem.''

# III

The huge living room was panelled in mahogany, real old-fashioned red-brown African mahogany, the kind my mother's furniture was made of, not the *luan* that's so common today. The fireplace was twice as big as the one in the dining room, but there was no fire lit. The curtains were drawn and the draperies almost closed. With the huge Fine Arts Museum across the street blocking out the sun, when Mr. Belmont closed the door, the room was almost dark. The walls were covered with small paintings in a line, one after the other, giving the room the feel of an art gallery.

A maid rolled in a cart of drinks. I chose green Chartreuse, the 110-proof liqueur you can't hardly get around here anymore. Other than cognac, Armagnac, and calvados, there were no hard liquors; not that I ever drank Scotch anyway, but I was beginning to read my host: nothing but the best for his friends and his guests, but his way, only his way.

Burton, seated on Mr. Belmont's right and knowing the secrets of the house, nodded at the beautiful little cut-crystal decanter on the table to his host's left, where Alexander was sitting.

"Wise choice," Mr. Belmont said. "This is a very fine,

*14*

very old brandy; very little left in the world. When this is gone . . .'' Although he never drinks, Alexander chose to taste the old brandy too. Mr. Belmont's hand shook a little as he poured, but nothing spilled. These cut-crystal decanters are heavy and I was afraid that Alexander, out of consideration for his host's age, would offer to pour. That was the way he broke my mother's decanter, similar to this, but twice as large, quart size. Alexander doesn't know his own strength and he grabbed the neck of my mother's decanter instead of holding it near the globular base. It snapped off, not from the weight, but from the speed of turning. Irreparable. Ever afterward, Alexander would hold anything glass by the base—his hands are big enough to go around any bottle—but I still feel better when he doesn't handle expensive things.

When we had all sipped, Mr. Belmont reached to the little table at the right side of his wing chair and pressed a button. The draperies closed silently and the room was completely dark.

Then, one by one, the lights illuminating each painting on the walls lit up, each light shining from a different angle, each a different intensity and shade of white, evidently designed specifically for the painting it was shining on. One by one, five seconds apart, the paintings flashed into life. Vermeers! They were all, it was clear, going to be Vermeers. When five were lit up Alexander jumped up and went to look at them closely. After a minute he came to me and said, ''Give me your reading glasses.'' He went back and examined the paintings carefully.

Alexander studied the paintings for several minutes, then called Pearl to join him and handed her my glasses. ''Well?'' he asked after she had inspected two paintings.

She hesitated, then said, ''They look very— It's hard to tell.''

Alexander turned to Mr. Belmont and said, ''Either you are the world's greatest art thief or the world's greatest forger or . . . Is this what you wanted to consult with me about? Burt must have told you; my only experience with art comes from museums."

"Sit down, Mr. Gold," the old man said. "You too, Mrs. Hanslik. I am not a thief and these are not forgeries. And if you knew more about art, this would be clear to you. They are copies, and I am sure you appreciate the difference. If you were to look at the back of any of them, you would see that it is painted on modern canvas, dated within recent years, and signed 'Becker.' If you x-ray it, the plate would show the same. After she prepared the canvas with a white ground, she painted her name and the date in heavy white lead paint on it, then put another layer of white ground over that. And so careful is she, so much does she hate forgery, that just in case anyone wished to remove the canvas from the painting— Don't look so surprised, Mrs. Gold, it not only can be done, it often is done by skilled conservators, where the support and the ground are in bad shape, in order to save the painting—so careful is our Hannele that, on the slight chance that someone could remove the canvas and the first ground, and then remove her white name and date from the white second ground—and all this just to pass off a stolen copy as the real thing—so careful is she that she has placed between the layers of paint, in the dark background areas of course, her initials and the date in lead paint, so that the most careless X-ray would show up the fake."

"Anal-retentive personality," Pearl said. "Practically obsessive-compulsive, almost paranoid."

"Of course," Mr. Belmont said. "All conservators should be like that. And that isn't all. Even when the original painting was on a wood panel, as was often the case in those times, she copied that painting on canvas. There is no way anyone could pass off these paintings as real Vermeers."

"But they are so perfect," Pearl said. "They could fool anyone. Other than an expert, I mean."

"That's why I have them," Mr. Belmont said. "There is no way any individual could buy a Vermeer today. There are none for sale, nor will there ever be. And even if he could buy one, no real art lover would, or should. All Vermeers must be in museums, where everyone can see them and where the conservators can take care of them properly."

"Do you mean to say," Alexander asked, "that this girl painted all these for you?"

"Hardly a girl," Mr. Belmont said with a smile, "she's almost sixty-five. No, she didn't paint them for me, she painted them for herself. It's her—I was going to say hobby, but Mrs. Hanslik said it better—it's her obsession. When Hannelore Becker leaves the museum, she goes home and paints. Copies, rather. She has a series of eleven-by-fourteen-inch color transparencies she took herself with a huge view camera, of every Vermeer in existence, with light coming from every angle, so that every tiny brush stroke is visible. Some of these slides are bigger than the originals, so you can be sure she has captured every detail. How she got permission to do this, I do not know, but she did. She's a very determined lady."

"You've been in her home?" I asked.

"Once. Probably the only person in the world she's allowed in."

"Because you are chairman of the Board of Trustees of the museum, where she works?"

"Hardly," Belmont smiled. "Hannelore has very little respect for position or title; contempt would be more like it. No, it was because I tried to buy a Vermeer for the museum; because she found out that I loved Vermeer and. . . . When my wife passed away—that was twenty years ago, hard to believe, twenty years already—I wanted to buy *Girl with a Pearl Earring* from the Mauritshuis. As a remembrance, you see. I am a very—money was no object. I explained to them that the painting would be treated with respect, with love; that many more people would see it in New York than in The Hague. They were very understanding, but pointed out that the portrait was a national treasure; that there were only seven Vermeers left in The Netherlands while America already had at least thirteen authentic paintings. I even offered to acquire any two Rembrandts for them in exchange, three if they wished, but they declined, regretfully."

"That was when she sold you these beautiful copies?" I asked.

"No, you don't know Hannelore. But I am digressing. I would like to present my problem to you, Mr. Gold, directly, rather than discuss my personal life."

"Mr. Belmont," Alexander said, "I have discovered that when people consult with me about their problems it doesn't matter where they start. The problems surface in a very short time. And sometimes, the problems they thought they had are not their real problems, and their real problems are revealed in what they think is background information."

"Psychiatrists and psychologists," said Pearl, "have found that to be true."

"Psychologists know that too?" Alexander was truly surprised. He thinks he discovered everything. Or invented it. Alexander turned to Mr. Belmont. "Burt told me that you wanted to discuss a forged, or rather, an unforged, painting with me. It's obvious that the painting is a Vermeer and that Hannelore Becker is involved in the problem. Why don't you go on with your story in your own way. We'll get there eventually and learn a good deal as we go."

"It's not the way I had intended to present it to you," said Mr. Belmont, "but you may be right." He settled back in his chair.

# IV

&&I got to see the inside of Hannelore Becker's studio, the
one in her home, not in the museum, because I had a
fight with her. Actually, all I said was that it was a pity that
there were only thirty-eight authenticated Vermeers around and
I wished there were more so I would buy the one I wanted—"

"That's all?" Burton interrupted. "I would have
thought that there were many more."

"Oh, no," Mr. Belmont said. "Vermeers are the rarest
paintings by a major artist since the 1600s. Some say he produced as many as seventy paintings in his lifetime, others say
fifty to sixty. Most experts put the number of existing real Vermeers at somewhere between thirty-four and forty-two, of
which at least four are very doubtful."

"My God," said Burton. "Picasso did that many in a
month. Less. How did Vermeer make a living?"

"Not by selling his paintings, you may be sure. He ran a
tavern and an art gallery, and didn't do too well with either.
When he died at the age of forty-three, he left a widow with
eight young children and a mountain of debt."

"No wonder you can't buy a Vermeer," I said.

"You can," Mr. Belmont said. "One. I'll come to that

soon. Anyway, when I said there were only thirty-eight real Vermeers known, darling Hannele jumped down my throat. There were thirty-seven, she said, and anyone who thought that *Girl in a Blue Dress and Yellow Cloak* was authentic was a fool and blind to boot; that it was obviously a copy by a rank amateur of *Head of a Young Woman* and you could tell a mile away it was a fake: the pearl was wrong, the ear was wrong, the pose was wrong, the skin wasn't transparent enough, and especially, the blue dress was at least fifty shades off Vermeer's perfect blue, and if I couldn't see that I should resign immediately as chairman of the Board of Directors of the museum and get a tin cup and a box of pencils.''

Mr. Belmont smiled at the recollection. "No one had ever spoken to me that way before," he said, "not even my grandfather, so I was amused rather than angered. I pointed out to her that Maurice Gröber-Eisenberg had said it was authentic in a recent monograph. She told me that Gröber-Eisenberg, although not as stupid as the rest of the so-called experts, was dead wrong on this painting, that he was incapable of distinguishing red from blue, better he should have become a butcher as God had intended him to be, and that when he got older, assuming he kept studying hard, he might learn to tell a Rembrandt from a Warhol, but he would never recognize a Vermeer if it bit him. Gröber-Eisenberg, you understand, was all of six years younger than Hannele, had just published a highly acclaimed analysis of Vermeer's works, and was the world's recognized expert on Dutch painting of that period.

"So, more to tease her than anything else, I mentioned that Vandermeis, Tabachnik, Spieler, Baliner, and many other highly respected experts all attributed *Girl in a Blue Dress and Yellow Cloak* to Vermeer. She became positively insulting, implying that, bad as Gröber-Eisenberg was, these experts weren't fit to— I leave it to your imagination. There is no museum in the world that would not accept the signed certification of any of these experts for a painting, as I would, and spend a million dollars, or more, with the absolute assurance of the painting's authenticity. But that wasn't good enough for this uneducated, opinionated little firebrand.''

"What do you mean, uneducated?" Burton asked.

"Well, actually," Mr. Belmont said, "I mean without credentials. She doesn't even have a baccalaureate degree. She's just a conservator; not even chief conservator.''

"Then why listen to her?" Pearl asked.

"In spite of that," Mr. Belmont said, "she may very well know more about Vermeer than anyone else in the world. After our little encounter I had her investigated through my European connections, and I was truly astounded at what I found. Hanna was born in Berlin in 1917, the only child of a Jewish father and a Catholic mother, not as uncommon as one might think, before Hitler. Her father was killed on the Western Front just before she was born. Her mother had a very bad time in the post-war years, but they survived. Hannelore was a beautiful, brilliant, talented child, involved in a great many activities and interests. All the nuns in her convent school predicted great things for her. She had just turned sixteen when her whole world was smashed.

"It was one of those freak accidents; nobody's fault, really. The driver had a heart attack and lost control of his truck. It mounted the sidewalk and smashed Hannele against a storefront. She was in the hospital for six months, and when she came out, one leg was stiff and shorter than the other, her spine had three vertebrae fused, and her face . . . well, they did their best, but she was no longer beautiful. The only thing that remained unchanged was her hair, her beautiful long golden hair, very much like yours, Mrs. Hanslik," he nodded to Pearl, "when I first saw her, and it served only to point up the"—he was going to say ugliness, I was sure, but clearly could not—"the incongruity of her appearance.''

Others have survived handicaps like that," Pearl said. "Charles Steinmetz, for one. Helen Keller. Toulouse-Lautrec.''

"Oh, she survived," Mr. Belmont said, "but she changed. Became withdrawn, stayed home all day and read.

Wouldn't talk to people and refused to go to school. She discovered painting and jumped in with both feet. Enrolled in an art school and apprenticed herself to a restorer to pay the tuition. She had the talent, and developed the skills rapidly, but, somehow, lacked the spark to become great. In her studies she had to copy the great masters and found she had a talent for this; found it easy. All except Vermeer. She couldn't copy Vermeer. Actually, no one could.''

"Didn't Hans van Meegeren copy Vermeer successfully?'' Alexander asked. "In the thirties?''

"Not successfully,'' Mr. Belmont answered. "He was sentenced to jail. His forgeries were not in the least like Vermeer, an amateur would laugh at them now, but the hunger to find a new Vermeer was so great at that time, that many experts accepted them.''

"Hannelore Becker seems to have copied Vermeer well,'' I said.

"Yes,'' he replied, "very well. You could put any of these next to a real Vermeer and I would be hard pressed to tell them apart, and I've been living with these for years. But, you see, Hannelore, frustrated by her inability to copy Vermeer, driven by her personality and probably by her physical problems, began studying Vermeer the way no one had ever studied him before: his life, his style, his techniques. She has devoted her whole life to . . . to becoming Vermeer, and this,'' he waved his hand at the paintings on the walls, "this is the result. The result of forty-five years of . . . When she came here in 'thirty-seven, on account of her father, you know, she started the life she now leads, and hasn't deviated from it since, as far as anyone knows.''

"What is her home like?'' Pearl asked.

"It's not a home at all; it's a huge loft studio with a bed in one corner and a kitchenette in another. The walls are completely covered with Vermeers, copies of course. Opposite her work table—she doesn't use an easel—is a huge screen on which she projects the picture of the painting she is working on, or a detail of that painting. She has a special projector, must have cost her thousands, for her eleven-by-fourteen-inch transparencies; the detail is enlarged so you can see every hairline of the brush.''

"Did she actually let you watch her work?" Pearl asked.

"Yes, and I felt as though I had been honored. She doesn't work like other copyists, trying to get the same sweep of arm movement and brushwork. She works like a miniaturist or an eye surgeon, with those long double lenses fixed to her head. While I was there she used a brush with a single hair, and copied each ridge and valley left by each hair of Vermeer's brush exactly. Not just the surface, either. Today's painters, they might slap a sizing on the canvas and fifteen minutes later start the finished surface in acrylic. Not Vermeer. His paintings are built up layer by layer, in different colors, giving depth and transparency to skin, to fur, to cloth. No sharp outlines, he would spread the glaze from one surface slightly onto an adjacent surface, like reflected light. And his light— No one handled light as well as he did, not even Rembrandt. It is said that one artist, on first viewing a Vermeer painting, looked behind the easel to see where the light was coming from.''

"That sounds like a lengthy process," Pearl said.

"It is. Very. As I said, Vermeer produced only a few paintings a year, and Hannelore was no faster. After watching her for an hour—it was so fascinating I could have watched all night—she stopped and took off the lenses. Her eyes were tired, and she had become very nearsighted with the years. She handed me a loupe, six power, and invited me to compare her work with the projection on the screen. I held the loupe to my eye and compared the wet area of the painting to the projection. I swear I could see no difference. She laughed at me, said I was a dilettante, not a serious lover of Vermeer.''

"To her, then, art was Vermeer and Vermeer was art," Pearl said.

"Exactly. Even at the museum she refused to work on

anything before Caravaggio or after van der Weyden. Of course, we have plenty of those to keep her busy.''

''Was that when she gave you these copies?'' Alexander asked.

''No. Yes. Well, actually what she did was give me a big magnifying glass and ask me to pick out—if I wanted *Girl with a Pearl Earring* I should have it—the best copy of it on the wall. I examined all four and for the life of me I could not tell one from the other. So at random I chose the farthest right, assuming it was the latest. She grudgingly conceded there might be some hope for me yet, if I applied myself, and told me that if I had picked any of the others, that one is what I would have gotten.''

''So,'' said Alexander, walking over to the tiny painting, ''this is it? It's beautiful.''

''No,'' said Mr. Belmont. ''In honor of my having picked the best copy, she was going to paint me a *really* good one, having just the previous year solved how to reproduce Vermeer's blue satin, she now thought she could do skin properly. Of course, the light would not be perfect, but I would just have to live with that. Then I almost ruined everything; I took out my checkbook. She told me she did not paint for money, especially not for Philistines. My mind was somewhat sharper then than it is now, so I immediately told her that I was going to donate two thousand dollars in her honor to Simon Wiesenthal in Vienna. I had picked an acceptable sum and an acceptable recipient, so the crisis passed. I am sure if I had said ten thousand dollars she would have thrown me out.''

''So every few months she brought you a new painting,'' Alexander said, ''and every few months you sent her a card noting an appropriate donation.''

''It's not that simple, Mr. Gold. Yes, she presented me a painting every few months. And hung it; my servants have instructions to let her in whenever she wishes. And she ordered and arranged the lighting. But, you realize, she is continuing to work, trying to duplicate Vermeer perfectly, according to her standards, and will keep working until she reaches perfection.''

"Which she will never do," Pearl said. "Her life would be finished if she did." Pearl may look like a dumb blond, but she isn't, really. In some areas. Some of the time.

"So every few months," Mr. Belmont continued, "she brings me a new copy, takes the old one away, adjusts the lights one degree, changes the bulbs that have darkened one shade, hands me a loupe, and for one hour points out the tremendous improvements in the new painting, stroke by stroke.''

"Which you can't see," Alexander said.

"Not if my life depended on it," the old man agreed, "but it costs me nothing and it makes her happy. Gives me a tax deduction, in fact. Actually, I make sure to. . . . People are always giving rich men gifts. Someone who would not give a starving man a dollar will fight to pick up the check when he dines with me. I do not embarrass such people by disputing this, but I always find a way to discharge the obligation. So I do not fight with Hannelore Becker. I have set up a fund, escrowed with my financial advisors. Each time I send a check to Wiesenthal, I put four times that amount into the fund. With compounding of interest, when she retires, she will be a rich woman. To her great surprise." He seemed to enjoy the thought.

"She may not take the money," Pearl said. "In fact, I am sure she would not."

"I had thought of that," he said. "Yet she has very little saved for her old age; I had it investigated. She spends all of her money on her obsession. Ultramarine pigment, for instance, Vermeer's famous blue, is made of finely ground lapis lazuli, a semi-precious stone. It is not cheap. One of the clues to van Meegeren's forgeries was the presence of cobalt blue in his paints. Hannah is not so careless. Although you can buy good ultramarine pigment now, made from finely ground synthetic lapis lazuli, Hannelore won't touch it. She buys real lapis lazuli and grinds it herself by hand in an antique brass mortar. Claims that the slight lack of uniformity in the ground powder, the slight impurities in the natural crystal, and the tiny dust of brass that grinds off the mortar into the pigment, gives the blue satin the same sheen that Vermeer achieved. All this, however, costs money and I feel some responsibility for her. So I set up the fund. Once the fund is hers, she can give it all to charity if she wishes. Knowing her, this is what she will do. The museum has a mandatory retirement rule. Hannelore will be sixty-five next week. I cannot let her starve. The museum cannot afford to lose such a skillful conservator. What would you do, Mr. Gold?''

"It's obvious," Alexander said. "Retire her in accordance with the rules, giving her the retirement pay, accumulated leaves, et cetera—I'm sure she didn't take vacations"— Mr. Belmont nodded, pleased —"and everything she is entitled to, and nothing more. Then retain her as a consultant conservator at an hourly rate which is slightly—say ten percent—higher than that of the highest paid free-lance conservators in the business— I am sure there are some—with adjustments for inflation. Give her back her old office, shop, whatever, but put a lock on it, for which only she has the key. Her name on the door, to show ownership, and Presto! Everyone wins.''

"She already has her locked private room; as for the rest, that is exactly what I have arranged, although she doesn't know it yet," the old man said. "We think alike, you and I. Good.''

"Did she live completely alone, Mr. Belmont?'' Pearl asked. "From her personality, I would have thought a cat, a canary?''

"She had a cat, Mrs. Hanslik. A big fat black cat that sat on her table as she worked. She had even put a light to shine on the cat, to keep her warm. I was reminded of a witch and her familiar. She actually introduced me to the cat. Mitzi.''

"I knew it wouldn't be a dog,'' Pearl said complacently.

"To get back to the problem. Mr. Belmont,'' Alexander said, "it is obvious that you, or rather, the Fine Arts Museum, is preparing to buy a Vermeer; you mentioned that there is one which could be bought, a while ago. By all rights it should be a forgery, since you are clearly not buying one from a museum. It has no provenance, there is no mention of it anywhere, but it has passed all the scientific tests. The experts who looked at it say it is from Vermeer's hand. The dealer claims he does not know the name of the owner. It is being offered at a very high price, possibly a record price for a painting. Is that right?"

The old man nodded wearily. "Ten million; almost our entire acquisition budget for the year."

"This room we're in, your memorial to your wife, you haven't invited anyone in here for twenty years, have you?"

Mr. Belmont nodded again.

Alexander went on. "So you're the only one who knows that Hannelore Becker is capable of painting a Vermeer that even he couldn't tell from his own."

"She would dispute that, Mr. Gold, but that is essentially correct."

"Hannelore Becker is one of the few people who know or remember your desire, need even, for a Vermeer. And knows how much it hurts you that the Fine Arts Museum, your own museum, does not have a single Vermeer."

The old man sighed. "True. I do not discuss my feelings with many people. All my old friends are gone."

"And you believe that Hannelore Becker may have forged this Vermeer, planted it somewhere, and is now trying to sell the forgery, using this dealer as a front." Alexander sat back confidently. "And you want me to find out if this is true."

"I'm afraid you have it backwards, Mr. Gold," the old man said apologetically. "Hannelore is the only one who says it may be a forgery." Alexander's mouth actually dropped open. "I'm afraid I presented to you badly, Mr. Gold. I should really have started at the beginning. The fact is—" The phone on the little table to the left of Mr. Belmont's chair flashed a faint light. He picked it up immediately and said, "I am with guests." After a moment he looked up and said, "Please forgive me, this seems to be important." He listened for a minute, then said, "I'll be right over," and hung up.

Mr. Belmont stood up, looking very upset. "Please excuse me," he said. "I must go to the museum at once. Pembrooke's been killed. Murdered," he said.

"It can't be," Pearl moaned. "We're not licensed yet."

"Don't go," Burton said. "You're not involved. The publicity will be terrible."

"I must go," Mr. Belmont said. "I am needed. Please come with me, Hanslik, I may need you. Mr. Gold, will you escort the ladies out? The servants will fetch your coats. I will speak with you later. Goodbye. Thank you for coming."

I knew it. I positively just knew it. Every time I trust Burton, it ends up in a murder. And me without a gun.

# V

"**S**tabbed in the back of the neck?" Alexander exploded at Burton. "Are you trying to be funny?"

Burton was busy schlurping up his second bowl of my terrific mushroom-barley soup which I had saved from Pearl and Alexander an hour ago at supper. I knew Alexander would be *plotzing* until he got the details of the Pembrooke murder directly from Burton, so I convinced Pearl to leave her husband a note saying she was next door at our house.

Burton calmly scraped the bowl; irritating Alexander might be fun but my soup deserved serious concentration, especially on a cold winter's night.

"All right, Alec," Burton finally said. "The killer stabbed Penbrooke in the left buttock and he died of humiliation. Does that make you happy?"

We had been waiting five hours for Burton to come home and Alexander is not famous for his patience, so I stepped in before his neck swelled. "I'll trade you, Burton. You talk straight, no fooling around, and I'll give Pearl the recipe."

"Nothing left out?" Burton, the lawyer, unnecessarily suspicious; I hadn't lied to Pearl in weeks.

"Complete, accurate, and detailed," I swore. "But my

genius I can't transfer, so don't get vicious if one bowl doesn't produce a high."

I served tea and *stollen* as Burton began. "Orville Marston Pembrooke, director of the Fine Arts Museum of New York, was found dead in his dining room at 2:30 P.M. with an oyster knife stuck in the back of his neck."

"What's an oyster knife?" Pearl asked.

"It has a short, stubby, pointed blade," I informed her. "You use it to open oysters."

"How does it work?" she asked.

"You hold the oyster in your left hand, stick the point of the knife into the hinge, and pry and twist. Experts can do it in two seconds; I never could. Julia Child says to use a metal beer-can opener, but I gave that up too. I take the coward's way out; break the edge of the shell off with a pliers and slip a plain knife in."

"Don't pieces of shell get inside that way?"

"Sure, but I wash them out. That's supposed to destroy the delicate flavor, but what the hell."

"You have one I could look at?" Pearl asked.

"Somewhere. I don't use it anymore; too easy to stab your left hand when you slip."

Alexander couldn't stand it anymore. "You want to give her your recipe for Oysters Rockefeller too?" he asked sarcastically. "Or am I allowed to find out about my next case?"

"Next case?" I asked stupidly. "You're sure?"

"It's obvious," he said. "Belmont feeds us lunch, shows us his Vermeer gallery, gives us the background on forging Vermeers, and is about to retain me to solve his problem—"

"Which you messed up," I pointed out, just to keep things straight.

"My analysis was perfectly logical," he said, "given the facts. *Belmont* messed up, the way he presented the information; even admitted it himself. Then he said he would get in touch with me tomorrow. What for? To have me work on the forgery while the police work on the murder? Nonsense. The two crimes are connected and he is positively going to retain me to solve them."

"But we're not allowed to," Pearl said. "We don't have a license to practice."

"That's why I was so late," Burton said. "Alec is right. Belmont intends to hire him. So after I left Belmont, I went back to the office and had an associate prepare the papers the way we discussed. While he was doing that, I called Art Kaplan to come to the office and sign them. As soon as Norma and Pearl sign and give me the checks, you're in business."

"Does Belmont understand how I work," Alexander asked, "and that I'm not a private eye?"

"I explained everything," Burton said. "He likes the idea of paying for results only. But are you sure you want this case? It's a real puzzler; the police don't even know where to start."

"That's why I want it," Alexander said. "Because it is a real puzzle. Besides, it's clearly soluble. An oyster knife in the back of the neck? There has to be only one set of circumstances to explain that and only one person who fits those particular circumstances."

"Like a Magritte painting," Pearl said. "It just looks irrational, but when you understand it, everything falls into place."

"Exactly," said Alexander. "So let Burt talk."

"They won't have the medical examiner's report till tomorrow," Burton said, "but I'll tell you what I do know. The fifth floor of the museum houses the executive and administrative functions: curatorial, public relations and publications, the registry, the library, the archives, data processing, accounting, et cetera, and the staff dining room and its kitchen."

"Does the kitchen serve the basement cafeteria too?" Alexander asked.

"No. That's a different level of quality. The upstairs dining room is fairly nice: tablecloths, waiters, and good cooking. Lunch only, but it's free. One of the perks for assistant curators and up. The museum doesn't pay tremendous salaries, but there are many benefits. No other museum has this.''

"Also a place to take big doners, right?'' I said.

"And members of the Board of Trustees, city officials, movie stars, and respected attorneys,'' Burton agreed. "The dining room serves many museum functions; that's why it's so big.''

"This is where Pembrooke was killed?'' Alexander asked.

"Pembrooke?'' Burton said. "Never. He had his own little dining room; had it built when he took over the position of director. At the end of the executive corridor, right next to the staff dining room.''

"You mean he never ate in the staff dining room?'' I asked.

"When he was entertaining big shots, yes, he sat with them. But he never ate there; he always ate before they came or after they left.''

"A drooler?'' I asked. "Palsy?''

"No. He was in perfect health, comparatively, for a man of sixty-five.''

"Mr. Belmont said that the museum had a mandatory retirement at sixty-five,'' Pearl reminded him.

"Pembrooke wasn't quite sixty-five. His retirement was scheduled for this June.''

"Then this insistence on eating alone,'' I asked, "was it a psychological problem or just a quirk?''

"I worked with him several times,'' Burton said, "but I really didn't know him well. I don't think he had any serious psychological problems. I have heard him called a megalomaniac, but that might have been the jealous reaction of a rival museum director who had been beaten out in the acquisition of a major painting.''

"Then what was the reason?'' I pressed.

"Have any of you heard of James J. Rorimer?'' Burton asked. None of us had, not even Alexander. "He was the director of the Metropolitan Museum of Art for more than twenty years. He rehabilitated the museum, made great changes, originated new concepts, raised tremendous sums of money, was one of the most respected and influential men in the art world and one of the strongest forces in making America art conscious. But you've all heard of Thomas Hoving, haven't you?''

We all had. "Hoving was a great director,'' Burton went on, "competent, innovative, even daring. But he took over a museum which was, essentially, what it is today and he was director for a much shorter time than Rorimer. No one outside the field knows of Rorimer, yet there is practically no cultured person who doesn't know of Hoving. Why? Hoving knew how to use public relations well; Rorimer didn't. It's my belief that Pembrooke, as part of his campaign for the aggrandizement of the museum, and of himself, decided to become a public character. Pembrooke was intelligent; he was not so foolish as to take on false characteristics, or to buy identifications, such as unusual pets. What he did was to enlarge those characteristics and tastes he already had, and to publicize them to the point where he was Pembrooke, the eccentric but brilliant director of the Fine Arts.''

"Oysters and champagne for lunch,'' Alexander said triumphantly. "That's the one. If I hadn't lost brain cells I would have made the connection right away.''

"Who doesn't like champagne?'' Burton said. "And I am sure he really liked oysters. But who can believe that a sane man would eat nothing but two dozen oysters and a bottle of champagne for lunch every day of the week? And insist that unless the oyster was eaten the instant it was opened it was not fit to eat?''

"Didn't he ever get tired of this diet?'' Pearl asked. "Bored?''

"If he did he never admitted it,'' Burton said. "I researched the subject once and asked him about it, pointing out that there were only four varieties of oyster in North America. He said that the location of the oyster bed, the temperature of the water, the mineral content, the seasonal variations, and a variety of other factors made each oyster type so different from another that each had a name: Belon, Wellfleet, Cotuit, Olympia, Chincoteague, and so on. He offered to bet me that he could identify, blindfolded, at least twenty different oysters, provided that they had been taken within the last twelve hours and opened within three seconds before he ate each one.''

"It still sounds boring," Pearl said.

"Maybe not, the way he did it," Burton said. "Counting foreign oysters, there are at least twenty-five different kinds available here and about the same number of champagnes. The chef kept records so that, by proper rotation of wines and oysters, Pembrooke could have a different combination of oysters and champagnes without repetition for two years."

"What about months without an 'R'?" Pearl asked.

"That's a superstition," I told her. "Oysters can be eaten anytime, if you know where to get them. One or two kinds aren't eaten for about a week, when they spawn; at that time you can eat others."

"The museum paid for this?" Alexander asked.

"Gladly. It cost them about fifteen thousand per year and the publicity was worth ten times that much to them. After Pembrooke became director, the attendance increased ten percent per year to the point where we are now second only to the Met."

"Just from oysters and champagne?" Pearl asked.

"He also wore only bowties and shaved his head, but those were just the outward characteristics. Pembrooke was unequalled in getting publicity and in originating special exhibits."

"How do you know all this?" Alexander asked. "Are you attorney for the museum, too?"

"No. Maxwell Korbin, the in-house counsel, handles the routine matters, and they use several law firms for whatever else they require. I am Mr. Belmont's personal attorney and attorney for the real estate holdings. But he asks my advice on many matters."

34

"Was Pembrooke killed with his own oyster knife?" Alexander asked.

"There is no question of that. For his sixtieth birthday, his staff chipped in and got him a custom-made oyster knife. It had a solid silver handle fitted to a special steel blade, similar to the usual one, but somewhat wider and longer. It had Pembrooke's initials engraved around the handle at the front end, where the thumb goes. That was the knife that was sticking in his neck when the busboy found him. There can't be another like it in the world."

"Do the police think the busboy did it?" I asked.

"They haven't said anything yet, but I don't see how the busboy could have done it. He went into Pembrooke's dining room well before Pembrooke entered it, and found Pembrooke dead long after Pembrooke was killed. The kitchen is on the opposite side of the staff dining room from Pembrooke's room and the busboy had to cross the staff dining room to get to Pembrooke's room."

"You're not describing it well," Alexander said. "Start from the beginning. Where are all the rooms in relation to each other?"

"The whole north side of the fifth floor is top-level executive offices. Pembrooke's office is in the middle of that side. Harold Wechsler's office, he's the deputy director, is in the northwest corner, facing both uptown and Fifth Avenue."

"Isn't that unusual?" I asked. "Most top executives keep the corner office and the best view for themselves."

"Pembrooke was smarter than most top executives. The power is always right next to the boss and Wechsler, as the logical replacement for Pembrooke, was placed as far from the boss as possible. And Wechsler's beautiful view was of the Metropolitan Museum of Art, a subtle reminder that Wechsler had, so far, failed to attain the FAMONY's goal of beating the Met's attendance record. Also, being right next to Pembrooke's dining room, but never having been in it, was another not-so-subtle slap in the face. And to top it off, Wechsler was not given a secretary of his own. He had to use one of Pembrooke's when she was available."

"Why were the top executive offices on the north side?" I asked. "Aren't they usually on the south side so they'll be light and sunny?"

"Pembrooke was attentive to detail and subtlety. All the people in the art world are aware that sunlight is bad for paintings. Pembrooke had, on his walls, some of the museum's best paintings, in monthly rotation. The paintings and the north light are reminders that he is both a connoiseur of the arts and mindful of the museum's property. Wechsler's office was decorated by Pembrooke, just after Wechsler was hired over Pembrooke's violent objections, in chrome modern, the direct antithesis of everything the FAMONY stands for. For Wechsler's walls, Pembrooke selected copies of contemporary paintings. 'He'll never know the difference,' Pembrooke told the decorator in front of several people. Two more slaps: One, against Wechsler's knowledge and scholarship, which, I am told, is at least as good as Pembrooke's, and two, against Wechsler's good sense. Anyone from the Board of Trustees who visited Wechsler's office would immediately get the idea that if Wechsler were to become director, he would immediately throw out the Rembrandts and fill the museum with piles of self-destructing bedsprings and paintings called *Purple on Purple*. In addition, on the south side, the view is of a big apartment house directly across the street, cutting off the sunlight for most of the day, while to the north there are only low brownstones, including Mr. Belmont's on the corner."

"Pembrooke really cut down the competition," I said, half admiringly. "Why didn't Wechsler change his decor and the paintings?"

"Pembrooke made sure he would be director until he died," Burton said. "Which he achieved, though not the way he planned it. Wechsler was helpless. If he changed the paintings now, everyone would say he was opportunistic, trying to curry favor with the board. He had lived with them for a long time, because like any new employee, he did not want to start a fight with his superior the first year. When he wanted to change the furniture, Pembrooke told him that he would gladly allow him to petition the board for this, but that, as director, Pembrooke would oppose it, since he did not feel that this was really the time to spend hard-gotten money for personal indulgence, especially after living with this decor and apparently being satisfied with it for several years.''

"Did he do the same with everybody?" I asked. "Or just Wechsler?"

"Wechsler more than anyone, but Pembrooke made sure that any of the top executives who knew art had no hope of competing with him. Konrad Dorner, the chief curator, was also kept far from the seat of power. For example, imagine yourself standing in the corridor in front of Pembrooke's office. On your left is his arts secretarial staff office; on your right is his business secretarial staff office."

"That sounds like overstaffing," Pearl said.

"More like overkill," I said. "Evidently Pembrooke didn't want even his secretaries to know the whole picture."

"Precisely," Burton said. "He was Machiavelli's Prince in modern dress. To the left of his arts secretaries was the comptroller's secretary and to the left of her office was the comptroller, Melville Gerson. To the right of Pembrooke's business secretary was the secretary of the director of Public Relations, and to her right was Ken Rand, the PR man."

"The picture becomes clear," Alexander said. "He had two secretaries' offices between him and any executive, and even the secretaries couldn't communicate too well with each other since there was always arts next to business. I take it this pattern continued throughout the whole fifth floor?"

"Yes, the chief curator's secretary was next to the comptroller's office and the chief curator was after her. Then came the in-house attorney and his secretary, and at the Fifth Avenue end was Wechsler. Going east, in the other direction, was the chief conservator and her secretary, and filling the rest of the space at the east end was the security chief and his set of offices. Three hundred feet of executives and their secretarial staffs, and no two compatible people were next to each other.''

"He really believed in divide and rule," Pearl said.

"Can we please get back to the murder?" Alexander asked.

"Okay," Burton said. "If you were to walk west from Pembrooke's office, toward Central Park, right at the end of the corridor you would come to Wechsler's office. A few feet directly to your left is the door to Pembrooke's dining room. Across the corridor from Pembrooke's door is a staff elevator, and just past that is the door to a stair. Opposite the stair door, recessed a few feet, is a pair of doors leading out of the staff dining room. You are now walking south, parallel to Fifth Avenue.''

"Wait," Pearl said. "I'm lost. Going from Pembrooke's office toward Wechsler's office we went west, right? Towards Fifth Avenue and Central Park. Then did we turn left?"

"Correct. At Wechsler's office, turn left. The staff dining room doors are on your right, the elevator on your left. Keep walking and at the other end of the building, the south end, the corridor turns left again, away from Central Park, to the middle-level executive offices. You've just made a big 'U.'''

"How big is the dining room?" Alexander asked.

"The full blockfront less Wechsler's office, Pembrooke's room, and the kitchen, say one hundred forty feet long by twenty-five feet deep."

"If it's that long, there has to be another pair of doors from the dining room to the corridor to comply with the Fire Laws.''

"There is," Burton said. "Just like the first pair, with a staff elevator and a stair opposite. Perfectly symmetrical. The mid-level staff usually enters and leaves the dining room through those doors and the top-level executives usually use the doors at their side of the dining room.''

"I'll bet they sit that way, too," Pearl said. "In the dining room, I mean."

"They generally do, although there are no hard and fast rules. Top staff is at the Pembrooke end of the dining room, mid-level staff at the kitchen end."

"The kitchen occupies the southwest corner of the building?" Alexander asked.

"Exactly. The same relative space taken up by Wechsler's office and Pembrooke's dining room. There are a pair of doors, an in and an out, from the kitchen to the dining room. Lunch is served from noon to 2:00 P.M. and the dining room is cleared by 3:00 P.M."

"There must be an exit door from the kitchen directly to the corridor," Alexander said. "A fire exit."

"There is, but no one can use it except in emergencies."

"What if someone has to go to the toilet?" Pearl asked. "Someone from the kitchen staff?"

"Lower-echelon personnel do not use executive bathrooms. There is a male and a female locker room just off the kitchen, with a lavatory in each."

"So that's why you say the busboy couldn't have done it," I said. "He had to go into the dining room to get to the corridor to get to Pembrooke's room. He would have been seen."

"Is the kitchen fire exit kept locked?" Alexander asked. "That's against the law."

"It's not locked, but there is one of those mechanical exit alarms on it. Also, there are people always working around that area; they all swear no one opened that door during the lunch period."

"Did Pembrooke keep regular lunch hours?" Alexander asked.

"Almost perfect. He would invariably go into his room between five to one and five after one every day he was in the museum. The day he was killed he entered his room a few seconds after 1:02 P.M."

"How do the police know it that exactly?" Alexander asked.

"Pembrooke always popped his head into the staff dining room just before he went to his own. Just a quick look around, paternal, he said. The younger staff said he was checking up; they made sure to smile when he looked at them."

"You haven't answered my question," Alexander said. "The time. Did someone look at his watch?"

"There is a clock over each pair of doors. The assistant curators have a daily pool; whoever draws the closest time when Pembrooke's head appears, wins for the day. And they check the clocks against their watches; no one would dare gimmick the clocks, even if he could."

"When did the busboy set the table in Pembrooke's room?"

"At exactly 12:30 P.M. he always brings in—wait, I have a list—the tablecloth, two napkins, one on each side of the dish, a champagne glass, a bud vase with a seasonal flower in it—all the tables get one—a dinner plate, Pembrook's oyster knife, perfectly polished, a plastic pail for the shells, and a clean plastic-reinforced canvas gardener's glove."

"For the other hand," I said knowingly. "So the sharp shells don't cut his fingers."

"No knife and fork?" Pearl asked. "And why two napkins?"

"A connoiseur eats the oysters directly from the shell," I explained. "And maybe you need two napkins when you schlurp oysters."

"Can we please get back to the busboy?" Alexander complained. "Did he go to Pembrooke's room at exactly 12:30 today too?"

"Yes," said Burton. "All the junior staff saw him. He came back in less than two minutes."

"When were the oysters brought in?"

"The chef himself scrubbed the oysters at 12:15 and put them in a big glass bowl with cracked ice. He put the champagne, which had been in the refrigerator for a half hour, into a silver ice bucket at 12:40 and two waiters took the oysters and the champagne into Pembrooke's room at 12:45.''

"The junior timekeepers again?"

"Yes, and the waiters said that the table had been laid exactly as usual. Tablecloth spread, bud vase center rear, with respect to Pembrooke's chair; that means towards the door.''

"Pembrooke didn't face the park?"

"Only later. He always dined with his back to the window, facing the door, so as not to be distracted from the oysters and champagne. Plate centered, a napkin on either side. Shell bucket on the floor to the left of his chair, oyster knife sitting on the left napkin, glove on the right napkin.''

"Are you telling me Pembrooke was left handed?" Alexander asked.

"Yes, everyone knew that. What difference does that make?"

"I don't know yet, but I asked you to tell me everything.''

"In due time, Alec; give me a chance. The champagne glass was in front of the left napkin, the champagne cooler to the left of the chair, the bowl of oysters to the right of the glove.''

"Was everything exactly this way when the body was discovered?"

"Exactly. The busboy and the waiters were brought in later and they agreed. Except that the glove had been moved and the knive was in Pembrooke.''

"Had the glove been worn?"

"The police think there is a good possibility of that. The glove is in the police labs right now.''

"What was the room like, Burt?"

"It's a narrow, deep room. You enter, the door swings in to the left, on the opposite wall is a wide picture window, almost ceiling to floor, overlooking Central Park. The walls are bare, painted a soft off-white.''

"You've dined there?"

"Are you kidding? I don't think Pembrooke would allow even Mr. Belmont to dine with him. No, I just looked in one afternoon when I was there on business. Curiosity."

"It wasn't locked?"

"No, just a 'Private' sign on the door. Everyone knew it was Pembrooke's."

"So anyone could walk in, anytime?"

"You didn't just walk in on Pembrooke; he'd fire you on the spot."

"But anyone could, couldn't he? As you did?"

"What's the point? Nothing to steal."

"He ate on the floor? Japanese style?"

"Don't get sarcastic, Alec. If you gave me a chance to talk without interruption. . . . There is a fine old wood table, dark oak, simple and beautiful. Behind the table is a wood and leather executive wing chair, swivel type, and behind that, a matching footrest. After he ate, Pembrooke would swivel his chair around, put his feet on the footrest, lean back and rest for half an hour contemplating the park and meditating. He claimed it made it possible for him to work at maximum efficiency the rest of the day."

"All this he told you, Burt?"

"He told a magazine interviewer. Another facet of the Pembrooke mystique."

"A workaholic?" Pearl asked.

"Museum director is a very high-stress job," Burton said, "with a crisis every hour on the hour. The workday has no end; when the daily routine is over, the nightly routine begins: parties, openings, meetings, fund-raising—you have no idea. Pembrooke had a small gym built in the cellar for the top executives; used it regularly himself. He claimed his regimen was the only way to withstand the rigors of his duties. In truth, he looked very good for his age, slim and trim, and he held the position longer than any director of a major museum in America."

"Leave the history for Norma and Pearl to research later," Alexander said. "So the busboy found him at 2:30 P.M.?"

"That was his regular time to clean up. Sensibly, he touched nothing and went right back to the kitchen to tell the chef. The chef called Sam Zager, the security chief, who then called Wechsler, the deputy director. Wechsler called Mr. Belmont and the police."

"Where was the body?" Alexander asked.

"Sitting at the table, forehead on the plate, arms hanging straight down."

"Knife sticking straight up?"

"I didn't ask that. Find out for you tomorrow, when I get all the reports."

"When was Pembrooke killed?"

"Indications are sometime before 1:30 P.M."

"Right after he entered his dining room?"

"Just about. The champagne had been opened and poured."

"Any drunk?"

"About one sip, it appears. We'll know the exact amount tomorrow."

"Had he eaten?"

"No oysters had been opened, but the glove had been moved. The presumption is that Pembrooke had put it on. When we get the lab report we'll know if he had picked up an oyster."

"Any fingerprints?"

"The expected ones plus— There's a problem here, Alec. There were clear fingerprints on the knife; Pembrooke's left hand, no others."

Alexander moved his closed fist to the back of his neck as though he were holding a knife in it and made stabbing motions. "Don't tell me," he said, "that Pembrooke committed suicide this way. I don't believe it."

"You're holding your imaginary knife the wrong way, Alec," Burton said. "The fingerprints were on it the other way around; thumb on top pointing forward, parallel to the flat side of the blade. Just as if you were going to open an oyster.''

Alexander tried to put his hand in that position at the back of his neck. Impossible. "It can't be done, Burt. Even by a contortionist. You said the fingerprints were clear?"

"Put it out of your mind, Alec. The police thought of that too. A person's hand can't even be forced into that position. And the prints weren't perfectly clear; they were consistent with Pembrooke's picking up the knife and shifting it slightly into the right position to open an oyster.''

"Burt, I don't believe it.''

"I'm reporting accurately, Alec. I'll have the complete reports late tomorrow.''

"Where did you get all this information?''

"Warshafsky told me.''

"My Warshafsky?''

"Who else? If you persist in getting involved with homicides in Manhattan, Warshafsky comes with the territory.''

"He doesn't still hate me, does he?''

"He never hated you, Alec. He appreciates what you've done and that you've let him take all the credit. With your help, if there are enough murders, he figures to make commissioner next year and be able to marry Roberta Baron.'' Burton was referring to Lieutenant David Warshafsky's not-so-secret romance with the daughter of a recent rich client who had too much money for Warshafsky to marry her, in Warshafsky's macho opinion. Meanwhile, neither of them was getting any younger. Men!

"When am I supposed to meet with Belmont?'' Alexander asked.

"Tomorrow, 2:00 P.M. At his home. And be nice, Alec, please. He's an old man and very conservative. No million-dollar betting like you did with Max Baron.''

"That was Baron's idea, Burt, not mine. I'm going to be myself with Belmont; I'm sure he would see through any phoniness. If he doesn't like the way I am, let him get somebody else."

"Alex is right," Pearl said. "No one gets to be that rich or to stay rich, being soft or stupid."

"I didn't mean to give you the idea that Belmont is either soft or stupid," Burton said. "I'm his lawyer, and I know how sharp he is. And don't let that sweet-old-gentleman appearance fool you; I've known him to be absolutely ruthless when the situation required it. But he is old-fashioned and he is a gentleman; his word is his bond and he likes the people he deals with to be straight."

"Do you want me to start researching Pembrooke?" I asked Alexander. "Get an early start on the case?"

He thought for a moment, then said, "No. We may not be retained. Mr. Belmont has to be a much tougher nut than he appears on the surface. All his life he's gotten things to go his way, that's clear, and had everyone dancing to his tune. Well, I'm just getting used to doing things my own way and I like it."

"All right, Alexander," I said. "Whatever you say. But without excitement, please. You know it's bad for you. Don't work yourself up into a mad on Mr. Belmont just on your own assumptions about him. So please, Alexander, quietly."

"Of course quietly," he yelled. "Go sign the Kaplan papers and stop worrying about me."

Of course I would stop worrying. Worrying was when you didn't know what was going to happen. After it happened you stopped worrying and tried suffering for a change.

# VI

Alexander was surprised. "The Inquisition?"

"You did ask me to start at the beginning," Mr. Belmont said dryly. He was seated behind his desk and we were seated around his study in deep, soft, leather easy chairs; another dominance/control ploy. Burton sat facing us in a hard straight-backed wooden chair near Belmont's desk, a subtle reminder as to whose side he was on and what his function was. Affable as Belmont appeared, there was a small but unmistakable difference between the way he had treated us in his dining room and the way we, potential hirelings, were treated in his study.

"An ancestor of mine was one of the early settlers of New Amsterdam. In most of Europe Jews were not allowed to own land, so fortunately for me, Eduardo Belmont, faced with the huge stretches of empty land, went crazy. He worked like a dog and ate as little as possible, buying every bit of cheap land he could. He couldn't afford land in the good areas, so he had to buy in the wild outskirts, what is now midtown Manhattan. This, of course, included the land the Fine Arts Museum is on. He left us with the injunction never to sell the land, no matter what, even if we were starving. Ever since then, regardless of the dispersion of the ownership, the oldest son of the direct line—I am the present officeholder—has been charged with the responsibility for the family real estate holdings.''

"Do you still own the museum land?" I asked.

"Unfortunately, we do."

"Unfortunately?" I said. "I would love to have that land. It must be worth millions."

"If you could sell it, yes. But for ninety-nine years from the day it was turned over, renewable for another ninety-nine years, it will bring in, as a net net rent, the magnificent sum of one dollar a year; somewhat less than the cost of the postage I use in managing the property. If Eduardo had not told us never to sell the land, I would have given it to the museum, taken its fair market value as a tax loss, and be done. But I had to honor my family responsibilities."

"So that's what Burton meant when he said you owned the FAMONY."

"It's worse than just the land; I own the building too, personally."

"Another dollar a year?" I said. "This could begin to add up."

"Another dollar a year," he agreed ruefully. "Because of my wife. It was built for her; I could not let it, even a hundred years from now, be turned into a department store or an apartment house, so I had to own it. It was not . . . not inexpensive."

"She must have been an extraordinary woman," I said. I wasn't jealous; Alexander would give his life for me, and had tried to do that, once.

"Helen . . . yes she was." He paused, then spoke in a different tone. "When I first saw her she was standing in front of the *Girl with Pearl Earrings*, my favorite Vermeer and his strangest painting. Vermeer's usual way was to place his figure against a white wall, sometimes with a map on that wall, with a light streaming from one direction, usually the left, the figure silhouetted against the wall by the light. Here the girl was light against a plain dark background. She was wearing a blue turban with a yellow scarf wound around the top part of the turban. The painting is sometimes called *Girl in a Turban*—we don't know what Vermeer named his paintings—and I have seen it called *Head of a Girl with Pearl Eardrops*. The name is not important. The girl's face is derived from light itself—even the X-rays show no lines—the paint built up, layer by transparent layer as if Vermeer were *creating* the girl from light. The edges are not sharp, but blend into the surroundings. And the model, if one ever existed, is the most beautiful girl Vermeer ever painted.

"Helen was standing in front of that painting, her hair bobbed short, almost a turban. If someone had told me she was a direct blood descendant of that girl of three hundred years ago, that beautiful girl made of light, I would have believed him. Helen was even more beautiful. . . ." Belmont drew a deep breath and let it out slowly.

"Helen was an art student working for the summer as a volunteer assistant curator in the Mauritshuis, unpaid but happy. Her father was a small manufacturer in Leeds who thought I was a fortune hunter and who opposed the marriage. But after he had me investigated—" I must have made a face because he said, "Don't jump, Mrs. Gold. It was quite common in those days to investigate a suitor; if more people did it today there would be fewer heartbreaks and fewer divorces. Afterward, of course, her father was all for the marriage. Somehow he got the idea, and I could never convince him otherwise, that I was related to the famous August Belmont."

"Did you investigate her?" I asked. "Your wife?"

"Of course," he replied. "It was required."

"What would you have done if she were a . . . uh . . . an unsuitable person? Of bad family?"

"I had considered that, of course. I was not a boy, I was a man of thirty, with responsibilities, the older son. What I had decided was . . . There was no doubt in my mind that I would marry Helen. No question at all. I had, in fact, proposed to her before I had even ordered the investigation, so that was that. If she . . . I would have had to give up my responsibilities for the family, of course, transferring them to my younger brother. I would then have moved to England so that Helen, at least, could have family, changed my name, and lived a quiet life with my wife. I considered the world well lost for her."

"She evidently checked out well," I said.

"Nothing bad. Her mother was distantly related to an eminent family, the D'Aguilars of Vienna and London, so Helen and I were very distantly related outselves."

"The museum, then, was your wedding present to your wife?" I asked.

"She had no interest in jewels or clothes. We already had this home. It is customary, among the wealthier members of our family—yes, Mrs. Gold, not all Belmont descendants are rich, some dissipated their inheritance—on very special occasions, to give a small, carefully selected personal gift, and make a large donation to charity in the name of the loved one. I thought it appropriate for my wife—the museum. The land, of course, was a gift of the entire family. She was very pleased at my thoughtfulness. The opening day was a long, long way off, but it was great fun to plan it together."

"Isn't it customary to name the building after the donor?" I asked. "Or after your wife?"

"We don't seek publicity. But I did have it designed as a specialized museum for the kind of art we both loved. It's in the original charter which can only be changed by a unanimous vote of the Board of Trustees, that the museum is for the acquisition and exhibition only of easel paintings and free-standing sculpture produced prior to 1920. No murals, no reliefs, no costumes, jewelry, utensils, temples, no Modern or Contemporary art. And I am proud to say that in our specialized area we are the best, I believe, and may also be bigger than the Met, the Louvre, and possibly even the Hermitage."

"No Modern art at all?" Pearl was clearly upset. The FAMONY was our favorite museum, but it had evidently never occurred to Pearl why. Just as the Museum of Modern Art is known as the MOMA, so the FAMONY is jokingly referred to as the NoMA.

"We do have some late Matisse and others of that kind; it's more a matter of style than date. But the acquisition of any late-date artwork or any work requiring more than five percent of the annual acquisition budget requires the approval of a majority of the Board of Trustees; Pembrooke's tame acquisitions committee can only have its way with relatively cheap old masters. And tell me, Mr. Hanslik, are you not concerned that the Modern specializes in Modern and Contemporary only? No? Then why should we not specialize too?"

Before Pearl could take us off on a tangent, I said quickly, "Did Mrs. Belmont work as a curator in the museum?"

"Certainly not. She was only a young girl, not qualified. A curator has to be an expert in a particular period or style, well educated, have an encyclopedic memory and a feel, a real feel, for his specialty. This takes years to develop. Making Helen a curator would have deprived a worthy person of the job."

"You could have forced the museum to do anything you wanted, couldn't you?"

"My grandfather once told me that force is the recourse of the weak and stupid. And it is wrong to—a gentleman does not use force and an intelligent man need not."

"You have never in your life—?" I stopped; why make trouble?

"I can usually accomplish what I want by arranging the situation so that. . . . Well, by some definitions it might be said that I *have* used force. What I meant was that to me force implies violence. I find that distasteful."

It took him long enough, but now he was definitely leading up to the murder. About time. "You're referring to Mr. Pembrooke?"

"I am. I was the one who brought him into the museum. As deputy director under Walter Brodmann Ludwig. I retained

Ludwig when I first conceived the idea—Helen had studied under him in England—because I wanted the best man in my favorite period, one who would command world-wide respect. The museum I had in mind would need a tremendous number of paintings which had to be acquired quickly, skillfully, and quietly. This required almost continuous fund-raising efforts, so a man of Ludwig's stature was the only choice. The Depression was at its height and providing money for the purchase of the works of art was beyond my ability; underwriting the construction of the museum had brought me close to my limit and I was terribly busy with the architects and other matters. The War, of course, delayed construction, and with one thing and another, it was late nineteen forty-seven when we finally opened.''

"I was there," Pearl glowed. "My father took me. It was wonderful.''

"Yes, thanks to Ludwig and Pembrooke. In late nineteen forty-four when it became clear we would be opening the museum in a few years, I got Pembrooke to help Ludwig with the administrative work. Ludwig and his team of curators were busy searching, studying, acquiring the art; they really had no time for mundane details.''

"Also you wanted a potential competitor for Ludwig in the organization," Alexander said. "A bit of 'divide and rule.' ''

"Perfectly normal," the old man said. "I'm surprised you saw fit to mention it. It's never good to give anyone too much power." I didn't think it was the proper time to point out how much power Mr. Belmont had. He must have read my mind. "Of course," he said, "I am constrained by family and by training to work for the maximum good. And I felt a strong responsibility for all the money I had raised from my friends.''

"Pembrooke took over as director in nineteen fifty-one, didn't he?" Pearl said, "I remember the occasion. It was combined with the opening of the Velásquez exhibition.''

"A typical Pembrooke touch," Mr. Belmont said. "I

am sure that this exhibition was an important factor in the appreciation of that great artist and the subsequent sale of his *Juan de Pareja* for six million, but at the same time, the success of the exhibition took everyone's mind off the way Ludwig had been betrayed by Pembrooke. From the day he was hired, Pembrooke worked at two jobs: the first was to do his work absolutely perfectly with his customary brilliance, and to make sure everybody knew it, and the second was to build up his own internal organization, absolutely loyal to him only, and to tear down Ludwig."

"I thought that Ludwig retired because of his age," Pearl said, "and his poor health. That's what the papers said."

"Factually true," Mr. Belmont said, "but the poor health was caused by Pembrooke's sniping, his hidden lack of cooperation, and above all, gossip and innuendo, leaking to the media exaggerated descriptions of minor mistakes—the only way an executive can avoid mistakes is by doing nothing—and undercutting what would have been Ludwig's triumphs. Finally Ludwig did something which, presented in the wrong way, could have been considered dishonest, and Pembrooke blackmailed him into resigning."

"What could Ludwig have done that was so terrible?" Pearl asked.

"He discussed a contemplated one-man exhibit with a dealer, an old and trusted friend who was an expert on that particular painter."

"That sounds perfectly normal to me," Pearl said. "What's so terrible?"

I answered that. "A one-man exhibition in a major museum is the surest way of building up the value of an artist's work. It could increase the price of that artist's works by ten times. A dealer who knew this sufficiently far in advance could buy up paintings by this artist and make a killing. A percentage of this money could end up in the bank account of the friend who tipped him off."

"Did Mr. Ludwig do this?" Pearl asked.

"Ludwig? Certainly not," Mr. Belmont said. "Some other museum directors may have done this, or worse, but Ludwig was a scholar, a man of the old school, born in Germany and educated in England. The consultation was confidential, for advice only. I am sure he was going to talk to other specialist dealers shortly afterward. The trouble was, he talked to his friend before he presented his idea for the exhibition to the board."

"How do you know this?" Alexander asked. "Did you have him investigated too?"

"Of course. Continuously. You don't hand over acquisition of, control of, hundreds of millions of dollars worth of art and property to a manager without knowing something about the person you place in charge."

"Didn't you investigate Pembrooke?" Pearl asked. "Didn't you know what kind of person he was?"

"I knew Pembrooke better than his mother did," Belmont said quietly. "He was the most brilliant young art historian in the country, very intelligent, very handsome, healthy, old New England stock, six generations, broad interests, good social graces, perfect as the second director of the Fine Arts Museum."

"It seems to me," said Alexander judiciously, "that in view of what you said about Ludwig's resignation, you have not mentioned several of Pembrooke's other characteristics. You also said 'second director.' As in Eric Hoffer's theory?"

Belmont beamed. "I see we'll get along, Mr. Gold. Eric Hoffer," he explained to the rest of us, "said that revolutions are led by three different types, in this order: the theorist first, then the man of action, and last the consolidator, the bookkeeper, the status quo man. Wechsler, of course, is the bookkeeper I have been grooming to take Pembrooke's place."

"So Pembrooke was not completely honest?" Alexander asked.

"Pembrooke was the most thoroughly dishonest man I have ever met. Even worse, he was completely unscrupulous.

Not amoral, he knew what was right and what was wrong, but it did not bother him one bit to do what was immoral.''

"How could you—?'' Pearl was flustered. "Did you know before you hired him?''

"Of course I did. Everyone who had any contact with Pembrooke for more than a few months had the scars to show for it. Not that Pembrooke was a psychopath; he did not hurt for pleasure. But if a situation came up where someone stood between him and what he wanted, Pembrooke always got what he wanted.''

"A perfect second director,'' Alexander said.

"Quite so, Mr. Gold. And the sarcasm is uncalled for. My grandfather once asked me, when I was very young and innocent— He presented me with this problem: I have to hire a manager for a big office building. The choice is between two men, both equally qualified and experienced. One is completely honest, but slightly stupid. The other is reputed to be somewhat dishonest, but very smart. Which do I hire? I immediately chose the honest man. I was wrong. A stupid man can put you out of business in one day, my grandfather told me. The smart one will continue stealing, but so small a percentage and so carefully that you can never be absolutely sure he is stealing. And, to cover his crimes, he will work very hard at his job, brilliantly. He will make a great deal of money for your company; treat his thefts as an increase in salary for his good work.''

"Did Pembrooke ever steal from the museum?'' Alexander asked. "Directly?''

"He was too smart for that. The museum's books were always perfectly accurate, the money was always there, to the penny. Only fools steal paper clips. Pembrooke stole outside the museum, using the museum as his weapon. It was well known in the trade that if a sale was to be made to the Fine Arts, it had to be through one of six galleries. They were all, sensibly, major galleries in major cities, London, Rome, Paris, Berlin, Tokyo, and, of course, New York. Even if the sale originated in some other gallery, the commission had to be split with one of the favored six. Pembrooke got a share of the profit. The price of the artwork was always about fair market value, Pembrooke was prudent, but who knows what fair market value means in the art world, especially in a period of inflation.''

"Well, at least he couldn't shake down living artists," Pearl said, "the FAMONY being what it is.''

"Oh, Pembrooke wouldn't miss that opportunity," Belmont said. "When Pembrooke found a little-known contemporary artist whose work he liked—he really didn't dislike today's art in spite of what he said to the papers—a deal was made. A dozen selected paintings were sold to Pembrooke—through an agent, naturally, the artist never knew Pembrooke was his fairy godfather—for a trifling sum. The artist would get a one-man show in one of Pembrooke's pet galleries and sometimes all of them. There might be an interview in the papers about this promising young genius who showed signs of becoming another Matisse and whose paintings were certain to increase in value soon. Naturally, with all this, they did.''

"He didn't miss a single trick, did he?" I said.

"Not one. For example, many people leave their collections to the museum; some even while they are still alive. Usually there is an agreement that the collections are to be kept together and not to be sold, to become part of the permanent collection of the museum. Pembrooke promptly sold what he wanted, when he wanted, always to one of his favored galleries at prices somewhat below what might be considered fair market value. He then used the money to buy big-name artists, popular names, again from his friendly six, at higher and higher prices, pushing the prices on some artists to the point where even the richest museums complained. Of course, he was smart enough to sell only the poorer works, and to buy only acceptable great artists, their secondary work only, so that at all times he stayed within his discretionary limits. And who on the board would object to a Renoir, even though not everything Renoir did was all that great. Pembrooke then used the paintings he bought to promote circus-type exhibits featuring interviews with TV soap opera ingenues, illiterate rock music superstars, famous gangsters, and even politicians. The lines would stretch around the museum for weeks; Pembrooke really knew how to bring in the crowds. Not necessarily crowds of people who understood art, or appreciated art, or even loved art, but crowds nevertheless. 'Bringing culture to the masses,' Pembrooke called it. And, of course, he used the size of the crowds to justify his sales and his acquisitions.''

"But isn't it illegal,'' Pearl asked, ''to sell a gift like that? If you agreed not to?''

"Not illegal, but the museum is presently defending several lawsuits on this very matter.''

"Why didn't you stop him?''

"The money from sales of any kind, other than of art acquired by vote of the trustees, is not under the control of the board. It is understood that such money is to be used for normal museum functions. Generally, the trustees are involved only in major purchases. Our original attorneys made a mistake; they envisioned only sales from the Gift Shop: prints, books, publications, and purchases of a similar nature. They assumed that there would be no purchases of art other than by vote of the acquisitions committee, and that no one would dare sell gifts and bequests which were, so to speak, entailed. That is why they no longer represent the museum.''

"Didn't you ever tell him to stop this?''

"Not at all. He was smart enough to sell only the poorer works of a collection and to buy only good, second-level paintings. No one ever questioned his taste or his skill.''

"You could have stopped him, but didn't. That's—''

"Dishonest? Immoral? Possibly. In a sense. But only in the service of a higher morality. I was preparing to destroy him anyway—don't twitch, Mrs. Gold, I didn't mean 'to kill'—and this would serve very well. You know the saying 'Would that mine enemy would write a book'? How much better it is if thine enemy, or rather the museum's enemy, does something which is certainly wrong and may be criminal, and at the same time irritates a lot of important and influential people.''

"Why destroy, Mr. Belmont?" Alexander asked. "Couldn't you have forced his resignation?"

"I'm sure I could have, Mr. Gold. But I don't like force, as you know. I prefer to have the evildoer destroy himself by his own weakness. It's more elegant. Pembrooke deserved to be destroyed for what he had done to Ludwig and to many other good people. A balancing of the scales, so to speak, and the perfect time to remove him, one way or another.''

"You knew that would happen when you hired him," Pearl said. "Wouldn't it have been easier not to hire him?"

"Easier, yes. But easiness was not my goal. He served his purpose; it was time for him to go. He was getting dangerous and time was short. Pembrooke had one great advantage over me, an insuperable advantage: his age. Statistically, I was sure to die before him, leaving my museum at his mercy without a single strong defender. So—"

"Mr. Belmont," I broke in, "since this is a business meeting and I don't take shorthand, I've been running a cassette recorder. In the open, not trying to hide anything. You've said some things, and I have a feeling you are going to say some more things, that you may not want recorded, especially now that Pembrooke's been murdered. What do you want me to do?"

"Record or not, Mrs. Gold, as you wish. It makes no difference.''

Pearl still seemed upset by Pembrooke's dishonesty. "What did he do with all this money?" she asked. "Wouldn't the IRS have noticed?"

"Pembrooke did live very well, right up to his recorded income, but not beyond it. He put his ill-gotten retirement funds into a small bank in the lovely city of Basel, which, conveniently, is also on the borders of France and Germany.''

"I thought Swiss banks weren't supposed to tell."

"Swiss banks don't, Mrs. Hanslik. But there are individuals in Switzerland who cooperate with me. Let me play a tape for you, one I made in this very room. It's an interview I had three months ago with Orville Pembrooke which bears directly on the matter I want you to look into, Mr. Gold."

I carefully and visibly turned off my recorder and put it into my bag. I didn't want Daniel Pereira Belmont to be annoyed with me. I particularly didn't like the way he had said, "to remove him one way or another."

"Do not be misled," Mr. Belmont said, "by the apparent affability of the conversation; Orville Pembrooke was as skilled in the use of the stiletto as I am. Almost. This was a battle to the death and we both knew it. For my part Pembrooke had to be severed from the museum and all his evil influence eliminated completely before I died. As far as he was concerned, my death could not come too soon for him, and I did not put it past him to help the process along.

"Some of the acquaintances he had picked up in his various dealings were, I am sure, not unacquainted with the ways and means to help Pembrooke in his goals, and I do not exclude murder. So I had to make sure that my plans were perfect, that my methods did not allow Pembrooke any way out, even if I were gone. It was the only way to insure my own life."

He reached into his right-hand drawer and pressed something. The recorder hummed, then we heard Belmont speak.

# VII

BELM: Ah, good evening Pembrooke, I am so pleased you could find the time to see me. I must be one of the few people who knows how hard you work; how much time and energy you put into projects outside your regular museum duties.

PEMB: Good evening, Mr. Belmont. You're looking remarkably well, all things considered, particularly in view of your age and the wide range of your interests.

BELM: Well, I do take precautions to preserve my health and I have so many people who look after my interests. There are even some who are concerned that I do not pass away suddenly, even if it appears accidental. The financial upheavals and the other ramifications would cause great damage to many people, even those who thought they were not directly involved.

PEMB: I am sure that such eventuality is highly improbable. Still, at your age, it might be prudent to temper your activities a bit.

BELM: I have tried to slow down, several times. But each time something came up which required my personal attention.

PEMB: Ah, Gladwin mentioned our little talk to you. I had hoped not to trouble you with petty details, so I asked him to treat the matter confidentially.

BELM: Evidently his sense of duty took precedence. And I know, from our many intimate talks, that he has no desire to take over as chairman of the board of Trustees.

PEMB: Don't you think the museum would benefit if the members of the board were less intimate with each other? The overlapping terms and the absence of community representation make it difficult for progressive views to be considered. I am sure that when the community becomes aware of the huge sums not paid in taxes by an organization which ostensibly is there only to serve that community but which actually serves the personal interests of only one man, actions might be taken which could result in a more democratic board.

BELM: My feelings exactly. I too do not want the museum run for the benefit of one man. What I had in mind was that you might resign at once, gracefully, rather than waiting until your sixty-fifth birthday.

PEMB: I would give that serious consideration if I were sure that a fully qualified person were to be my successor.

BELM: I'm afraid that Howard S. Alford is not acceptable to the board. Harold Wechsler has been groomed as the new director and is fully acceptable to the entire board. Unanimously. However, I understand that you might find it difficult to live on your pension; you have such expensive tastes. With your cooperation, and in view of your so very long service, I am sure I could convince the board to increase your pension somewhat; say ten percent?

PEMB: Thank you for your well-known charitable instincts, but a small increment would not be of interest to me. I have little need for it, having always felt that it is up to each individual to provide for himself.

BELM: A wise view, but sometimes difficult of accomplishment. I am gratified you refused my well-meaning but clumsy attempt to make your retirement a bit more comfortable; had you acccepted, it would have meant that I had misread you. So sure was I that you would refuse, the board has already proceeded to implement some decisions which we had been considering in executive session for the past several months. With my own secretary taking the minutes, of course.

PEMB: It is highly irregular to hold meetings without the director.

BELM: But within the charter. You will be informed officially in due time, but it will be my pleasure to tell you about them now. I know you are all ears.

PEMB: If my cooperation is needed in implementing these schemes, surely my input would have been helpful.

BELM: I don't think your cooperation is required, Pembrooke. These are mostly negative actions which Wechsler will handle while you are busy with your regular activities. I am sure you are aware that Wechsler has been underutilized of late.

PEMB: I've always had a lack of confidence in his abilities and his loyalties.

BELM: You were right to be concerned about his ability; it is so much superior to that of any other person in the field. Fully equal to that of the late Dr. Ludwig in scholarship and much his superior, in spite of his low profile, in modern . . . uh . . . business administration. As far as loyalty is concerned, he is absolutely loyal to the museum rather than to any person, unlike so many of our other executives.

PEMB: My staff functions as a perfect team which is naturally centered around the director.

BELM: Exactly as it should be, and when Wechsler takes over, he will release them, one by one, to follow their leader wheresoever he leadeth, so that there may be assembled a staff which is loyal to the museum. Fortunately you used a technique employed by some weak directors to insure personal loyalty: keeping all the key people in very short-term contracts. I am sure Harold Wechsler will be less precipitous in letting people go than you were in eliminating Dr. Ludwig's staff, but then, it is understandable, you were so very young.

PEMB: Many of my staff are quite important and influential in the art world, with strong connections to some very big people. It may not be so easy for little Harold to accomplish everything he wants.

BELM: You think the control you command would endure after you drop the reins? Certain loyalties—bought loyalty and fear loyalty—these weeds wither in the hot sun of exposure, especially when the water and fertilizer have been cut off.

PEMB: I'm afraid I don't understand barnyard metaphor.

BELM: We are going to settle all claims by estates and donors; admit liability and pay the damages and costs.

PEMB: That's crazy. It will cost a tremendous amount of money.

BELM: I'm afraid so, but it will serve several good purposes at once. First, it will restore our honor. Second, it will insure that no museum, ever again, will break its contract with a donor. Third, it will insure that no director will ever work against the interests of his own museum or his Board of Trustees, regardless of what the fine print permits. Fourth, it will insure that the director who caused all this trouble will never work in this field again. At last and best, we will, of course, request that all the trustees be given immunity from prosecution, but we will not ask that the true culprits, the chairman of the board and the director, be freed from the threat of prosecution. This will keep both of us, and our lawyers, busy for a while, but justice must be served.

PEMB:   I was within my authority in making those sales.

BELM:   My dear boy, are you panicking already? Resorting to "within my authority" in this business? A business as dependent on trust and faith as, say, the diamond business? But you are spoiling my pleasure, panicking so soon. There is more to come.

PEMB:   Keep talking, old man, have your moment of triumph. You may be in for a surprise yourself.

BELM:   Good. I was afraid you'd fold too quickly. Next, we have been talking to attorneys. Not the museum's attorneys nor my personal attorneys, but a firm well-known for its all-out-attack-on-all-fronts technique, one which asks no quarter and gives no quarter. We're asking them to sue the galleries which bought those paintings from you—there were six such galleries, were there not?—and sold them to other art lovers for an unusually high profit.

PEMB:   Those galleries bought these paintings in good faith. They can't be held liable.

BELM:   My, my, such a surprising concern for these crass commercial enterprises. Did not the galleries ask for the provenance of each painting? Did not the provenance include the contracts under which these gifts or bequests were made? Why were these galleries so sure that no one would make any difficulties for them? Interesting, is it not?

PEMB:   It's foolish to bring suit. There is no way such a suit can be won. Other museums have done the same thing.

BELM:   These attorneys are so confident that they

have taken the suits on contingency. And when they work on contingency, they are like tiger sharks; someone's blood will flow. They also feel that once they start, other donors and estates will retain them in similar suits. They envision huge fees. Of course, the galleries, all six of them, will have, at best, rather heavy expenses and may have to delay the payment of, say, other obligations, possibly indefinitely. Certainly it will take a great deal of their time and energy, time which might have been spent in profitable enterprise. I would not be surprised if they were a bit upset with the man who got them into all this. But you, my dear boy, you will have achieved what you always wanted: world-wide fame. Or, if not world-wide, at least in London, Paris, Rome, Berlin, Tokyo, and New York.

PEMB: If that's all, old man, I'll be running along. I do have work to do.

BELM: You're free to go anytime, of course, but there's more, much more. You'll stay? Good. With the burden of these expenses, the museum, of course, will not be able to make any new acquisitions for at least two years; will even have to cancel those purchases agreed to but not yet consumated. I'm afraid certain galleries will have heavy costs for a while, unanticipated costs such as interest, insurance, and so forth, and may even find themselves a bit short of capital for a while, to pay their heavy expenses and overhead.

PEMB: The paintings we bought are all good works; they can be sold anywhere.

BELM: Of course, but not for a while, and not for the same price you agreed to pay for them. Further, we work openly; we will announce to the press that, considering the doubts some of our people had about these paintings—and there are always doubts about any painting—with an ever-so-slight intimation that these respective galleries may not be used by us in the foreseeable future—

considering all this, and that we felt the prices were so heavily inflated that we preferred to wait until the prices came down to a reasonable level—

PEMB: My god, you'll destroy the whole art world.

BELM: Not really, only these few dubious enterprises will suffer. And, of course, the people who depend on commissions from these particular galleries. The ethical galleries will do even better than before, especially when we start buying again, and favor them with our custom. Of course, as part of our retrenchment program, we will have to cancel the special exhibitions for the next few years.

PEMB: You can't do that. It takes three years to set up a special exhibit. There are other museums and other governments involved. Agreements have been made, contracts signed.

BELM: Unfortunate, but we really can't afford them now. And my investigations show that certain formerly fortunate galleries have bought heavily in the artists we were going to exhibit. Must have been a leak somewhere. Well, they'll just have to take their losses.

PEMB: You're biting off your nose to spite your face. The museum will suffer if you do this.

BELM: Knowing Wechsler, I am sure he has made some quiet preparations for substitute exhibits which will be ready to go shortly after he becomes director.

PEMB: Are you quite finished, sir?

BELM: You seem remarkably calm, Pembrooke. Are you thinking, perhaps, of your hoard of contemporary art? Sixteen artists, wasn't it? A dozen from each?

PEMB: I occasionally invest in promising young artists. Who doesn't?

BELM: I don't, usually, but in the past few years I have seen the wisdom of doing so. For investment purposes only, you understand; I keep them where I don't have to look at them. I have hundreds upon hundreds, thousands, in fact; these young people are so productive. But then it's so easy for them: a few splashes of acrylic from a five-gallon can and presto! Another great painting. I bought them when you did, Pembrooke, I have such faith in your judgment. Quite cheap, then, fairly expensive now.

PEMB: I'm pleased to have been of service, sir; to have helped you increase your assets, if ever so slightly.

BELM: But I am ashamed that I have done this, Pembrooke: allowed the public to believe that these splotches have any artistic merit, solely to make money. So I will atone. There will be an announcement in tomorrow's paper—too late for you to unload your little collection; the word will have gone 'round already—that these thousands of desecrations will go on sale at . . . I forget the name; one of those miserable places that sell genuine oil paintings for four-ninety-nine plus frame . . . at a reasonable price, one dollar a square foot or make an offer. Cheaper than prints.

PEMB: That's absurd. No one will believe it.

BELM: Of course they will. There will be columns and columns in papers all over the country, news as well as commentary, about how the public has finally shown its good taste and about the pitfalls of investing in junk. Plus carefully selected interviews with interested collectors, such as myself, who will carefully explain that they made a mistake and want to get out before it is too late. People will start unloading and the whole house of cards will come tumbling down.

PEMB: You're spending millions just to make sure I can't retire on the proceeds of my art?

BELM: Not really; much, much less. And that, only temporarily. First, I bought these paintings for investment only, that's on the record and not one has hung in my home or anywhere else after the purchase. So that when I sell at a loss, there will be a capital loss which will offset my capital gains. The IRS will not be able to prove otherwise, so my losses are down to thirty percent of the investment. Second, there are some very good contemporary artists working today. In the rush to unload, some fools will sell good work by these artists at a very low price. I do not care for most contemporary art, but I do recognize skill, talent, and honest workmanship. I will buy all these bargains I can; my agents are on the alert all over the world. I may very well end up making money on the overall transaction.

PEMB: You are hurting innocent artists. Some galleries may even go out of business because of you.

BELM: Is this the Pembrooke we all know? Concern for others? These sixteen got lots of undeserved money for years; any of their paintings sell now for more than Vermeer earned in an entire lifetime of painting. As for the galleries, if my agents know of an ethical gallery in distress, they have instructions to buy any of their good paintings on my account for a fair price, to keep them going. The agents are even authorized to suggest that, if the gallery has some really good work, the museum will buy it directly from that gallery in the near future and not only through the favored six.

PEMB: You've spent years planning this, haven't you?

BELM: Not quite as many years as you have building your little empire. If you had been straight, none of this would have come about. What gives me even more amusement is that you have pledged these paintings to your bank as security for the loans for your commodity speculation. You should be getting calls from your bank for repayment of these loans tomorrow, and for more security, otherwise they will liquidate your commodity positions. Your commodities are not in such good shape right now, are they? Why didn't you stay in a field you understood?

PEMB: You chose this time carefully, didn't you. Well, do your worst; it won't be enough. I can take all these losses. And after I do, I'll go to work on doing what I have to do with regard to Wechsler, the museum, and you. Assuming you're still around, old man. I still have six months to go on my contract and even you can't stop me.

BELM: Are you referring to your little hoard in Basel? The code is . . . I can't remember the code, my memory isn't what it used to be, but it was Rembrandt spelled backwards. Don't look so shocked, Pembrooke, every franc is still there.

PEMB: There's supposed to be absolute secrecy in Switzerland. What are you implying, "every franc is still there"?

BELM: There isn't absolute secrecy in Switzerland, read the banking laws, just relative secrecy. There isn't absolute secrecy anywhere, not even in Russia. And I do have many friends, relatives, connections, people I have helped in the past. Cast your bread upon the waters, you know.

PEMB: What have you done with my money?

BELM: Very sensible of you to keep it all in Swiss francs. Though the Swiss franc is no longer backed totally by gold, it is still a very sound currency. And I haven't stolen your money. I could have if I put my mind to it, but stealing is so very inelegant, no pleasure in it. I am not a thief; I merely recorded the numbers.

PEMB: You entered my vault? My valise? How did you—? What did you want the numbers for?

BELM: My dear boy, you have a very limited imagination. Anything with a lock on it is meant to be opened, given time and privacy. It was opened by someone who was obligated to someone, and in his presence only, to insure that not one franc was taken. No, no heroin was found, the Swiss are very nervous about drugs, you know, and everything was put back exactly as before. However, the numbers of many of the notes were copied, not necessarily those on top.

PEMB: The heroin bit was clumsy. If any was planted— No, you wouldn't do anything as stupid as that; no one keeps heroin locked up in a bank. I'm going to Basel at once to remove the valise. And to lodge a complaint against the bank and its manager.

BELM: For what? With whom? There is no record of anything. And surely, your mad dash to Switzerland can wait until I finish the story.

PEMB: Go on. I'll wait.

BELM: It seems there was an elderly clerk in another bank in Basel, a most unfortunate man who had a sick wife and an even sicker daughter. The poor fellow was very close to retirement, he had no money left and was desperately facing the prospect of not being able to take care of his family. Contemplating suicide, it turned out, so that the insurance would provide for his family. This terrible situation was called to my attention by one of my many friends who was aware of my small, personal, anonymous charities. A few days later a stranger—it doesn't take much to fool tired old nearsighted eyes, just a tall slim man with a shaven head, a small moustache, a bow tie, gray-tinted glasses, speaking German with an American accent—a stranger, as I said, approached the old man with a solution to his problems. Coincidentally, this was at a time when you were in Basel.

PEMB: Isn't that an awful lot of trouble to go through, not to mention the cost, for a practical joke?

BELM: Not at all, my dear boy. There is no trouble so great I would not endure it for a friend. And after all, what is money for if not to enjoy? At any rate, the next day the stranger appeared at the old man's station and walked away with a valise full of francs. After he left, the old man claimed armed robbery, but no one had seen a gun and the police were about to arrest the poor old man. I happened to be in Basel at the time and a friend who, coincidentally, was employed in that very bank called me. I rushed down at once and explained to the bank manager that I would be responsible for the old man. He was quite satisfied with a check for ninety percent of the loss, and given that the insurance covered the rest and that the old man was fired outright and lost his pension, the bank made a profit on the deal.

PEMB:   I take it the rest of the money was never recovered?

BELM:   None of it. Sad to say, the stranger cheated the old man, never showed up to share the spoils. I took full responsibility for the old man's pension and arranged for medical attention for his wife and daughter. Familial responsibility, you see. It turned out that the old man was distantly related to me. Sometimes, from the letters I get, I have the impression that I am related to half of Europe. Well, we the more fortunate must do what we can to help those less fortunate.

PEMB:   And the numbers of the bills?

BELM:   The old man always kept careful records of the numbers of the larger bills. Knowing he would find it distasteful to go back to the bank that had fired him, I brought the bank and the insurance company a copy of that list. If any of these bills turn up again—well, the Swiss are very serious about bank robbery.

PEMB:   So if I were to try to remove my valise—?

BELM:   If anyone were to visit that box, even just to try to change the notes for others, certain people would call the police right away.

PEMB:   You think you've thought of everything, don't you?

BELM:   I do think so, but I may have missed something. So just to keep you occupied for the next six months— It seems certain people have given the Internal

Revenue Service, here, and Inland Revenue in England, and the equivalent organizations in France, Italy, Germany, and Japan—they give rewards, you know, precisely to encourage such communications—have given them lists of certain large art transactions which, by their very nature, were not reported with absolute accuracy, if they were reported at all. You should have some interesting visitors soon, as will your associates.

BELM: You're not immune to this kind of harassment, you know.

BELM: Pembrooke, you are definitely panicking. Good. I am immune. I do not pay any more taxes than I have to; my consultants see to that. But I am not so foolish as to break the law; my attorney sees to that. And for the cherry on top, Pembrooke, I give you a minor matter, but an amusing one. I checked with my tax people: all that champagne and oysters? It's income. And you've not declared it. Not all that much per year, but you've been doing it for a long, long time. If you had eaten in the staff dining room regularly, anything you ate, even oysters and champagne, would have been passed over. But this was for you only; never even with a trustee or a donor, or even a lowly curator. Definitely not a business lunch. Taken together, it's enough to cause you considerable pain and problems. You may go now, Pembrooke, and contemplate your sins.

PEMB: Mr. Belmont, you may think you have won, but we are going to meet again, possibly under different circumstances. You, *I* assure *you*, do not know everything, as you will soon find out. Assuming you are still around.

BELM: My demise won't save you; others are ready to carry on. You are not universally beloved, dear boy. And wait, before you close the door, that cassette recorder in your pocket you may have been tempted to use against me, its tape has been wiped clean even as you passed through the door. Goodbye.

Mr. Belmont shut off the machine. He looked at me apologetically and said, "You can understand now, Mrs. Gold, why I was so unconcerned about your cassette recorder. If any of the information you just heard is of any use to you in your investigation, I will provide you with a transcript. Somewhat edited, of course."

"Your revenge on Pembrooke," I said, "seems too extreme. Overkill. After all, Mr. Belmont, you knew what he was when you hired him."

"Yes, Mrs. Gold, I did. And he did what he was designed to do, but he hurt too many people in doing it. What I did to him was not too extreme, it was exceedingly careful and complete. Pembrooke was very intelligent and resourceful, very powerful, well-connected at many levels, and completely unscrupulous. I had to make sure that every loophole was closed, that every nail available was driven fully into his coffin, so that the evil spirit might not rise again."

"So you want me to clear you of suspicion," Alexander said, "by finding the murderer of Orville Pembrooke?"

Mr. Belmont looked surprised. "Certainly not, Mr. Gold. I have no wish to find Pembrooke's killer. Why should I? In fact, I specifically request that you do not find him. I am not under suspicion; I was with you here when he was killed. If you have the slightest idea that I had him killed, put it out of your mind at once. I will tell you what I want you to do shortly. You will then decide whether or not you can do the job. Hanslik, I understand you have given AIK Inc., in the person of Mrs. Hanslik, a retainer?" Burton nodded. "And that Mr. Gold is here as an agent of AIK?" Burton nodded again. "Then all I have said to you today, and all you have heard, is privileged. If you cannot handle my work, or if you do not wish to, the retainer will pay you for your professional time and I will look elsewhere."

Mr. Belmont looked slowly around the room, stopping, assessing each of us in turn. "I hope I have intrigued you sufficiently," he said, "so that you will accept the challenge. I believe you have the talents, Mr. Gold, to solve my problem. But I do not want you wasting precious time on finding Pembrooke's killer."

It was no great pleasure to find I was right about Daniel Pereira Belmont. Of course, I was absolutely sure he wouldn't tell a lie, especially about something as important as having Orville Pembrooke killed, except in the service of a higher morality. I think those were the words he used. Murder is so very inelegant, is it not, Chumley? On the other hand, a custom-made solid silver oyster knife in the back of Pembooke's neck, with Pembrooke's own fingerprints on the handle—that's sort of elegant, isn't it? As I understand the word? I'd check the dictionary when we got home, then I'd know. Assuming, of course, that I really wanted to know. I think I'd rather not; Mr. Belmont might find it annoying.

# VIII

"If you don't want me to solve the Pembrooke murder," Alexander said, "what do you want me to do?"

"That will become clear shortly, Mr. Gold," Belmont said. "You see, I didn't delude myself that Pembrooke was finished. A lesser man might have been crushed and would certainly have left the field of combat, spending his time trying to salvage what he could from the ruins. Pembrooke, I was sure, would counterattack, but I did not know from which direction he would strike. His parting words were not just bravado. He seemed to know something. What happened then, Mr. Gold?"

"You've given me enough hints, Mr. Belmont, although you carefully buried them in seemingly aimless ramblings. I'll make an analysis, but I want something in exchange."

"Wasn't the retainer sufficient?"

"As a retainer, too much. But what I really want is for you to stop acting like a doddering old man who can't remember where he put his glasses and who *happens* to have friends who *happen* to find out things he *happens* to be interested in. Stop hiding, at least from me. I might get the idea you have something to hide."

"I do have things to hide, Mr. Gold. Many things. But

none, I assure you, which have any bearing on your assignment. I was not trying to mislead you as to my—capabilities; I assumed they would be obvious to you. It used to be, when I was younger, that I would have to, almost be forced to, act in a way which would not alarm the people I was working with. I am sure you have done the same. Today it is partly habit and partly real for me. I do look to the past a good deal; that was the time of my life when I was happy. And it gives me pleasure to play a role; one of the few pleasures left to me. Please forgive these minor lapses. I will be more forthright if that is all you want."

"I also want you to stop testing me," Alexander said. "If, by now, you don't know that I am the right man, tell me."

"Of course I'll stop," said the old man with a twinkle. "As soon as you stop testing yourself. Let us agree that you are here because there are some things you can do that I cannot."

"And, implicitly, vice-versa?" Alexander said. The old man spread his hands resignedly. "Very well then, Mr. Belmont, I'll complete the pattern. Pembrooke attacked you at your point of greatest vulnerability: your wife. There is a Vermeer for sale, one which has something to do with *Girl with a Pearl Earring*. Pembrooke controls the sale and is asking an exhorbitant price for it plus the lifting of all the pressures you have applied to him, otherwise the painting disappears into some palace in Saudi Arabia. You want the painting so badly that you are willing to pay the price and let Pembrooke off the hook, but you want to be sure that the painting is authentic. By all calculations, the painting should be a forgery. There is no provenance, but several experts, the ones you mentioned yesterday, are willing to certify that it is a Vermeer. Hannelore Becker, who, you alone know, is probably the definitive authority on Vermeer, says it is not a Vermeer. If it is a forgery, there is only one person in the world who could produce one which would fool these experts: Hannelore Becker. Hannelore Becker, having been hired by Dr. Ludwig, is not beholden to Pembrooke. For that reason, if no other, Pembrooke has been trying to get rid of her and she is fighting him. You have been protecting her, so it is highly unlikely that she would produce a forgery for Pembrooke to use against you. As you describe her, she would cut off her right arm rather than forge a Vermeer. So, if it is a forgery, who made it? And if she did it, why does she say it is a forgery? You have a limited time to make a decision: to buy or not to buy. Pembrooke's death has made life easier for you since you do not have to undo the events you started as his punishment and as a defense against his actions, but it has also complicated the transaction since you don't know whom to deal with. Pembrooke's heirs, if any, do not know of the existence of the painting or of Pembrooke's relationship to it. His agents, or whomever you have been dealing with, may now change the terms. You want me to find a way to assure you that the painting is genuine, because you dearly want it to be genuine, and you want me to find a method of insuring that the transaction will be consumated, to make sure that you do not end up with neither the painting nor the money.''

"That is a logical set of conclusions, Mr. Gold. It is not quite accurate, but it is close enough.''

"Where am I wrong?''

"Orville Pembrooke visited me two weeks after our little talk. As director of the Fine Arts, he had been offered first refusal for a limited time of a newly discovered Vermeer. Oil on wood panel, eight and one-half by seven and one-quarter inches; tentatively called *Girl in a Blue Kimono*.''

"Kimono?'' Pearl looked surprised.

"Oh, yes,'' Belmont said. "After Philip II closed all Spanish and Portuguese ports to Dutch ships, the Dutch merchants had to go to the Orient directly. So successful were they that there came a time when they were the only Europeans permitted to trade in Japan.''

"Was the blue kimono from that period?'' Alexander asked. "In Japan, I mean?''

"Yes, authentic. Everything else checked out too, all the scientific tests: X-ray fluorescence, X-ray, ultra violet, craquelure—that's the little lines made as the paint dries and cracks—everything. Even destructive testing.''

I really jumped at this. ''Are you serious?'' I asked.

He laughed. ''The painting wasn't . . . You take a tiny bit of paint, say two-tenths of a millimeter in diameter, from a background area, and a tiny bit of wood from the back of the panel, and test those. It all checked perfectly.''

''Scientific testing,'' Alexander said, ''doesn't guarantee authenticity. It can only prove something is not authentic.''

''That's well known in the art world, Mr. Gold. That's why I placed such store on the statement of the experts, Tabachnik, Vandermeis, Spieler, and Baliner. In art, the eye of the expert is far more important than anything else, assuming, of course, that the scientific tests show no problems.''

''What happened to Gröber-Something?'' I asked. ''The maven of all mavens?''

''Unfortunately, he is in Australia in the middle of a major assignment. He will be here three days from now, by chartered plane. However, that is getting ahead of the story. On May 16, 1696, a sale was held in Amsterdam which listed—one of the few written records we have that even mentions Vermeer by name—three paintings by Vermeer under the collective title *Portraits in Antique Costume*. Many believe that *Girl with a Red Hat* and *Young Girl with a Flute* were part of that group. A few experts think that *Young Girl with a Flute* was done by a contemporary of Vermeer's, but both Hannelore and I know it is authentic. The two have much in common. Both are tiny, fifty to sixty square inches in area. Both are on wood panels, the only times Vermeer used wood. Both are heads and busts of young women in costume, rather than in Dutch clothes. They are seated in chairs with carved lion-head finials. Both are wearing unusual hats. Both have relatively dark-colored figured backgrounds unlike most of his others, which posed the figure against a lighted wall. And both were probably made with the aid of a *camera obscura*.''

"What's a—?" Pearl asked.

"Like a big box view camera with a ground glass on the back," Alexander said impatiently. "Some artists used it to compose, to copy, to capture highlights. Let Mr. Belmont talk."

"This painting," Belmont went on, "had all the characteristics of the other two. If authentic, it had to be the missing third painting for *Portraits in Antique Costume*; it had to be the Third Vermeer. Then Pembrooke showed me a color photograph, full size, of *Girl in a Blue Kimono*. It was just as described. Head and bust of a young girl wearing a broad-brimmed yellow fur hat and a blue silk kimono, seated in an arm chair with lion-head finials, looking directly at the artist. The one thing he forgot to mention, deliberately, for shock value—and he succeeded, my heart almost stopped—was that the model was the *Girl with a Pearl Earring*. Helen. Evidently I didn't control myself and he saw—although I'm sure he knew anyway—no matter. He knew he had me; knew he had won."

"That's when he told you the price and terms?" I asked.

"I didn't mind the price. Actually, in constant dollars it was cheaper than the Met's *Aristotle Contemplating the Bust of Homer*. And, while I love Rembrandt, *Girl in a Blue Kimono* was by far the greater work of art. Much more important too, not just for me but for the world of art and the museum. The Fine Arts does not have a single Vermeer, not one, though our collection of Dutch Masters is the finest in the world. Actually, it was my fault. My grandfather always told me that when you win you should always leave the loser a way out, a way to save face."

"The Chinese have a saying," Alexander added, "'Take the rice but do not break the rice bowl.'"

"Yes, I should have left him the Swiss money." The old man stopped for a moment. "Maybe not. I doubt if he would have been any easier on me even if he had money. Pembrooke had a sadistic streak."

"What were the terms and conditions?" Alexander asked.

"The painting was offered exclusively to Pembrooke and the museum for a period of thirty days. The sale would be processed by the manager of a Zurich bank who dealt only with the owner's representative, a Liechtenstein attorney who had met the owner only once, and then in a dark café. At that time the owner gave him written instructions and a sealed envelope. The attorney was to give the proceeds of the sale to whomever presented him with the ten-number code which matched the one in the sealed envelope."

"Why not send your actor friend to the lawyer," I asked, "with any old code. Once the envelope was opened you could find out what the code was."

"If the wrong code was presented," Belmont explained, "the attorney was to turn over the money to some unsavory political groups. The same was to be done if the owner died."

"If the attorney didn't know who the owner was," I objected, "how would he know when he died?"

"Presumably, when Pembrooke's will is probated, there will be instructions to wire the Liechtenstein attorney a simple message, such as 'The owner of the painting is dead.'"

"And now that Pembrooke has been killed," I said, "the money goes to these fascists?"

"Or communists, terrorists, whatever," Alexander replied.

"Maybe one of them killed him," I said. "To get the money."

"Nobody knew about these provisions but the Liechtenstein attorney," Alexander said. "And a bomb would be more their style."

"But Pembrooke made a mistake," I said. "What would prevent Mr. Belmont from going to the attorney with a false code while Pembrooke was alive and making sure that

Pembrooke would lose all that money, even if these evil people got it?"

Mr. Belmont started to answer, but Alexander raised his hand and stopped him. "If that were done, Pembrooke would have no compunction about killing Mr. Belmont, burning all the Dutch Masters in the FAMONY, or something equally horrible to have his revenge on Mr. Belmont." He looked at our host.

Mr. Belmont nodded. "Or something worse. He would have no reason to hold back."

Alexander addressed Mr. Belmont again. "You were talking about the owner of the painting, then you started calling him 'Pembrooke.' I take it that the mysterious owner was tall and slim, had a shaven head and a small moustache, a bow tie, tinted glasses, and spoke German with an American accent?"

"However did you guess, Mr. Gold?"

"Wouldn't it be an automatic reflex for Pembrooke to change the code in his Basel bank in the same way he did in Zurich, using the sealed envelope technique so you could not get that code again?"

"This is exactly what happened the day after my little talk with Pembrooke."

"Why did the Liechtenstein attorney tell you all this?"

"To show us that he did not know who the owner was, that he would not tell us even if he did, and that he had no authority to make the slightest change in the terms or conditions."

"Why such an elaborate procedure," I asked, "for a simple thing like the sale of a painting?"

"Pembrooke respected my abilities and resources, and wanted to make sure I could not thwart him in any way. Also, I think, he wanted to show he could best me. He did not suffer defeat lightly."

"Did he expect you to buy such an expensive painting just from a photo?" Pearl asked.

"Up to four recognized experts would be allowed to inspect the painting in the bank's vault in the presence of the bank manager. Any non-destructive portable equipment could be used. No provenance would be given.''

"What happened at the end of the thirty-day period?" I asked.

"The entire price in gold, at that day's London market, had to be deposited in the Zurich bank, in escrow. If not, the owner's representative would sell the painting to, presumably, a wealthy Arab. If the deposit were made, the Swiss bank would issue an unvalidated draft to a specified Liechtenstein bank to the order of the owner's representative on account of the owner, for the total sales price less fees. This draft would be validated automatically in forty-five days unless otherwise instructed by the Zurich bank in writing.''

"Sounds like a very careful planner," I said. "When did the museum get the painting?"

"After the gold was deposited in the Zurich bank, the bank manager and the Liechtenstein attorney would get releases and transfer the painting to the museum's representative. The museum would then be responsible for insurance, transportation, security and so forth. We had forty-five days to examine the painting, make our own tests, and so forth. If the painting was shown to be a forgery by a recognized expert, it could be returned to the Zurich bank. If it was returned within the forty-five-day period, there would be a full refund, less fees. If the painting was lost, stolen, damaged in any way, or not returned in time, 5:00 P.M. Swiss time, on the forty-fifth day, the transaction was completed and the money gone without recourse.''

"How much time is left before the deadline?" Alexander asked.

"Oh, that passed a week ago, Mr. Gold," Belmont said calmly.

Alexander turned red. "Then what am I doing here?" he asked, very softly and politely. I got ready to step in, fast.

"Ah, youth, youth," Belmont said. Alexander will be fifty this May. "So impatient. I'm not playing games with you,

Mr. Gold. I'm trying to tell you the whole story in sequence, but your mind jumps ahead very quickly."

"Go ahead, Mr. Belmont," Alexander said. "Tell it your own way. I presume you investigated a bit and know the name of the Liechtenstein bank?"

"I would have been remiss in my duty if I had not. But that is irrelevant; the transaction is completed and the money is gone. I do not renege on a business deal. A week ago we were sure the painting was genuine; we accepted the price and the terms."

"What made the change in your opinion?"

"It's not necessarily a change, yet. Just a precaution. Hannelore Becker was cleaning the painting and she said she found evidence that, to her, indicated the painting was not what it should be, as she put it."

"You bought a painting that was so dirty that you could not see evidence of forgery?" I asked.

"No, no, Mrs. Gold. The dirt had been carefully removed before the experts ever saw the painting. What Hannele was doing was removing the yellowed varnish and repairing the warped wood and things like that. Normal conservator's work. And very carefully. In fact, when she first saw it, she was as thrilled as I was; even she was sure it was a Vermeer. She actually said so, at first look."

"And now she's changed her mind?"

"After the varnish was removed, she said that there were things she saw in it that were not painted by Vermeer. She tried to show them to me, but I could not see anything wrong. That's why we're waiting for Gröber-Eisenberg."

"You seem very unconcerned about ten million dollars of the museum's money, Mr. Belmont," I said. "Don't you have certain responsibilities as the chairman of the Board of Trustees?"

"I'm sorry, Mr. Gold, but I have to test you again. No museum can act as fast as this Vermeer's unknown owner required. The Board of Trustees spends a month in assessing a million-dollar acquisition with full provenance. Major museums generally buy on a six-month return basis if anything is found wrong during that period. The Fine Arts has no painting by Vermeer, the greatest painter, in my humble opinion, of our specialty period. Nor is it ever likely to get a chance to purchase one again. The painting is almost certainly genuine, but there are still more tests we can do and still more experts to call in. The analysis and the testing, the evaluation of the opinions, all this takes months. The painting has a strong emotional significance for me. What do I do, Mr. Gold?''

"Put that simply, Mr. Belmont, I would apologize for my wife's question." He never in his life apologized for his own. "You bought the painting with your own money with the intention of donating it to the Fine Arts. Although I am sure it did not escape you that Uncle Sam was your partner. After tax deductions the painting cost you only—please excuse the only—only three million.''

"Exactly. Of course, I allowed no publicity. I did not wish to become known as the ten-million-dollar fool if I had made a mistake.''

"And just as important," Alexander said, smiling nastily, "if it is not genuine, you cannot take a ten-million tax deduction.''

"That had crossed my mind, Mr. Gold. But I assure you that it is more important that the museum not be held up to ridicule. Look how much trouble the Met had with that Etruscan horse. And there is still controversy over the de la Tour *Fortune Teller*.''

"I assume, Mr. Belmont, that at the same time you were checking into the Liechtenstein bank, you also managed to look into the origin of *Girl in a Blue Kimono*.''

"It pays to be thorough, though this was a little more difficult. I could not ask too many questions in one place; my friends are not fools, you know. And some areas are more difficult to work in than others. But I did manage to put together a fairly clear picture.''

"I take it you have obtained point information and have filled in the story with high-probability assumptions."

"I got information in bits and pieces from friends and business associates, and other sources in Europe and Russia. It was far from complete, but it did make sense. There is a good deal of conjecture involved, naturally, but nothing far-fetched. Even if it's wrong in some particulars, I've found sufficient corroboration from diverse sources to know that, in general, the story is reasonably accurate."

"Could wishful thinking have warped your judgment?" Alexander asked.

"Judge for yourself, Mr. Gold." He cleared his throat. "This dirty little wooden portrait, just the right size for a souvenir, was stolen from some Dutch farmer's house in the first days of the Nazi invasion by a soldier who slipped it into his knapsack. When the soldier was killed, an ignorantly zealous security man set the picture aside for Herman Goering, who wanted to acquire, personally, all the artwork in Europe. The painting went into a packing crate to one of Goering's treasure caches, unnoticed among the bigger, more spectacular works. The Russians captured the warehouse and shipped the crate to the Tretjakov Museum in Moscow. Since Stalin and Hitler between them had killed most of the competent curators of Europe, the little wooden panel gathered dust in the museum's storeroom.

"Last year a young art lover, working as a janitor because the State had decided that it had enough curators, found the painting, recognized it for what it was, and trying to use it as a stepping stone to a better job, reported it, not to a curator, but to a KGB officer. For the same reason this officer bypassed his immediate superior and got the message to a KGB general. The general, recently widowed, saw the painting as a passport to a new life in the decadent West. After the young art lover and the KGB officer died in widely separated accidents, the general took the painting personally to Split, where he arranged to have the little sealed package shipped by the usual KGB routes to

Zurich. There it went into a Swiss bank; not the one he kept his mad money in.

"An Italian art historian was secretly brought in from Rome to examine the painting in the bank's vault in the presence of a bank officer. Based on this limited inspection, the expert stated that the painting was probably genuine.

"This was enough for the general. Coincidentally, a terrorist attack at the Fiumicino Airport in Rome managed to kill the art historian the next day. Far from Zurich."

"Why did he give the Fine Arts a thirty-day option free?" Pearl asked.

"He didn't," Alexander growled. "The rest is obvious."

"Correct," Belmont agreed. "Orville Marston Pembrooke's reputation by now having reached the Urals, a sealed envelope containing a Polaroid photo and a short note was delivered to him in the UN dining room. The deal was similar to the one offered to us, the only difference being that the gold was to be in Krugerrands and Maple Leafs, and the price to the museum was four million. There was only one problem with this from Pembrooke's point of view: he could not make any money for himself from this kind of transaction.

"The problem was easily solved. Pembrooke would buy the painting himself and then sell it to himself as the director of the museum, for ten million. A tidy little profit, and, at the same time, dotting my eye. However, just as he was about to close the deal, I had my little talk with him and had cut him off from his money. He had very little time left before the general got upset and sold the painting elsewhere, and, under this time pressure, did something quite foolish, although, to be honest, he didn't have much choice. He knew the certain people who always had four million laying around for just this sort of sure-fire cash deal and who were not too concerned with legalities. I am sure that they were particularly entranced with the beauty of a proposition where one protagonist apparently controlled both sides of the deal. I say 'apparently' because Pembrooke, I am sure, did not disclose to them his recent fall from power. This might have been dangerous for Pembrooke, but he was sure that I would knuckle under, and he was right. What he did not realize in his anxiety to regain all he had lost, and more, was what a vulnerable position he was in."

"Vulnerable?" Pearl said. "It seems to me he had everything and everyone under his control, including you, Mr. Belmont."

"Look at it this way, Pearl," said Alexander patiently. "The four million the general got was gone with the general. Eugene, would you say, Mr. Belmont?"

"Interesting, Mr. Gold. Most people would have said Windsor, Winnepeg, or Vancouver. A smaller number might have chosen Detroit, Sault Sainte Marie, or Seattle. Actually I didn't bother following up the general. It wasn't my money he had and it was sure to be very dangerous. But why Eugene?"

"New York is too close to the UN; too easy to meet someone who might know the general. Same for Washington. A university town would not find a foreign accent unusual. The Mexican border is too easy to cross and its government calls itself revolutionary. If the KGB came looking for him, Southern Canada would be the first place to look; after that, the American cities bordering Canada. Eugene, Oregon, is within driving distance of the Canadian border, and also not far from that other foreign state where strangeness is not strange: California. The Pacific is quite close, if you want to take a sea voyage, or a plane to faraway places. It was obvious."

I hate when Alexander says "obvious" and it is, but in front of Belmont, I didn't scream. Alexander continued, "Pembrooke had invested four million dollars of money which was not his on the assumption that he could force the Fine Arts, through Mr. Belmont, to buy the Vermeer. But what would he have done if, on the forty-fourth day, the museum had returned the painting to the Zurich bank stating publicly that it was a forgery and taken the money back? Actually, it would have been easier than that, since Mr. Belmont put up the money. All he had to do was to buy an expert, and there are some I am sure who would be amenable to such suggestion, who would state that he would not certify this painting because of doubtful authenticity. In fact, Mr. Belmont said before that there are still some experts who claim that several generally accepted Vermeers are not authentic, so this expert could do his job with a clear conscience. No museum, no collector, no one, likes to be taken for a fool. Pembrooke couldn't have sold that painting for four cents after that. His associates, the ones who advanced him four million dollars on his assurance that this was a sure thing, would have had a few words with him; his body would never have been found.''

Pearl turned pale. "I never thought of that. But then Mr. Belmont wouldn't have gotten the painting he wanted.''

"Sure he would," Alexander replied. "Two weeks after Pembrooke disappeared, Mr. Belmont could have announced that another expert, three experts if necessary, had convinced him that the painting was authentic and he was willing to close the deal. Who would have objected? Pembrooke's ex-partners, or rather ex-Pembrooke's partners, who now got the whole pie? I doubt it.''

"That little ploy had crossed my mind, Mr. Gold, but I decided against it. If I attacked Pembrooke again, who knows what the consequences would have been. I didn't want to take the risk of losing my Vermeer. So I just went through the deal as agreed. Let Pembrooke have his fund for retirement in Switzerland; I would find a way to eliminate his influence from the museum.''

"Why did you call us in, then, Mr. Belmont?" I asked. "You seem to have everything under control.''

"Three days ago Hannelore Becker told me she found things on the painting she was certain Vermeer didn't do: the pearls, the ear, the *pointillés*—"

"What are *pointillés*?" I asked.

"They're the little dots of light that are reflected off

shiny convex surfaces, such as the lion-head finials on the chair.''

"And these little details are enough to cast doubt on a painting that experts say is real?''

"Painters may change their style, but the technique usually stays the same. And Hannelore knows more about Vermeer than all the experts put together.''

"But she herself said it was genuine at first.''

"You must remember its condition. She's been cleaning it ever since she got it, and she now says there is strong evidence it's a forgery. Other background work looks dubious, too.''

"This long to clean a tiny painting like that?''

"She works very carefully, Mrs. Gold. Each square inch is insured for two hundred thousand dollars. Better safe than sorry.''

"Why did Pembrooke pass up the opportunity to make a big deal at its arrival?'' Pearl asked. "Big ceremonies, TV, publicity?''

"He was furious when I didn't allow it, but after all, it was my painting still. I told him that if a single word leaked out I would ship it back to Switzerland at once, publicly, as a fake. He got the message.''

"So when Gröber-Eisenberg arrives,'' Pearl said, "you will know for sure if the painting is genuine or not.''

"Not quite,'' Alexander said. "If Gröber-Eisenberg says it is a fake, then it's a fake. But if he says it's real, Mr. Belmont has to decide whether Gröber-Eisenberg is right or Hannelore Becker is right. That's where I come in. I have to tell Mr. Belmont which one is right.''

"Not quite, Mr. Gold. If there is a disagreement, I will make the decision, not you. I want you to get me more information, if you can, but most important, I want you to look at the problem from angles different from mine; from your own individual viewpoint. You may see something I do not merely because you are not an art expert but are an expert puzzle solver. And I do want you to solve this puzzle."

"You mean that if it's a forgery so good that Gröber-Eisenberg accepts it, who could have done it other than Hannelore Becker? And if she did make the forgery, why is she now saying it is a forgery? And how did she arrange to build up the history your friends gave you? And if some associate of hers could have planted the painting in the Tretjakov cellar, how could that person make sure each participant would play his role exactly as he did? And to what profit? And if there is, on this earth, another forger as good as Becker, why only this one painting? And why now? Why start with Vermeer rather than an easier painter to copy? And why the one picture on earth that would make Mr. Belmont part with ten million on a hope? And how does that forger profit? And—?"

"Stop, Mr. Gold. You have the idea. Do you want the commission?"

"I am troubled by your insistence," Alexander said slowly and carefully, "that there is no connection between the forgery problem and the murder of Pembrooke. What is the name of the murderer, Mr. Belmont?"

Mr. Belmont flushed. "Is that the only way to satisfy you that the two problems are not connected?"

"Show me another way, Mr. Belmont. I'm not rigid."

Belmont thought for a moment, then said, "Let's put the murder problem aside for a while and attack the simpler problem. Can we strike a mutually acceptable agreement for the forgery solution?"

"Certainly, Mr. Belmont. I will undertake to determine whether the *Girl in a Blue Kimono* is real or not for ten percent."

"Ten percent? Of what?"

"The purchase price. Ten percent of ten million dollars."

"That's a lot of money, Mr. Gold."

"What percentage do you tip a waiter, Mr. Belmont?"

Belmont thought for a moment, then said, "Who will decide if your determination is accurate?"

"You will."

"I alone?"

"You alone. Or your estate. If you either keep the painting or donate it to the museum after I advise you it is authentic, or if you discard the painting or sell it for very little to an arms-length purchaser after I advise you it is a forgery, you have accepted my evaluation and I get paid. Anything else, and I have earned no fee."

"What time limit?"

"I will give you my determination, and the reason for that determination, within ten days after Gröber-Eisenberg gives his considered professional opinion in writing to both of us in front of Burt Hanslik and a video camera."

"It must be no later than 11:00 P.M., six days from today."

"But Gröber-Eisenberg won't be here for three days. That's unreasonable. Why?"

"The scientific tests were mailed to him weeks ago, as were full-size and even enlarged photographs, the kind Becker takes, in all kinds of lighting, so he has had ample opportunity to do his homework on the routine examinations. He says all he needs is to see the cleaned painting for one day or less. I must tell you that he believes, as of now, that the painting is by Vermeer. That's why I called you in."

"Did Becker take the pictures you sent him?"

"Do you take me for a child? They were taken by a professional photographer who didn't know what he was photographing, and were processed in his own lab. I have all the negatives and all the prints."

"Give me a full-size photo taken with straight-on lighting so I know what I'm talking about. You didn't explain why there is such a rush. You've already paid for the painting."

"This is completely off the record. Ever since I first

heard of the Third Vermeer—even Pembrooke didn't know this, or Wechsler—I retained Alan Davidoff, the president of the finest art exhibition-coordination company in the business, to work full-time on one project. When all was ready, the Fine Arts would take the position of lead museum, in cooperation with the Mauritshuis or the Amsterdam Rijksmuseum, on the greatest exhibition ever conceived: the complete works of one painter, Vermeer. We already have interest in financing the project expressed by a big Dutch oil company provided that the Dutch government acts as a sponsor. An audience has been arranged for Davidoff in The Hague for 10:00 A.M., their time, seven days from now. He will be waiting for a call from me to tell him that he can announce the existence of the Third Vermeer, which will floor the Queen, guarantee the sponsorship of The Netherlands, and make this the biggest news item of all time in the art world. If this opportunity is lost, it may take six months or longer to arrange another audience. After that, it will take two or three years to complete all the arrangements before the exhibition opens. I am eighty years old, Mr. Gold; every day is precious to me. I would like very much to be at the Mauritshuis on the opening day of this exhibition."

"By your reckoning I should have until 4:00 A.M. on the seventh day, not 11:00 P.M. on the sixth. There is only a six-hour difference between New York and The Hague. Or, if you want to give Davidoff a full hour to get to the Palace, make it 3:00 A.M."

"I need the five extra hours to implement another approach to the problem if you fail."

"If I fail, Mr. Belmont, no one could do the job, and the extra few hours won't help. But I'll accept the time limit. It's a deal."

"Do you also agree not to investigate the murder of Orville Pembrooke?"

"Mr. Belmont," Alexander said in measured tones, "you're afraid that I will find the murderer."

"Of course I am, Mr. Gold. It has to be one of the

senior executives. The museum needs all of its people now. I never intended to let anyone go precipitously, even Pembrooke's closest allies. A slow process is better, especially now that Pembrooke is gone. We might even keep some of them; they're all very competent, and several, I'm sure, would like to work with Wechsler, if they're allowed to.''

"You're afraid that Harold Wechsler is the killer.''

"Pembrooke was particularly nasty to him. It took all my persuasion to make Wechsler stay. I gave him my word that he would be director when Pembrooke left.''

"He's also in the best position, geographically, to be the killer.''

"I'm aware of that, Mr. Gold. And he is, by far, the smartest man in the museum; the one most likely to have figured out how to commit this apparently impossible crime. If he killed Pembrooke, I will do my best, everything I legally can, to see that he gets away with it. Pembrooke deserved to be murdered, you know.''

"Does that include not retaining me if I refuse to lay off the murder?''

"I am depending on you, Mr. Gold, to solve that little difference between us.''

"How about this, Mr. Belmont? I give you my word that I concentrate on the painting and investigate the murder only where it intersects with my work on the painting.''

"Are you certain, Mr. Gold, that the two crimes are connected?''

"Yes. So are you, otherwise you would agree.''

"What I am certain of, Mr. Gold, is that you are trying to provoke me into retaining you to investigate the murder. Try Column B, Mr. Gold.''

"I'm trying to persuade you, Mr. Belmont, that it is in your interest to retain me to solve both puzzles. I offer my services to the museum gratis, in return for everyone's cooperation in the murder investigation, and look into the painting problem only as it impinges on my work on the murder.''

"I'm afraid that's even worse, Mr. Gold."

"I'll put this offer into the newspapers. You'll find it hard to refuse."

"I wouldn't think of refusing so generous an offer, Mr. Gold. But it takes so long to convene a meeting of the board . . . and to come to a decision. . . . Do you have a Column C?"

"You would like it even less, Mr. Belmont. That's where I do my investigation as a public-spirited citizen, not responsible to anyone, and treating everyone connected with the museum as an adversary. Including you."

"You're really fascinated with this problem, aren't you, Mr. Gold? So fascinated that you would solve both problems for nothing, wouldn't you?"

"You spent a lot of time fascinating me, Mr. Belmont, and you succeeded very well. Yes, I would investigate both problems without a fee. It's really one problem I am sure, the most complex I've ever come across."

"Go ahead, then, Column A it is. At least I have some measure of control that way. I do trust your word that you will not look into the murder except where it may be part of the painting forgery problem. And, as you said, no fee. Agreed?"

"Agreed. I investigate the painting and try to avoid the murder. And, of course, at no fee, I am not obligated to tell you the solution to either."

Mr. Belmont studied Alexander for a moment, then laughed. "You'd never have been able to keep it to yourself. All right, Mr. Gold, you win. Column A with a million-dollar fee if you meet the deadline. Hanslik will write the agreement. You solve the forgery problem; my actions to determine if you've succeeded."

"It must include complete cooperation from the museum staff. And from you."

"It will. But I reserve the right to try to get the forgery solution from you without a fee, that is, to delay you one minute past the deadline. It won't hurt my plans, but it will teach you respect for my gray hairs. And it's not for the money, I'll give twice that to charity, but because—it may sound callous with a man dead—but I haven't had so much fun in years, jousting with you. If I were ten years younger you'd never have been able to twist my tail like this."

"I've learned a few things from you too, Sir. Is chess too easy for you?"

"Not too easy, too limited. I like this better."

"One more question, Mr. Belmont. You kept close tabs on Pembrooke. Did he have atherosclerosis?"

"Well, at that age, we all have some hardening of the arteries, to some extent. He suffered a very slight stroke two years ago. Didn't even know he had it; it was caught by the doctor at our required annual examination. As far as I know, it didn't bother him and didn't leave any visible effects. Why?"

"Just a passing thought. Are you an accurate reporter?"

"I'm not sure I know what you mean by that."

"Someone calls you up and says, 'He said he will be at the café at exactly 12:00 P.M.' I ask you what the message is. Would you say, 'He said he'd meet me at midnight at the restaurant'?"

"Of course not. I would repeat the message verbatim. And so would anyone I work with; I insist on it. Most people edit or transpose messages; that was one of the problems I had with my old attorneys. They used to put what they thought I should have said into contracts and leases instead of what I had actually agreed to, word for word."

"So everything you told me which you heard from other people is reported accurately."

"I guarantee that, Mr. Gold. And so is what they told me."

"That's good to know. Then before I leave, since you like games so much, I'll offer you another amusement. I'll bet you one hundred thousand to your million that you will not only have to pay me the million for determining whether the painting is authentic or not, but that you will *beg* to pay me a fee of *another* million for solving a problem you aren't even thinking of now.''

"Related to the painting, or the murder?"

"Both."

"Mr. Gold, you're on. I don't need your money, but the pleasure of taking it from an arrogant young pup like you is worth the risk. Part of the bet is to give me a copy of your cancelled check to hang on my wall, next to the Vermeers. No one has *ever* heard me beg before, in my life. If you can make me *beg* you, Mr. Gold, beg to pay you a fee of one million dollars to solve a problem I don't even know exists, then you have earned another million dollars." He smiled like an old gray wolf.

Alexander stood up as if to leave. Then, in apparent afterthought, he turned to Belmont and said, "You kept the Third Vermeer secret, didn't you?"

"Only Pembrooke, Hannelore, and I knew about it. If it turned out to be a forgery, I didn't want anyone else to know."

"Where is Miss Becker cleaning it? Her home?"

"God forbid I should risk that treasure in her neighborhood. No, it's in her room in the museum. She always keeps it locked anyway and never allows anyone in, so there's nothing to arouse the suspicions of the other conservators."

"Is that safe?"

"There's a security guard with a registrar's sheet at the entrance to the conservators' area. No strangers are allowed. There are tens of millions worth of paintings there on any normal day."

"Good. Will you please have Wechsler arrange appointments for me, about an hour maximum each, with all the top executives of the museum, the ones in the North Wing on the corridor leading to Pembrooke's dining room."

"We distinctly agreed, Mr. Gold, that you were to investigate the painting, not the murder."

"Of course, Mr. Belmont. I only put it that way for convenience. Let Wechsler select the order of the meetings, including his own meeting with me. I don't know enough at this stage to decide whom to see first. Why don't you come along, Mr. Belmont? You could then be certain that I am not investigating the Pembrooke murder unnecessarily."

"I have already accepted your word, Mr. Gold. And I have already trusted you with information no one else, not even Hanslik, has heard before today."

"Please come, Mr. Belmont. You might find it amusing." Alexander had that teasing tone in his voice, the one he used when, in a political discussion, his opponent had just propounded an unusually stupid idea. I hoped Belmont wouldn't pick it up. I should have known better.

"I sometimes find it *interesting*, Gold, to stop in front of a building excavation to watch experts at work, but I rarely find it *amusing*."

"Then visualize this, Mr. Belmont: I meet with Harold Wechsler and say, 'Mr. Wechsler, if there were a work of art in the museum which you don't know exists, and which I cannot tell you about, which may or may not be a forgery, and it is important to know this very quickly, would you give me your opinion as to its authenticity?' Surely, Mr. Belmont, you would find my difficulties amusing. And Harold Wechsler's face when I asked this question? Side-splitting. As for the chief curator? I am sure even he might find it funny."

Mr. Belmont glared at Alexander, then his face softened a bit. Not much. "Very well, Gold, nothing, it seems, will stop you from investigating the Pembrooke murder. You have made your point. You are hereby authorized to appear to be, I repeat, to *appear* to be investigating the murder, but you are really to concentrate on the authenticity of the painting."

"Thank you, Mr. Belmont. I knew you would see it my way once it was explained to you." Alexander didn't know when to stop. As usual.

"It is now clear to me," Belmont said, "that you think, in spite of my assurance to the contrary, that I don't want you to investigate the Pembrooke killing in order to protect myself; that in spite of, or even perhaps because of, my presence here with you at the time Pembrooke was killed, I am involved with, and might even have ordered, his murder. And when I am finally brought to justice I will beg you—those were your exact words, were they not?—beg you to accept another million from me to exonerate me, thus increasing your already exhorbitant fee by two more million.''

"That is a possibility, Mr. Belmont.''

"Then, Mr. Gold, you have not understood what I have shown you today. Tell me, if you were playing chess, and were losing, would you kill your opponent to insure that you would win? Of course not; it would spoil the game. Such a win would not give you any pleasure, any feeling of victory. Would you not prefer to lose to a better player than to win by this means? Well, so would I, Mr. Gold. So would I.''

"At this stage, Mr. Belmont, I cannot exclude anyone. I know too little. I do know that, given enough incentive, enough pressure, people may do things which are completely out of character for them. I would kill for the sake of my wife, for instance. You would have, too.''

Belmont smiled calmly, too calmly. "Gold, it will give me great pleasure to receive your solution to the forgery problem a minute too late—you will never be able to keep it to yourself, will you, driven as you are to show the world, and especially yourself, how very clever you are—and thus avoid paying you a penny of fee for that. And it will be my even greater pleasure to take your hundred thousand dollars; it may teach you humility. I have lost many battles, Gold, but I have never lost a war.''

Alexander, Pearl, and I left. Burton stayed behind, promising to bring the police reports over right after supper.

So Alexander had done it again. Not satisfied with taking on the most complicated puzzle of his career, where an impossible murder was only the side dish to the main course of determining if a painting, which should have been a forgery but almost certainly wasn't, is really a forgery as claimed by the only person in the world capable of producing such a perfect forgery. All this in a field where Alexander is, at best, only a looker. With a time limit so that even if he comes up with the right answer we get nothing if the bulb lights up too late.

And as if that were not enough, my brilliant husband deliberately—I was watching, I know—deliberately goaded the smartest man I ever met—Alexander is extraordinarily intelligent, but not very bright, as witness that stupid bet—deliberately goaded the smartest, most dangerous man I ever met, a man who has plenty of time and nothing better to do with it than to play stupid games with my husband; a man who has plenty of money and lots of friends to put obstacles in Alexander's path—has bet this combination of Fu Manchu and Professor Moriarty that he, Alexander, could make him beg—did you get that "beg" part?—beg Alexander to pay Alexander a million dollars, make that two million, one for the fee and one for the bet, for doing something which—what it is nobody knows—which is related to *both* the is-it-forged-or-not painting and the impossible murder, which murder the very-smart Mr. Belmont assures us is not related to the painting and even if it is he does not want the murderer caught—and has cleverly set the terms of the first deal, on which all other bets hinge, so that the honorable (maybe) Mr. Belmont has it in his sole, repeat, sole power to decide if Alexander has correctly determined if the painting is authentic or not and Alexander has, in addition, sworn not to investigate the murder except as it connects to the forgery—Alexander keeps his word; Belmont? who knows?—and has further made it worthwhile financially for Mr. Belmont to bend the rules a bit, if necessary—money in lumps, say a million and up, interests even rich people—and has given wily old Daniel Pereira Belmont an additional incentive to fool around, as if more were needed, by challenging this very rich, very smart, very ruthless old man to a duel, so to speak, *mano a mano*.

Fortunately, the most we could lose this time was one

hundred thousand dollars. God, did I say that? If my poor mother could hear me talk like that, she would *plotz* in no trump. One learns, very quickly, to breathe in the higher altitudes, but I still feel guilty about having lots of money. So, hold on to your hats, boys, Alexander the Great rides again! Now I know how Bucephalus, his horse, felt.

# IX

"Not stabbed in the neck?" Alexander looked incredulous. "How could you mess up something that simple, Burt?"

We were sitting around my kitchen table drinking tea with *malyines*, the tiny dried raspberries you can still get in a real apothecary shop of which New York has maybe two left, tops. On account of the weather. Amateurs push chicken soup when it snows, but it takes a real maven to even know from *malyines*. Chicken soup, even from a kosher chicken, a) is not for social drinking, b) is a broad-spectrum antibiotic which lacks the potency of a specific magic potion, and c) is therapeutic, which means you have to get sick first for it to work. *Malyines* on the other hand, one heaping teaspoonful in a glass (not a cup because there is a threshold effect: six ounces irritates a microbe; eight ounces ruins him; besides china absorbs the secret active ingredient) in a glass of tea (only Swe-Touch-Ne; Earl Gray is thrown-out money), drunk properly (a *half*-lump of sugar held between the front teeth, the tea *sucked* through it to distribute the wonderbrew evenly throughout the upper respiratory tract; also breaking the lumps is good exercise, although I have to do Pearl's) is the absolutely perfect prophylactic to protect you from catching sore throat if you are so foolish as to step outdoors on a damp day without, God forbid, wearing your rubbers.

"I didn't make a mistake, Alec," Burton said, "that's how the police reported it. The medical examiner was just more specific. The oyster knife entered between the atlas and the occiput, so where would you say he had been stabbed?"

"What's the atlas and the oxy-whatever?" Pearl asked.

"The occiput is the back part of the skull," Alexander answered. "The atlas is the first cervical vertebra."

"Detective stories?" I asked.

"Whodunits," he replied with a shrug. "Where else?"

"I get it," Pearl said. "It's called the atlas because it supports the skull like Atlas supported the Earth."

"I suppose so," Burton said. "The knife was driven in with terrific force; chipped part of the posterior arch of the atlas and part of the occcipital bone before it entered the medulla oblongata, the lowest part of the brain which is the nerve center where the spinal cord connects. Death was instantaneous."

"Just like pithing a frog," Pearl said. "I had to do that in Biology. Yuch."

"Find your oyster knife, Norma," Alexander said.

"I knew you would want it, so I already did, Sire." I put the little knife on the table.

Alexander took out the little architect's scale he always carries and began measuring. "Cylindrical handle one inch in diameter at the blade end, one-sixteenth inch less at the other end, three and three-quarters inches long with a slight concave curvature to provide a grip for prying. Blade two and one-half inches long by nine-sixteenths inches wide, one-sixteenth-inch thick, flat on one side, with the other side ground off in a curve to each edge. Tip angled upward toward the flat side; edges and tip are not sharp. Not quite the ideal instrument for stabbing."

"Well, it was handy," Burton said, "and Pembrooke's knife was longer, wider, and thicker, as I told you."

"Handy?" Alexander asked sarcastically. "Are you suggesting this was a sudden crime of passion?"

"That's what the police think," Burton replied. "After all, if you plan to stab someone in a private room, no one around to see you, why not bring in your own knife? A long, sharp, pointed knife that can fit into your breast pocket or your sleeve? Pembrooke's room was easy to get into and out of. The only worry was being seen, and with everyone at lunch that was no big problem."

"Was everyone at lunch when he was killed?" Alexander asked.

"More or less," Burton said. "The time of death can't be pinpointed within seconds, you know. The executives and the conservators entered and left the dining room at one- or two-minute intervals."

"Why do you say executives and conservators, Burt? Just because they are both in the North Wing?"

"If a junior executive or a curator or a preservator left the dining room by the north door it would have been so unusual as to have been noticed."

"What's wrong with the killer leaving by the south door and walking along the corridor to Pembrooke's room?"

"It's about one hundred fifty feet from door to door. He could be seen going the wrong way for at least half a minute."

"So? If it was a crime of passion, he didn't know he was going to kill Pembrooke."

"No one is supposed to disturb Pembrooke during his lunch period."

"If anyone saw the killer going up that corridor, Burt, he could always just keep going and say he was going to see the chief curator."

"The chief curator was in the dining room."

"So he was going to drop off a package or something. No, I won't rule out anyone at this stage, junior or senior. And why would anyone want to disturb Pembrooke at lunch? Whatever he wanted that couldn't wait, he would not get Pembrooke's approval this way.''

"How about something that couldn't go through normal channels, Alexander?" I asked. "An assistant curator discovers his boss is stealing, or her boss has made her pregnant, or whatever goes on in a museum?"

"Even if it can't go through channels, is this junior curator going to ruin his chances for getting what he wants by interrupting Pembrooke at lunch, or is he going to find a better way? I'm not saying it couldn't have been a junior, but the act-of-sudden-passion killing is ridiculous. Try this scenario: Junior walks into Pembrooke's room just as Pembrooke— Burt, did the police lab determine if Pembrooke had worn the glove?"

"He had not only worn it but had picked up an oyster with it.''

"Okay. Junior walks in and finds Pembrooke with an oyster in one hand and the knife in the other. Pembrooke looks up and tells him he's fired. This so enrages Junior that he walks around the table to Pembrooke's left side, wrenches the knife out of Pembrooke's hand and—''

"Wait a minute, Alexander," I protested. "Couldn't Pembrooke have put down the knife first?"

"It's unlikely but possible, so I'll accept it for the moment. Burt, did Pembrooke take off the glove himself?"

"Yes. There were traces of salt found on his left hand and on the left-side napkin, which had been used.''

"Okay. Pembrooke carefully puts down the knife, removes his glove, wipes his left hand, and then tells Junior he's fired. Junior walks around the table and picks up the knife, while Pembrooke, seeing an angry Junior approaching, does not pick up the knife to defend himself, and—''

"Obviously," I said, "Pembrooke knew well whoever came in and did not think that person would kill him. That's why he put down the oyster and took off his glove. Then they talked. Pembrooke said or did something that upset her and she killed him.''

"You're still thinking of people killing each other over pregnancy in this enlightened age, Norma?''

"By me, Alexander, passion is passion.''

"Okay, we'll go that way. Junior walks in, highly pregnant. I'll make it even better, pregnant by Pembrooke. That's why he doesn't fire her on the spot and stops eating so he can tell her his mother objects to his marrying a lowly assistant curator but that he will contribute to the abortion. This so enrages her, she is already standing on Pembrooke's left, the natural position because of the way the door swings, that she stabs him in the medulla oblongata. Several little problems: One, she had better be a big strong girl to stab him there, to go through two pieces of bone and some very tough ligaments. Two, she had better be very lucky to have grabbed the knife at exactly the right angle so the flat blade could slip between the atlas and the skull. Three—''

"When people are emotionally upset, Alex, they can perform tremendous feats of strength. Like the little woman who lifted a car off her son.''

"I'll believe that when I see it, Pearl, but let it go for the moment. Third, she had better be very smart, to stab Pembrooke, wipe off the fingerprints, and then find a way to get his fingerprints on the knife. There's more, but let's chew on that for a while.''

"Let's try it, Alexander,'' I said. "Lean your forehead on the table while I try to get your hand around my oyster knife.'' I held the knife to Alexander's neck and tried to lift his hand to the handle. Nowhere near. "Your muscles are so big they get in the way,'' I said. "Let's try with Burton.'' Again no luck. "It's not impossible,'' I said, "because it was done somehow. We just don't know how, yet.''

"Do you really believe this was figured out on the spur of the moment by some hysterical pregnant female who had just murdered the father of her unborn child?'' Alexander asked, and before I could answer he said, "Because if you do, I have another little problem for you. Was Pembrooke sitting, standing, lying down, running away, or what, when he was stabbed?"

"If it was an act of passion— I see what you mean, Alexander. He would be sitting in his chair. The back of the chair would be in the way."

"Not only the back, Norma. It was a wing chair; the wings would be in the way too. Burton, put your forehead on the table the way Pembrooke's was."

"Let's make it accurate, Alec. I'll put my head on the saucer, in its normal position."

Alexander probed the back of Burton's head and neck with his hand, then lightly held the oyster knife at the top of Burton's neck at a forty-five-degree angle. "This is about how the knife would have to enter to go into the right spot."

"Whoever did it knew anatomy," I said.

"Everybody in a museum knows anatomy," Pearl said. "Even the security guards."

Burton sat up again. "All right," he said, "it was a premeditated crime. But was it planned in the few minutes that the killer was arguing with Pembrooke or days before?"

"It would take an extraordinary mind to plan this in a few minutes," I said. "After all, how long does it take? Pembrooke sat down, opened the champagne, took a sip, put on the glove, picked up the oyster and the oyster knife; maybe two minutes, tops."

"Not even that long," Alexander said. "You're figuring from the time Pembrooke entered the room; I'm figuring from the time the killer entered the room. It's extremely unlikely that Pembrooke would have continued eating and drinking with a visitor there, remember his passion for privacy, so you have to assume Pembrooke put down his knife and glove when the killer came in. The killer said something that caught Pembrooke's attention, such as 'I'm pregnant,' and they started arguing. Do you believe that anyone could figure out how to kill Pembrooke in such an unusual way during such a conversation?"

"Pembrooke wasn't necessarily killed one minute after the killer entered the room," I said. "They could have talked for five or ten minutes first."

"True," Alexander said. "Once inside, it made no difference when the killer left, as long as it was before the busboy came in to clean up. As a matter of fact, the killer could have spent an hour arranging things after the murder just to confuse the police. He could have put the glove on Pembrooke's right hand, picked up an oyster, everything we think Pembrooke did, except drink the champagne."

"Why not that too?" Pearl asked.

"Stomach contents," Burton said. "Unless he brought a tube and forced an ounce of champagne down the dead man's throat, which seems pretty pointless and would have shown some trauma at the autopsy."

"What about being seen leaving Pembrooke's room?" Pearl asked.

"Same odds as being seen entering," Alexander replied. "Better, because he could open the door a crack and see if anyone was coming down the executive corridor. Two steps and he could be in that corridor, in the stair enclosure, or in the elevator if it were at that floor then; that is, if someone had just come up or down the elevator to go into the dining room."

"How about just standing in front of the elevator waiting?" I asked. "It's normal to be standing there."

"Possible, but dangerous," Alexander said. "If the killer had spent one or two minutes in Pembrooke's room, no problem. Ten minutes, and whoever came out of the staff dining room might have noticed when the killer left it and wondered why it took so long for an elevator to come. I'm inclined to believe that the killer spent only a few minutes with Pembrooke, then opened the door a crack and waited for the elevator to come. As the door was closing, if no one was there, he just zipped across the hall into the elevator and was safe."

"I agree," I said. "If he took an hour getting back to his office, there'd be too much explaining to do. Someone might have noticed that he wasn't in the toilet and he wasn't in the storeroom or whatever excuse he had to use."

"So there is no point," Pearl said, "in checking the time each person was out of his office or left the dining room."

"Or entered the dining room," I pointed out. "There's no law saying that the killer couldn't go into Pembrooke's room before he ate lunch. Two steps and he's in the dining room. A lot safer than taking the elevator after the murder, or any other technique, since no one could say how long it took someone to walk to the dining room. Also, it's easier to see when someone leaves the room than enters it. I'll bet that's how it was done."

"I think we should check all the times as well as we can," Alexander said. "It may not help tell us who the killer is, but it may be possible to rule out some people, those whose location was known during the period in which Pembrooke could have been killed."

"I thought you promised not to investigate the murder," Pearl said.

"I'm not investigating it, Pearl, I'm analyzing it. Don't you want me to help Warshafsky make commissioner? Besides, I know the murder is connected to the painting."

"Know from evidence or know from intuition?" I asked.

"Just know. We have to ask about the murder because we can't talk about the painting, and we better be able to ask sensible questions."

"So I'll ask a sensible question, Alexander. How did Pembrooke's fingerprints get on the knife?"

"If I knew that, I'd know who killed him."

"I read once," Pearl said, "that you can transfer fingerprints with some kind of sticky tape."

"Without leaving a trace? Maybe an expert could, but not an amateur. Besides, how do you get that slight smearing or rolling Burt described before, of Pembrooke shifting the handle in his fingers to get it into the right position? No, somehow Pembrooke's hand was either placed on the knife after he was killed or he was stabbed in such a way as not to smear the original prints."

I had a sudden flash. "I know now, Alexander. It's simple. The killer brings his own oyster knife with him, it's small enough to fit into a pocket, or even a lady's bag. He stabs Pembrooke, pulls out his knife, and with a handkerchief, carefully slips Pembrooke's silver knife into the hole left by the other knife."

Burton answered this one. "Warshafsky thought of that and had the medical examiner inspect the wound very carefully. First of all, it would have taken considerable effort to pull out the first knife and some blood or other fluids would have come with it. There was no sign of this. Then, the tip of the oyster knife is bent up. As it goes in, it rips tissue and bone in one direction. As it goes out, it pulls some bone spicules in the other direction. There was no evidence of this. Further, a handkerchief, or plastic, or anything wrapped around the handle of the knife would have dulled and smudged the sharp appearance of the prints; just picking the knife up that way would have done it. There was no evidence of this. Also, the silver knife was longer, wider, and thicker than a regular oyster knife. To drive it in through additional bone and tissue would have taken a good deal of force, enough to make the handkerchief slip. The medical examiner stated flatly that the knife found in the wound was the knife that had originally been stuck there."

"It seems to me, Burton," I said, "that all you're doing is shooting down our ideas. Why don't you contribute some of your own?"

"I'm doing it deliberately, Norma. I don't want to influence Alexander to think along the lines the police have already thought of."

"There's the position to consider too," Alexander said. "Burt, put your head back on the saucer. See? His head is sort of tilted back, which would close the space where the knife had to go in. Did the medical examiner say what Pembrooke's head position was?"

"Pembrooke's head was tilted forward as far as it could go, as if his head were on his chest when he was stabbed."

Alexander studied Burton for a while, then he went into the living room and brought back a wing chair, which he set at the table. "Sit here," he ordered Burton, "and put your chin on your chest." He then held the oyster knife at the base of Burton's skull. "See? The angle is such that the knife would have to pass through the back of the chair first. It won't work."

"Why does it have to be a downward stab?" I asked. "Couldn't it have been sideways? Or gently slid in, you know, wiggled in to get through the space between the bones?"

"No. A sideways blow couldn't deliver the power and the wings of the chair are in the way. Wiggling in wouldn't chip the bones, and do you think you would hold still while someone was wiggling a knife into your head? It had to be a downward blow, like a karate chop; that's how the arm delivers the most power."

"Why are we talking about the killer standing at Pembrooke's side?" I said. "How about from across the desk? Like this?" I stood opposite Burton and reached across the table with my left hand as I picked up the knife with my right. I grabbed Burton by his hair and pulled his head forward until he was leaning across the table. "Now watch this," I said, still holding his hair. I pushed the front of his head down and forward. "This opens the space where I have to stab him, and— SCHLOMM—I stab down in the perfect position and the perfect angle."

"Perfect," Alexander said. "But Pembrooke shaved his head. And not everyone is as big as you, Norma."

"There are plenty of men as big as I am, Alexander, and as strong. And if your hands are big enough you could hold his head instead of his hair. You could do it, Alexander, if you stood on your toes."

"I could get my hand around his forehead," Alexander said, "but it would be a tough grip to hold, round and smooth. I doubt if I could hold him if he pulled back and twisted, as anyone would in that position. Also, if you stabbed him that way, his forehead would slam into the plate. Any abrasions on his forehead, Burton, or scratches? Anywhere?''

"None. But if he were killed immediately after, there would be no signs of bruising unless the skin were broken.''

"How about lividity? Did the blood collect in the position he was found?''

"Yes. He was either killed in that position or placed there immediately after he was killed.''

"Alex said he could have pulled away," Pearl said. "What if he couldn't? What if he were drugged?''

"There were no signs of any drugs in him, liquid, solid, or gaseous. No needle marks anywhere. The medical examiner looked very carefully in all the non-obvious places.''

"Wouldn't the champagne bucket have been in the killer's way if he stood on Pembrooke's left?" I said. "We're assuming the killer was right-handed. If he were left-handed, he could have stood at Pembrooke's right and stabbed down with his left hand.''

"The shell bucket was on Pembrooke's right," Alexander said, "but you're right, Norma. Either could have been moved and later put back into position. What did the carpet show, Burt?''

"Pembrooke's chair rolled around a little and moved back and forth, in the normal movements a man would make in settling down and moving towards the table to eat. His own footprints under the desk were undisturbed. The areas from the door to the table and all around the table and chair had been smoothed out. No footprints of any kind left.''

"Perfect," Alexander said. "Another clue. That had to have been done by the killer right after the murder. Was it done by his foot, a brush, or what?''

"It was done by a long, hard, smooth object that didn't pull out any carpet fibers. The police think it may have been a ruler or something like that.''

"That doesn't help," Pearl said. "Everybody in the museum has a ruler or some kind of straightedge."

"True," I added, "but maybe the killer had unusually large feet or small feet or special shoes or a peculiar walk. Or wore high heels."

"It's more likely that the killer was as careful in this as in everything else he did," Alexander said. "Was the champagne bucket or the shell pail disturbed, Burt?"

"Nothing showed, but that doesn't mean the champagne bucket or the pail couldn't have been moved away and back again and the carpet straightened out afterwards."

"We're missing something," Alexander said. "Pembrooke was a tall man in good condition, worked out regularly in gym. Why didn't he fight back, struggle? How did he let himself be killed so quietly, so easily? You didn't mention any sign of a struggle, Burt."

"There wasn't any. Everything was exactly as it had been left except what Pembrooke touched. You can tell if a freshly ironed napkin has been refolded or if a tablecloth has been wrinkled and later smoothed out by hand."

"Then Pembrooke knew the killer very well," Pearl said, "and didn't expect any violence from him. They were probably even friends. Or her. Men don't expect violence from a woman."

"Women don't usually slam a knife into a person's head from behind," I pointed out, "that's why men don't expect it. We're the gentler sex; poison is our game."

"That bring up my next point," Alexander said. "Why was Pembrooke stabbed in the medulla oblongata, of all places? It's hard to reach, protected by heavy bones and ligaments. It's hard to find, few people even know what it is, much less where. There's a great risk of missing the right spot; a half inch lower you cut the spinal cord and Pembrooke would have been a paraplegic, but alive and able to name his killer. A half inch higher and you'd be trying to cut through the heaviest bones of the skull. Why stab him there?''

"Well, if you hit the medulla, it's instant death," Pearl said. "Absolutely painless. Maybe the killer didn't want to hurt Pembrooke. I mean, cause pain."

"Wouldn't it have been easier to stab him in a more accessible place?" I asked. "If you know anatomy, as the killer plainly did, there must be a dozen better places to stab him. Even with an oyster knife. Or shoot him."

"Shooting is noisy. Poison is out; how do you poison a closed oyster or a bottle of champagne? Club? Could be noisy, not certain, and how do you carry one around in a lunchroom? Or an executive corridor? Choking? It has sounds of struggle, and who knows who will win? So a knife fits the situation, but why an oyster knife?"

"Aside from being handy, and we disposed of the crime-of-passion, sudden-rage bit, I can think of several reasons why an oyster knife would be the worst choice. It's very short, not sharp, its point is bent up—very hard to kill someone with an oyster knife. And if you don't bring your own, how do you know the intended victim won't grab it before you do? It's really a rather rotten choice."

"If you bring your own knife," Pearl agreed, "it could fit into a pocket or bag; you could buy one in a supermarket so no one could identify you, and you could pick where you wanted to stab or cut your victim. Anything would be better than an oyster knife."

"And why in Pembrooke's room?" Alexander asked. "Weren't there a hundred better places, inside and outside the museum, to do him in? Why pick a place where people can walk past at any time, see you going in or coming out, and hear noise? Why pick a room where, the moment you enter it, the victim can see you; where you don't belong, where no one ever enters, where the victim is angry with you just because you're there, where, if you're an enemy, as you must be, by definition, he has a table between you and a knife at his hand? The very knife you intend to kill him with? It's ridiculous! You want to stab him? Lure him into a storeroom, a dark corner of the museum, your bedroom, or his, if you're an attractive woman. Or better still, in the street, in a movie, any place else but in his private dining room.''

"It's very clear that this was a premeditated murder,'' Pearl said. "Otherwise why do it in the hardest possible way.''

"I know why,'' I said, tired, really tired, because I knew what would happen; could see the whole scenario now. Alexander would be lucky if he got just another heart attack, and I would be a widow. "I know why. An oyster knife was used because it's perfect for stabbing into the medulla; short, strong, thick, tip turned up just the right amount. The medulla was perfect because it would kill silently, instantly, without causing pain, like a kosher slaughterer. The room was perfect because it was the hardest place to kill Pembrooke; you don't like easy puzzles either, Alexander. The time was perfect because anyone in the museum could have done it except some poor innocent busboy or the man who was telling us stories at the time Pembrooke was killed. Using Pembrooke's own solid silver knife added a really elegant touch. And, of course, Pembrooke's own fingerprints on the knife? Triply elegant: to make sure no innocent person could possibly hang for the murder, to increase the difficulty of the problem, and to—how did he put it?— 'I prefer to have the evildoer destroy himself by his own weakness'? Well, Pembrooke's own silver knife and his own private dining room and his own fingerprints on the knife that killed him—what could be more elegant?''

"Are you saying Mr. Belmont did it?'' Pearl asked. "But he couldn't have. And he's one of Burton's clients.''

"Not with his own hands,'' I said. "He never does anything himself. He has people who . . . who are obligated, who owe him, who have eaten of the bread cast upon the waters. He accomplishes what he wants by arranging situations so that people make happen what he wants to happen. Just as he manipulated you, Alexander.''

"Nobody manipulates me, Norma. I manipulated him."
My simple, honest, straightforward husband. My husband who
depends so much on his intelligence that even I can manipulate
him, thinks he put something over on the shrewdest puppet-
master in the world. I would do whatever I could to save him,
but I didn't know what I could do or how to do it. If I had a
gun. . . .

"If it makes you feel any better, Norma," Burton must
have been watching my face, "I have never known Mr. Belmont to lie. Never. And he said that he was not involved with
the murder."

"I wish I had my tape, Burton. He didn't say that. All
he said was that if we thought he was involved we should put it
out of our minds. Think back."

"If you think Mr. Belmont . . . instigated Pembrooke's
murder," Pearl said, "who did the actual killing?"

"It had to be Wechsler; motive, means, and opportunity
was there. He owes Belmont. He gains from Pembrooke's
death. He has to hate Pembrooke himself. He's very smart,
even by Belmont's standards. And I'll bet a nickel he's big and
strong, without even meeting him."

"You'll have a chance to meet him tomorrow at 10:30
A.M.," Burton said. "He's not very big, but he's very smart.
You'll find he's a sweet guy. I can't imagine him killing any-
one."

"Isn't that what they always say on TV, Burton? Such a
nice boy, who would imagine he'd kill his whole family?"

"If he did it, how did he do it?" Pearl asked.

"Don't worry, Alexander will figure that out," I said
dully. "Guaranteed." And get himself killed in the bargain by
some other nice sweet guy who owes Mr. Belmont. Nothing I
could do to stop it. Nothing. I can't even stop Alexander from
solving the puzzle; that would be like stopping his heart. I wish
I had a gun. Or a knife. But I've got a knife. I'll carry it in my
bag, always, and stay with Alexander, next to him, every minute, wherever he goes. Anyone tries to hurt Alexander, I'll
know what to do. With an oyster knife. Belmont isn't the only
one who can be elegant.

# X

"I took over this office," Wechsler said, "immediately after Pembrooke's body was found." Harold Wechsler: about forty-five although it was hard to tell his age, sandy hair slightly gray, brown eyes behind silver-rimmed glasses, a little above average in height, a little below average in weight; the kind of man who, if the police asked you, you would very accurately describe as average. If you looked into his eyes as he spoke, and listened carefully to what he said in his soft careful voice, you would not be at all surprised if, when all was ready, Darth Vader unzipped the Wechsler skin and announced that henceforth Earth would be a minor vassal of the Empire.

"I would have preferred to stay in my corner office," Wechsler continued, "but in people's minds Pembrooke's office was the throne, so it was necessary for the smooth transfer of power that I occupy it. Also I wanted to make sure Pembrooke's secretaries, out of a misguided sense of loyalty, did not remove any of his papers."

"Are you keeping his secretaries for your own?" I asked.

"No, I had them assigned to other jobs on the sixth floor. In order for rewards to work, there must be punishments as well. I'm using temporaries until I can acquire the right people for myself."

"How is assignment to the sixth floor a punishment?"

"Any change for the executive secretaries of the head of an organization is psychologically a demotion. The assignment to the work areas, working with conservators, preparators, storage, is clearly a humiliation. Further, I placed them in a steno pool set-up, which is even lower down the scale."

"Won't they all quit?" I asked.

"That's the idea. The sixth floor is now very overstaffed secretarywise," he smiled briefly at the word, "and they know it. Every one of Pembrooke's secretaries is looking for a job right now and the regular sixth-floor secretaries are sweating, albeit unnecessarily. I've made it harder for them to get new jobs by ordering no personal use of telephones; in two weeks, I'll lift that order."

"Did you fire anyone yet?"

"There is a saying that a king, to be a king, must visit a prison once a month, march down the line of prisoners, select two at random and say, 'Free this one; kill this one.' I fired one of Pembrooke's secretaries, one who was particularly nasty to me, within the first hour."

"And for a reward?"

"I announced that a new division would be created, Dutch and Flemish Seventeenth-Century Painting, which is, after all, our specialty. It will require a new curator, at least two new assistant curators and support staff, all to come, if possible, from within our present staff. Selections to be announced in a month."

"How did the chief curator take this?"

"Dorner? He was very upset; said I should have consulted him. I asked him how many times he had consulted me about anything. Dorner had been promised by Pembrooke that if all went well with his acquisitions, Pembrooke would recommend Dorner to succeed him as director when he retired. Dorner never opposed a single acquisition Pembrooke wanted."

"Wasn't there someone else that Pembrooke wanted?"

"An outsider, Alford, was the one Pembrooke really wanted. But Pembrooke kept lots of people on the hook with vaguely promised promotions."

"Did Dorner know about this? Did he resign?"

"He didn't know, but he heard rumors. Dorner made the mistake of threatening to resign, but since he had been relying on Pembrooke's promises, he hadn't really prepared any other place to go, so he had to back down. This put him in an even weaker position with Pembrooke."

"Did he resign when you took over?"

"I should have taken him up on it, but for the near future, I didn't want to lose too many people at the top at once. Looks bad. So I told him that I felt he was overworked and I was going to give him a deputy chief curator. Selected by me from outside the museum."

"Deputy, not Assistant?" Alexander asked. "Is there such a job?"

"A subtle but important difference which you picked up, Mr. Gold, and I am sure Dorner did too. It's a job I invented."

"Do you need the approval of the Board of Trustees for changes like this?" I asked.

"In effect, I have it already. But in any change of position like this, anything I want to do for the first year, I can do. All mistakes will be blamed on my predecessor."

"Presidents do it, why not you?" I said. "But you will have to produce after that."

"I will," he said. I had no doubt about that, or about anything else Harold Wechsler might undertake. Or had already undertaken.

"So, Mr. Wechsler," Alexander said, "you are carrying out Mr. Belmont's wishes?"

Wechsler looked coldly at Alexander. "Mr. Gold," he said, "in a short time the idea that I am here to serve Daniel Belmont personally will be laid to rest. He selected me because we are in agreement on most things, including art and administration, but I am not his carbon copy nor his servant. He knows it and he likes it that way. If you think otherwise, don't waste time talking to me; go ask Mr. Belmont what I think.''

Alexander has the idea that challenging other people, playing devil's advocate, is the quickest way to learn things. It may be, with some, but I know it doesn't work with others. Wechsler was definitely not a carbon copy of Belmont. He lacked Belmont's money. Which meant that he had to be tougher than Belmont in some ways.

"I can see that Pembrooke's death was beneficial to you," I said.

"I was overjoyed when I was told. If Sam hadn't warned me not to go near that room, I would have peeked in, just to make sure."

"Sam? The head of security? Zager?"

"Zager. I called him first. He told me to call the police, to stay in my office, and to say nothing. He even sent Korbin to stay with me."

"Why did he think you needed a lawyer?"

"He wanted an attorney present when anyone from the museum was questioned, but your assumption was right. He thought I was the most likely suspect."

"And still he tried to protect you?" I asked.

"The Roman centurions, if they did not kill the new emperor, served him. Sam decided to serve me as well as he served Pembrooke."

"Why did Sam think you were the most likely suspect?" Alexander asked.

"Are you telling me you did absolutely no research before this interview, Mr. Gold?"

"I'll put it another way, Mr. Wechsler. Who do you think killed Pembrooke?"

"I'm sure you've come to the same conclusions yourself, but since you want to see how I think, I'll go through the exercise."

"Before you start, Mr. Wechsler," I said, "would you object if I stop you if there is something I don't understand?"

"Very politely put." He smiled. "What you mean is if there is something you disagree with. No, I won't mind." He leaned forward in his chair, a leather, swivel wing chair, executive type. Pembrooke's favorite, evidently.

"By the way," I said, "is that the same chair that was in Pembrooke's dining room?"

He looked at me wryly. "Mrs. Gold, I've never been in that room. And if I were, this is not the way to find out." He put his forearms flat on the desk and began. "The killer is one of the top executives of the museum; there were no visitors on this floor at lunchtime and a junior has too little to gain to take the risk of murder. If Pembrooke had any personal relationship with any assistant curator or junior executive, he kept it very quiet. It's hard to keep things secret in the little world of art, and impossible to keep a secret within a museum."

"He never fooled around with any of the girls in the museum?" I asked. "Or any of the boys?"

"He was too smart to do that, Mrs. Gold; something like that cannot be hidden. He never appeared at formal museum functions with a date; he always escorted one of the donors, usually elderly ladies. The only sexual innuendo I ever heard was that he romanced wealthy old potential donors, but I am sure that was exaggerated. It is part of the director's job to be attentive to potential donors. I'll have to do it too. And I believe he was strictly heterosexual."

"He was unmarried, then?"

"I can't imagine Pembrooke being close to anyone."

"Even his murderer?"

"It was not a crime of passion in the classical sense, Mrs. Gold. The only emotion involved was passion for money; something like that."

"Couldn't someone from the outside have hired someone from the museum to kill Pembrooke?"

"If you wanted to hire a killer, would you hire an assistant curator or a chief comptroller? There are plenty of outsiders for hire to push a person under a train or to put a bullet in his back. No, the killer was an executive, almost certainly one of our top people, male, in good physical condition—"

"Do you use the basement gym?" I asked.

"Regularly. I am relatively strong for a pencil pusher."

"Why do you say male?"

"The way he was killed; that took strength."

"Couldn't a big woman, someone such as myself, do the job?"

"The only big female we have on North Fifth is Freya Larsen, our chief conservator. She could easily have killed him, but she would more likely have broken his arms first, then his legs, then his neck. Besides—" He stopped.

"Besides a knife is not her style?" I asked. "She could have picked it up because it was there."

"It takes a lot of brains to become a chief conservator. It takes scientific knowledge, art knowledge, great technical skill, tremendous patience, good judgment, decisiveness— All these, but Freya does not have the kind of mentality, the speed of thinking that would allow her to plan this murder in a few seconds."

"Because she's slow thinking, methodical?" Alexander asked. "If she has that much patience, those qualities, couldn't she have planned this killing for months, worked out every detail, then executed it with precision in seconds?"

"If she planned it for months, Mr. Gold, why not entice him into the storeroom to look at a painting and stab him there? Or drop a weight on his head in the gym? No, Mr. Gold, a planned murder would not have taken place in that room, with that knife, next to the staff dining room. This was a spur-of-the-moment killing by a brilliant, fast-thinking, physically strong, probably male, museum executive."

"Who are the other executives in that wing?"

"Sam Zager is in good shape, even though he's sixty.

But his mind? He's good at what he does, but he sets up systems, routines, works by the book. He's definitely not an improvisor."

"What about the chief curator you mentioned? Dorner?"

"Konrad Dorner is fairly big and strong, but he had nothing to gain by Pembrooke's death and everything to lose. As far as I know, he had no motive. And he's not too smart. At least compared to some of the whiz kids around here."

"I thought a chief curator had to be very knowledgable in all fields of art and very good in his own area. And a good administrator to boot," I said.

Wechsler looked at me pityingly. "Do you think Pembrooke would have allowed anyone with those qualifications to get anywhere near the throne? After me, and Pembrooke would never let me take over, the chief curator was the logical next director."

"Are you telling me Konrad Dorner is not competent?"

"Oh, he knows his field, all right. I didn't mean to imply he is a dope. I was only comparing him to Pembrooke. Besides, the nerve has been removed. Pembrooke treated him so badly, he broke his spirit."

"So Dorner hated Pembrooke?"

"Come on now, Mr. Gold. Everyone hated Pembrooke."

"You too?"

"More than anyone else, I think, other than his killer."

"Who else is there on North Fifth?"

"Melville Gerson is a tub of lard. I don't mean he's all that fat, but he's very soft; probably never did a day's exercise in his life and lives on junk food."

"Any man, stabbing downward, can produce enough force to have done the job," Alexander said.

"So you've figured that out already, Mr. Gold," Wechsler said in mock congratulation. "Melville is very smart, especially with numbers, but also with space, time, and probability. The kind of whiz kid that called out the answer before the teacher finished asking the question. You'll love him; reads British mysteries, the kind where someone catching one train and switching to another can commit the murder and be back at the castle in time for tea. He solves them halfway through the book and tells you the solution.''

"Who else is there on the floor?"

"Maxwell Korbin, our house counsel. He's the opposite of Gerson, so skinny I don't think he could lift Pembrooke's knife. He's left-handed, if that means anything to you.''

"It sure does," I said. "Is Maxwell smart?"

"Maxwell? Oh, sure. Everyone who makes it to North Fifth is super-smart, in one way or another. Maxwell is wise too, cautious and conservative. I can't imagine him going to the toilet without researching all the precedents first.''

"Could he have figured out how to commit this murder?"

"If anyone could, Korbin could. He can juggle twenty incompatible concepts in his head at once. But decisions? He left them all to Pembrooke. If he were capable of committing this murder he could also have been, by now, a senior partner in one of the prestigious law firms instead of working for salary here.''

"Is that it?"

"Ken Rand, our PR guy, he's a possible, physically, and very bright in his own way; imaginative and clever rather than highly intelligent.''

"Could he have committed the murder?"

"It's possible; he's used to handling emergencies and wild variables. Almost as good as Davidoff, our outside exhibition consultant. But murder? His personality just doesn't fit. He's too happy a soul.''

"You know where that leaves us, don't you?" I asked.

He smiled ruefully. "I'm not only the logical suspect, I'm the guy I would have picked if I were the detective.''

"Harold Wechsler, did you kill Orville Pembrooke?" Alexander asked.

"No." That flat.

"You had the motive, you had the opportunity, the means were there."

"But I'm too smart to do anything that stupid."

"Stupid, Mr. Wechsler? Not immoral?"

"Sometimes killing can be a moral act, Mr. Gold. Killing Pembrooke, for instance."

"Where were you when Pembrooke was killed?"

"Either finishing lunch, on the way to my office, or in my office."

"You left the lunchroom a little after one?"

"So I was told. I didn't look at the clock."

"Even though it was right over the door?"

"Ten feet up, Mr. Gold. Sorry."

"Was that before or after Pembrooke looked in?"

"After, I'm told. I was sitting facing the park."

"Don't you get enough of the park from your own office?"

"My desk faces the Met. It's screwed to the floor. Another of Pembrooke's little touches."

"You could have had it changed."

Dead face. "I decided not to."

"Did you see anyone else leave?"

"Becker, our old lady, she's one of the conservators, was just going through the door as I was getting up."

"The conservators eat with the top executives?"

"They're North Wing too, one flight up."

"Did you see her near Pembrooke's office?"

"All I saw was the elevator door closing."

"Which way was the elevator arrow pointing?"

"Up, naturally."

"Did you go directly to your office?"

"Once I was in the hall, yes. But on the way out of the dining room I stopped for a moment to talk to Ken Rand and Freya Larsen."

"What did you talk about?"

"Ken was going to make an event of Becker's retirement next week; newspapers, TV, a nice gift, that sort of thing. She had been here longer than any of us, from Ludwig's day, in fact. Even before Pembrooke. It was a natural. Ken was keeping it hush-hush so the old lady would be surprised, break down in tears, the kind of stuff the seven o'clock news loves."

"How could you keep a thing like that secret in the museum?"

"Becker's a loner; doesn't mix with the others. Eats by herself, keeps her door locked, sneers at everybody."

"Was everything all set?"

"Oh, sure. Ken's good at that sort of thing and Freya keeps her gang under very tight control. Wait till you meet her. I was just checking that everything was ready."

"How long did that take?"

"Less than a minute, I'm sure."

"Did you hear anything while you were in your office?"

"Not a sound, but that doesn't mean anything; the walls here are fairly soundproof."

"When you were talking to Ken Rand, which way were you facing?"

"Sort of parallel to the park, but I could have seen anyone going out the door peripherally."

"Did you?"

"No, but I got the impression Sam Zager, he was only a few tables away, was getting ready to leave."

That seemed to be about all. We got up and shook hands, so I took the opportunity: "Mr. Wechsler, would you measure your hand against my husband's, please?" They put their palms together. Alexander's was twice as big; all right, maybe thirty percent bigger. Another theory shot to hell. Wechsler gave us the list of appointments he had set up for us. It was perfect; dates, times, full names, titles, office numbers, location, extension, and secretary's name. He was going to make a great museum director, that I was sure of. From all I had learned, it took the same skills as being a great murderer.

He also gave us a key to the staff elevators and a chit for lunch in the staff dining room.

Very thoughtful of him.

It was time for lunch, so we started walking toward the dining room, but unfortunately, Pembrooke's dining room had been sealed by the police. I was only going to peek in for a minute, honest.

We were the first people in the dining room and the waiter handed us the menu of the day as soon as we sat down. For service like that alone, it pays to be an executive. I was going to wave the menu aside and order, there had to be plenty left, oysters and champagne, but one look at Alexander's face convinced me otherwise, so it was bay scallops and Riesling. I had deliberately chosen the corner table overlooking the park, with our backs to the door. Why spoil everyone's appetite with Alexander playing Lombroso and trying to pick out the potential murderers by the way they walked? Besides, we both needed the relaxation.

I did not allow any business talk until after dessert, then I started. "So, did he do it, Alexander?"

"I don't know yet. That reverse psychology business, that he's the prime suspect, doesn't mean he's innocent. In TV the most likely suspect is guaranteed innocent; in real life it's the other way around."

"I got the message he was pushing: that everyone on North Fifth should be on the list of possible killers. Did you notice?"

"Absolutely. If he was too fat, he was super smart. If he was too plodding, he was strong enough. If he had nothing to gain, he was strong and smart."

"Wasn't Wechsler taking an awful chance telling us all the reasons he is the prime suspect?"

"Maybe he thinks he's so super-duper smart it doesn't matter. Maybe he doesn't know how good I am. I'll bet he didn't talk to the police that way."

"You're right, Alexander, I'm sure he shows a different

set of characteristics to everyone he deals with. He looks so nothing, he's a perfect chameleon.''

"I'm not denying he's bright, if only because Belmont said so, and Belmont should know if anyone does. The question is not could he have done it, it's did he do it.''

"Isn't it too soon to be breaking your head over this? We have a lot of people to interview and a lot of information to get yet. Pearl has started making a report on Pembrooke; that may provide a clue.''

"I don't know if we need a report in this case. Maybe Pearl would be more useful circulating among her friends in the art world to see what she can pick up.''

"You're certain that the murderer is from within the museum and has nothing to do with Pembrooke's past?''

"The killer is one of the museum's executives, that's obvious. As for the past, I'll bet that the last three months is as far back as we have to go.''

"The Third Vermeer? What makes you so sure that the murder and the painting are connected?''

"They have to be; I know it.''

'Have to be?' From my Alexander? Not 'It's obvious'? And why didn't he ask Wechsler about the painting? Did he want Belmont to think he wasn't investigating the painting? Never. I knew why: it was because he couldn't think of a way to word the questions. When my husband is at a loss for words, when Alexander depends on hunches instead of cold logic, I know we're in trouble. Deep trouble.

# XI

I'm usually kidding when I accuse Alexander of looking like a bald gorilla with glasses. Aside from being so broad, short, and muscular, if he lost another thirty pounds he could look rather nice, in a rugged sort of way. Konrad Dorner, although tall and thin, really looked like an ape. He had huge hands at the ends of arms so long he could have scratched his knees while standing at attention. His feet were big too, although his legs were short and bowed. But it was his head that really did it: bald on top with a big underthrust jaw, sunken eyes, a tiny nose with big nostrils, and huge ears that stood straight out sideways; the missing link between man and chimp.

Dorner's soft voice spoiled the picture, making me think of a philosophy professor emeritus at a small exclusive prep school. "Actually," he said, "there is so much administrative work that I don't function as a curator at all. The curators come to me for authorization for proposed acquisitions and deaccessions, for changes in the permanent exhibitions, for budget increases—everyone wants a budget increase—for additional personnel, and for new exhibits."

"And you decide what to approve and whom to refuse," I asked, "so half of them are sore at you at any given time?"

"All of them are, Mrs. Gold, all of the time. You see, the way the museum works, Pembrooke makes—made all the decisions, but told the lucky ones the good news himself while I had to tell the others the bad news."

"Didn't you feel uncomfortable in that position, Mr. Dorner? It seems to me that your major function was to be a buffer and a lightning rod."

"Short of resigning, I had to do what the director ordered. I felt that when I became director, I would have the opportunity to run the museum the way I felt it should be run."

"What about Harold Wechsler? Wasn't he the obvious successor to Pembrooke?"

"Mr. Pembrooke assured me that Wechsler would soon resign and that I would be the next director."

"Then who is Howard S. Alford?" Alexander asked brutally.

"So you know about that." Dorner seemed to shrink. "I found out only a month ago; a friend told me. It seems everyone in the art world knew but me. Alford is the son of one of the biggest art dealers in New York; he's supposed to be a brilliant businessman but has only a superficial knowledge of painting and sculpture. He never worked in a museum before and he's only forty."

"Why didn't you have it out with Pembrooke then? Threaten to resign?"

"I did, but it was an empty threat and he knew it. Where could I go? Everyone knew I had been passed over, fooled. I hadn't functioned as a curator in ten years, so busy doing paperwork that I couldn't even keep up with the literature, much less know what's going on in the art world."

"You seem very free with these admissions, Mr. Dorner."

"What's the difference? Any curator in the museum would have told you the same, or worse, with pleasure."

"So you began to hate Orville Pembrooke?"

"Began? No, Mr. Gold, I hated him from the beginning. Everyone did."

"Enough to kill him, Mr. Dorner?"

"I dreamt of it many times, but I could never bring myself to do the deed."

"Where were you at the time Pembrooke was killed?"

"In the dining room, I believe, but that depends on the exact time he was killed. I may have been in my office."

"Isn't your office a short distance from Pembrooke's dining room?"

"Right after Max Korbin's secretary."

"So it would have been easy for you to jump into Pembrooke's room, kill him, then continue on the way to your office. The whole thing could have been done in one minute."

"I suppose I could, Mr. Gold, but what about the risk of being seen? There were always people leaving the dining room at odd intervals."

"But the dining room doors are recessed. If they were opened, the person leaving would have to take at least two steps before entering the corridor. Do the doors squeak?"

"A little."

"Then if you were standing near Pembrooke's door you could have heard if anyone was coming and either entered quickly or continued on the way to your office?"

"I suppose so. And to get out, you could open the door a slit and if the coast is clear, just walk to the office. No one would have known it took the extra minute to get to my office."

"So you have figured out how to do it, Mr. Dorner."

"What about it? If you asked anyone here, and he answered honestly, you would find that everyone in the museum had fantasies of killing Pembrooke. Torture too, I'm sure."

"Did you kill him, Mr. Dorner?"

"I've never killed anybody, not even in Korea."

I decided to get off this fruitless task. "Did you see anyone leave the dining room ahead of you, Mr. Dorner?"

"Sam Zager, he's the security chief, left a minute or two before I did."

"Did you see anyone in the hall? His office is at the far end of the floor; it must take one or two minutes to get there."

"I didn't see anyone, but Sam walks fast, so that doesn't mean anything."

We had to ask about the painting sooner or later, so I tried. "As chief curator, you were involved in acquisitions, is that correct?"

"It was my function to present the request for important acquisitions to the Board of Trustees, but the decision as to which ones to present was strictly controlled by Mr. Pembrooke. That way he took credit for the ones presented and approved and I took the blame for those not presented or disapproved."

"Couldn't you have found a way to avoid being put in that position?"

"No way. As far as Pembrooke was concerned, this was one of my major functions. And I did it very well. I was once a respected authority on seventeenth-century European paintings."

"Pembrooke wanted you to take the blame in case his choice of dealer and acquisition was questioned?" Alexander asked bluntly.

Dorner seemed to shrink even more. He licked his lips before he spoke. "So you know?"

"Don't you, Dorner?"

"I didn't really know, but I sort of knew. There was an unmistakable pattern there. It took me time to see it but I am not a complete fool. I could also see that I was being set up as the fall guy in case anything went wrong."

"You could have left," I pointed out gently.

"Then I would have had no control of the situation at all, and would have been in an even worse position to defend myself. How do you prove you don't take commissions?"

"So you decided the only way out was to kill him?" Alexander asked.

"I never decided; I only thought about it."

"At length, it's clear."

"My hobby, Mr. Gold," he said wryly. "I'm grateful to the man who killed him, but that's my only crime."

"Don't you gain tremendously from Pembrooke's death?" I asked.

"Only in the pleasure that justice has been done."

"The museum gains too, now that Alford won't be the new director."

"Wechsler won't renew my contract. He'll get rid of anyone he thinks was close to Pembrooke."

"You could prove to Wechsler that you weren't," I said. "That you've done him a great service."

He looked blank for a moment, then smiled wanly. "By admitting I killed Pembrooke? That would hardly improve my position."

"If you didn't kill him, Mr. Dorner, who would you pick as the most likely candidate?"

Dorner thought for a moment, then said, "Harold Wechsler. He's a lot tougher than most people give him credit for. Don't let his pleasant manner fool you."

"I'd like to get back to acquisitions," I said. "If there were a major painting for sale now, seventeenth century, say Dutch or Flemish, you would know about it, wouldn't you?"

"That's my meat, Mrs. Gold. By major, I presume you mean an important painting by a major artist, not just a sketch or a study; one which had artistic as well as historical merit."

"Yes, and one that costs—" I hesitated for a moment, trying to pick the right figure, "over two million dollars."

"Mrs. Gold, that kind of painting is our specialty. Mr. Belmont would like us to acquire every such painting that exists, even if it is overpriced, and the dealers know it. We have standing orders to keep our eyes open for any Vermeer offered, you know. Unfortunately, there is no such painting as you describe on the market right now. If there were, I would know about it.''

"How can you be so sure?"

He drew himself up slightly. "I am still chief curator of the Fine Arts Museum of New York, and that period is my period. I have contacts all over the world who would call me the moment such a work were offered. I assure you, there is none right now.''

"If there were, how would you handle the situation?"

"Is this a hypothetical question, Mrs. Gold?" He searched my face excitedly. I could see he grasped at this as a means to save his life. If he could come up with a major seventeenth-century Dutch painting, and if he played his cards right, Mr. Belmont would see that he was not fired. "Do you know of any such work?"

"The question is hypothetical," I answered.

His face fell again. "I would fly out immediately," he said, "and take the curator with me, and an assistant curator too, to do the paper research, check the provenance. If we were all satisfied, I would negotiate for the purchase, make a deposit, and arrange for the scientific tests.''

"You'd make a deposit without consulting the Board of Trustees?"

"In a case like this, yes. I don't think the board would refuse, but in this business you cannot always play safe, you have to take chances. And when the situation calls for it, you have to back your judgment with everything you have.''

I glanced sideways at Alexander; he didn't meet my eyes. He knew what I was going to do, he wanted me to do it, but he didn't want to share the responsibility if it went wrong. A typical wife's function, so I went ahead. "Mr. Dorner," I said, "another hypothetical question. Suppose you were offered, from an unorthodox source, a Vermeer. What would you do?"

"A museum," he said, "cannot acquire stolen art. How could we exhibit it? Only a private collector, a crazy one like

Mr. Belmont, would buy it. Put it in his vault and gloat over it. Useless to me."

"I worded it badly, Mr. Dorner. I should have said a new Vermeer, newly discovered."

"With good provenance?"

"With no provenance. You don't even know the present owner."

He laughed bitterly. "This sounds even worse than the Bury St. Edmunds Cross. This is not a hypothetical question, Mrs. Gold; you're talking about a real painting, aren't you?"

"My question is hypothetical," I said carefully.

"I understand your caution, Mr. Gold, and I'll respect it. To answer your question, without knowing any more than you've told me, I would say the painting is a forgery. I don't care how well it tests, forgers find new ways every day of aging paint, producing craquelure, and fooling the instruments. There are more forgeries than you could imagine in museums all over the world, including this one, careful as we all are. In private collections, forgeries are even more prevalent. Even the greatest experts have been fooled, as I am sure I have been. You can't imagine the huge sums of money involved. Your best bet is to deal with an ethical gallery and to get full provenance. Even then, there is no absolute guarantee of authenticity, but a good dealer stands behind his sale; if it proves to be fake, you get your money back. But what you said, no provenance and an unknown owner, almost guarantees a forgery. Add to that the painting's a Vermeer; no one can copy a Vermeer so that an expert would be fooled, even if the scientific tests show no anomalies."

"What would you say if I added that several highly respected experts say the painting is an authentic Vermeer?"

"The odds against finding a new Vermeer are so great. . . . People have been searching for a hundred years for a new Vermeer. If under these circumstances these experts are willing to sign a certification of authenticity, I would very much like to acquire that painting for the museum. I presume that Gröber-Eisenberg was one of them?''

"No, he was unavailable.''

"Then I would put a deposit down and let— I see by your face that a deposit is unacceptable. Very well, I would pay the full agreed-upon price into escrow subject to Gröber-Eisenberg's written certification.''

"How much would such a painting sell for, Mr. Dorner?''

"It depends on many things. Was this an early work or when he was at his peak?'' I nodded. "Peak, then. It would, it's hard to be exact, but it would have to be one of the highest-price sales ever, might even break records. Certainly over five million today.''

"For that kind of money, couldn't Gröber-Eisenberg be bribed?''

"Some others, maybe; it's not likely though. Most are very careful of their reputations, and are ethical people who are truly art lovers. The most any of them might do, and I repeat, might do, and for a big enough fee, is to shade the judgment one percent of doubt, so that if a work is that close to the borderline it can be pushed a tiny bit in the direction the dealer or the owner or whoever is paying the expert, requires. But not Gröber-Eisenberg, he's a fanatic about forgery, goes crazy when he finds one, as though it's the vindication of his whole existence. If he said, or rather, signed a certificate, I would buy.''

"He's that good?''

"He's the best. Have you ever met him?'' I shook my head. "Well, if you ever do, if you ever see him operate, you'll know what I mean. He's Swiss, you know, and very. . . . Once when I was in Geneva I bought a new pair of glasses. Two blocks away I was stopped by the cashier, an old lady completely out of breath. She discovered that she had overcharged me one penny. She apologized and gave me the penny. Well, if the executioner who was going to hang Gröber-Eisenberg's mother had lost his copy of the execution orders, Gröber-Eisenberg would have searched for the papers, found them, and run ten miles to give them back to the executioner.''

"I know what you mean," I said. "There was a sort of joke going around when I was a girl. The Nazis had issued a proclamation in Berlin. All Jews were to report to the nearest police station at nine the next morning to be shot. Bring your gun and make sure it's clean. One rebellious soul told his wife that he had had enough of blindly following orders; he would report to the police station at exactly 9:00 A.M. sharp, set the clock, and he would bring his gun, after all, *Befehl ist Befehl*, but he'd be damned if he was going to clean it.''

Dorner nodded. "I know the type. Gröber-Eisenberg would have cleaned his gun. Carefully. And been worried that the Nazi might have criticized him for a speck of dust.''

There was nothing more to discuss, so we left. Alexander was thoughtful. This time, he asked me, "Did he do it?''

"I don't know, Alexander. He certainly could have. And his present attitude . . . he had nowhere to turn. Remember what Belmont's grandfather said: even a mouse will kill if it has no way to escape.''

"What about the painting?''

"Obviously we have to wait until G-E gives his opinion.''

"G-E must say it's a fake.''

"How do you figure that? The other four said it was real.''

"That was before it was cleaned; that gives him his excuse.''

"How can you be so sure?''

"It's obvious. When he hears the price, G-E has to figure . . . If he says it's real and it isn't, he loses all credibility from now on, and may even get sued for his past decisions. Ten million is a very potent opinion swayer. If he says it's a forgery, who's going to complain? Pembrooke?''

"But four others said it was real. He can concur with them easily."

"They're more likely to concur with him. They can always claim that when they saw it after the cleaning, certain minor but important aspects were revealed which were not visible before. The ears, the pearls, the *pointillés*, remember?"

"You must have thought this way yesterday too. Why did you make those stupid bets?"

"Because the painting is real."

"How do you know, Mr. Berenson? You've never even seen it."

"Pembrooke knew that Belmont didn't trust him, particularly now that war had been declared openly. He would never have tried to foist a forgery on the old man, especially for that high a price. And especially not after borrowing four million from the Mafia."

"Pembrooke was desperate for anything that could save him. All this just means that Pembrooke thought it was real."

"He was also an expert on painting."

"Hannelore Becker is also an expert. Don't you believe her?"

"I believe her. But there has to be a solution that will accommodate all these factors, and I'll find it. What's our next appointment?"

"Freya Larsen, the chief conservator. We have time, let's walk slowly."

There *has* to be a solution? That's what we bet a hundred thousand on? And after he finds the solution that fits all the mutually exclusive factors in the painting problem, he's going to find the other solution that *has* to be? The one that ties the painting to the murder? Well, of course he will, as soon as he solves the murder case. Isn't it obvious?

# XII

"**I** always did what the director wanted," she said. "That's my job."

Freya Larsen could have been typecast as Brünnhilde, the chief Valkyrie, without additional makeup, just add one spear. Even without the spear. Although three inches shorter than my six-one, she made it up in breadth and weight, and there wasn't much fat on her either. She wore her white-blond hair in a plaited crown around her head, and her skin could have topped a Devonshire clotted-cream cake. Freya wore a wedding band on her right hand, European style; it would have been interesting to see what her husband was like. Maybe it wouldn't; he was probably a scrawny professor who bullied her. We big girls tend to atone for our sins by mortifying the flesh.

"But what do you think that involved?" Freya Larsen asked. "Cleaning one painting ahead of another? Is that bad? Shouldn't the director have his priorities respected?"

"That wasn't what I meant," I said. "Since he hired you, he might have expected you to bend over backwards to— Isn't it also the chief conservator's job to help determine if a painting is authentic or a forgery?"

"It is, and we do it, although we're not as well equipped

as we should be. There is some new equipment I would like to buy, an energy-dispersive X-ray flourescence spectrometer and its subsidiary equipment, for instance, but it was taken out of my budget.''

"You avoided my question, Ms. Larsen.''

"At home, I'm Mrs. Piccoli. Here, I'm Larsen, just like the male executives. I didn't answer your question directly because it was insulting, and I was being polite. No, the director never asked me to fake a report; he knew better. I know it's your job to ask questions like this, but you should do your homework first. Ask anyone in the field about me; see if you can get even one professional to say I am not honest.''

"I didn't mean dishonest, Larsen. But aren't there times when a work of art is a borderline case, where the curator is not absolutely sure of its authenticity? And where the technical evidence is as much one way as the other?''

"You have the mistaken idea, Mrs. Gold, that my word is final. It is not. There have been such instances, yes, but in that case, in all cases, I report what I find, and if it is not conclusive, or even self-contradictory, I report on our findings as we find them. I turn the results over to the curator and he gives them, along with his research and other evidence, to the acquisitions committee. Since we don't have a full laboratory, where an important acquisition is concerned we go to an outside consultant. The curator can go to outside experts too.''

Alexander tried to make nice. As usual, he did it clumsily. "The position of chief conservator seems to require an unusual combination of talents, Mrs. Piccoli.''

"Not at all, Mr. Gold," she said. "Any woman can do it. Aren't we all genetically programmed to be good cleaners, preservers, and conservers? Cleaning a painting is like cleaning a floor, only smaller. Repairing a hole is like darning a sock; nothing to it.''

"I didn't mean—" he tried to recover.

"Yes you did, Mr. Gold. You were patronizing, and I resent it. It is not unusual for a woman to be chief conservator and it requires a hell of a lot more skill and talent than almost any other job in the museum. You have to be a competent artist, a good technician, an art historian, a carpenter, tailor, mechanic, and anything else that is needed. You have to have unbelievable patience and the courage to act on your decisions. One slip and you could ruin a masterpiece forever. You want to try it? Put a million-dollars deposit and I will give you a small painting to remove the varnish, that's all, just the old varnish. You spoil the painting, you bought it for a million dollars. Well?''

Alexander is too old-fashioned to fight with a woman, so I had to smooth things down. ''Don't educate him, Larsen; he still thinks women should be worshiped and I like him that way. Do you still get your hands dirty, or does administration take all your time?''

''Both. Once a week I do something upstairs, just to keep the touch. And I'm trying, testing, the effects of ethyl chloride on a cheap painting with a varnish I can't budge. Ethyl chloride is so volatile that doctors use it as a freezing agent, not as a solvent, and my hope is that the slight dissolving of the varnish followed immediately by the sudden freezing contraction of the surface will cause the varnish to flake off. If it works I've found a new tool. If it causes the paint layer to peel, I have a lot of explaining to do.''

''The curator whose painting it is, he approves?''

''I talked him into it. He's scared too, but sometimes you have to take a risk.''

''So you had good relations with Pembrooke?'' Alexander asked.

''Not very,'' Larsen said. ''He was always cutting my budget. He wanted to acquire, always acquire, and didn't give a damn about conserving. After all, who can see what we do? Some fools even like the look of old yellowed varnish on a painting; they think it is a real masterwork only if it is old, faded, and brown. If you show them a clean painting, fully restored, looking the way the artist originally painted it, they'd think you were fooling them. And God forbid if you filled in the big cracks. They really believe that an artist purposely put cracks in his paintings.''

"What else did you disagree with Pembrooke about?'' I asked.

"Everything. He stuck his nose in my business all the time, telling me who to hire and who to fire, how to speed up production and cut costs, foolish things like that.''

"You refused?''

"No, I compromised. Every time he wanted a ten percent cut in my budget, I agreed, since I had built in already an increase to take care of such foolishness.''

"Did he ever ask you to fire Hannelore Becker?''

"All the time. He hated her.''

"Why? What did she ever do to him?''

"Nothing worse than she does to me. She doesn't take orders, has no respect for anyone, and expresses herself too freely. Also, she's very slow.''

"Why do you keep her, then?''

"She's very good. When she's finished with a job, I don't have to check, I know it is perfect. And I can trust her with our most costly work, she will never hurt a painting. Mr. Belmont likes her, she's from the old days, and what Mr. Belmont wants, he gets. That's another reason the director wanted to get rid of her. There was an antagonism between the director and Mr. Belmont.''

"But you kept her in spite of Pembrooke's pressure.''

"I run this division; nobody tells me what to do. Although there were times I was tempted to let her go for professional reasons.''

"She did something wrong?''

"She is very old-fashioned. The modern school of restoration is like the doctor's oath: *Primo, non nocere*; first, do no harm. That means, as we interpret it, don't do anything to the artwork that cannot be undone. If you restore an area, underpaint with a layer of varnish and use only acrylics, use different brushwork so that under a tangential light, anyone can see where you made the restoration. That way, if you want to remove what you have done, it comes off easily. Becker has the philosophy that restoration means make it exactly like the artist did it originally, use the same pigments ground by hand, the same substrate, the same binding agents and solvents, the same brushstrokes; to paint like the original artist. She is so good at it that— I have a Rembrandt she finished last year, even I couldn't tell where Rembrandt stopped and Becker started.''

"Isn't that good?'' I asked.

"In some ways, yes,'' she admitted grudgingly. "but there are dangers in this method too.''

"I understand that you are planning a big party for her retirement,'' Alexander said.

"Rand is planning it, I am cooperating. I think, in some ways, it is foolish, she is a poor old woman; give her the money it costs as a gift, make her last years more secure. But in other ways it may be good to bring to the public the awareness of what we do, and to the Board of Trustees too, so I can get my Macroanalyzer.''

"Didn't Mr. Wechsler speak to you and Ken Rand about this in the lunchroom,'' Alexander asked, "the day Pembrooke was killed?''

"Yes, he stopped at our table for a few minutes.''

"How long?''

"One or two minutes. Why do you ask?''

"We're trying to see who had the opportunity to kill Pembrooke,'' I said.

"And you suspect Wechsler?''

"We are checking everybody at this stage. When did you leave the dining room?''

"Rand and I were the last executives to leave. I think it was about ten after one.''

"You don't know the exact time?''

"I didn't know it was going to be important, Mr. Gold.''

"Did you go directly back to your office?"

"I dropped Rand off at the Men's Room, it is across from Korbin's office, and I went to the Ladies' Room next door."

"Couldn't Rand have popped out of the Men's Room as soon as you went to the Ladies' Room and gone into Pembrooke's dining room? It's only a few steps away."

Her eyes narrowed. "What you are really asking, Mr. Gold, is could not I have popped into the director's dining room as soon as Rand went into the Men's Room. Certainly I could, Mr. Gold, but if I did, why should I tell you?"

Quickly I asked, "Who left the dining room before you did, Larsen?"

"Korbin and Gerson. Aren't you going to ask me if one of them could have popped into the director's dining room, Mr. Gold?"

"No," he said, "I'd rather have you tell me why you hated Orville Pembrooke."

"I didn't say I hated him."

"Sure you did, Mrs. Piccoli. Everyone else you call by his last name, even Wechsler, the acting director, just as you want to be called. Pembrooke is always the director. A formal relationship, denoting position only. What did he do to you?"

She looked at me questioningly, like what was a Nice Jewish Girl like me doing with a Male Chauvinist Pig like him, and would I beat her brains in if she really told him off. I looked back as though I wouldn't, since he really had it coming, but to be gentle since he was a good guy at heart and could even be cuddly.

"Mr. Gold," Larsen said calmly, "to you women are weak creatures who should be coddled and protected, to be guided and taken care of by the superior male. There were times when I needed this, such as when I had small babies, and I liked it then. But in other circumstances, in my professional life, I do not carry with me these attitudes, attitudes which apply only to certain specific personal situations and times. I do not appreciate, however well-meaning, your talking to me, unconsciously, as though I were a swooning Victorian maiden. I say this in explanation, without anger, because you are not bad, just blindly rigid in your beliefs, to put in perspective my answer to your question. The director hated women. Really hated them.''

''Then why did he hire you?''

''I was the best available at the time, and in this job you don't take chances on anything less than the best, he knew that much. He thought because I was a woman he could control me, and at the same time, because of my size, he did not look on me as a real woman. So as long as he did not overstep my limits, I did what he wanted. But when he discovered that I was not a simpering fool, he went out of his way, took every opportunity to make my life hell.''

In certain areas, Alexander never learns. ''Why didn't you tell your husband to—'' I quickly stepped on his words. ''Why didn't he fire you?'' I asked.

''By that time I had proven my ability, and the trustees liked me. Also, I was very careful to give him no cause, and it's very difficult to fire a woman executive these days, especially for a tax-exempt institution. He knew I would file suit, make a public case of it. And I knew where lots of bodies were buried. The museum would have suffered greatly if he fired me, and he would have been blamed by the trustees. So I was careful to give no cause for complaint and he was careful to keep his torturing private.''

''What exactly did he do, Larsen?''

''When we were alone he would call me Dolly, Babe, Honey; annoying if it comes from ignorance, hateful if it is done with malice. In my office he would run his finger across my desk and comment on my sloppy housekeeping. He would come up behind me and whisper that my seams were crooked or my slip was showing, even if I were wearing seamless stockings or slacks. But the worst was at the staff meetings. We have disagreements there, naturally, and when the men get emotional, nothing happens. If I raise my voice, even slightly, he sweetly, very sweetly, says that if I had told him I was indisposed, he would gladly have put off the meeting a few days as a courtesy. What do you do, scream that you are not menstruating? I did nothing, and many good ideas went unused. But I remembered."

"Did he do this to every woman," I asked, "or just you?"

"I think only to me, because I stood up to him. But he did it to my people in my presence, deliberately. Three quarters of my conservators are women. Everytime he goes up there with me, he makes believe he is worried about the mental states of my women. He figures out that a period is five days, and he asks me to check his arithmetic, with all the women we have, on any day there are several we shouldn't trust with valuable paintings, statistically. Can you imagine what this does to someone who is working on a Rembrandt? Several quit on me every year, I am sure, because of him; good conservators can always get a job. Can I argue with him in front of the whole room? When I tell him privately to stop this nonsense, he laughs and asks why I am so sensitive this day."

"So you had reason to kill him?" Alexander asked.

"Surely I did," she replied, "but I was waiting for my shining knight on a white horse to do it for me. As he did."

"You're sure it was a man?"

"Everyone else on North Fifth is a man. Unless you think a secretary did it."

"Which man do you think did it?" I asked.

"I don't know and I don't care and I hope you never catch him."

"Do you think Harold Wechsler will be a better director?"

"He couldn't be worse. Wechsler will be bad to everybody equally, but he will act nicer."

"Can we visit your work area?" I asked. "I'd also like to talk to Hannelore Becker, if you don't mind."

"Right now?" When I nodded, she said, "Let's go."

"Wait a minute," I said and turned to Alexander. "Go check out the Men's Room. We'll meet you at the elevator across from Pembrooke's dining room."

Larsen was astounded. "He just does this when you tell him?"

"There's a big advantage to a loving M.C.P. type husband. When I really want something, he does it, even if he thinks it's illogical."

"I must try that with my husband. Joseph will do anything I want provided it is logical. This is not always possible."

"The reason I wanted to talk to you alone," I explained, "is that I felt you would be more open with Alexander gone, although I must tell you I intend to tell him everything you say." I carefully did not mention my cassette recorder.

"I don't mind him; I just thought that it would help you if I opened his eyes a little. Was I too harsh on him?"

"On Alexander? Forget it. What I wanted to know is, did Pembrooke make any advances to you? Did he try to pressure you sexually?"

"The director?" She laughed. "I told you before. He never thought of me as a woman that way. I have a feeling his only outlet was prostitutes; little young helpless-looking girls he could dominate. I'll bet he was a sadist in that too, a whipper. What made you ask?"

"I just thought— You're a very handsome woman, so it would only be natural."

"Thank you, but your opinion doesn't count. I'll prove it. When was the last time you were propositioned, Mrs. Gold?"

"July 7, 1955."

"I thought so. I met *my* husband on May 28, 1961. Why are American men so afraid of flirting, so afraid of big competent women? That's why we always vacation in Europe. I love especially Rome. Once a year I feel like a woman; not that I ever would, but it is nice to be wanted."

"I know what you mean, Larsen. Try Jerusalem for a

change. Better than Rome and without the pinching." We both laughed.

"Sounds good; maybe next year," she said and got up. Then she sat down again. "As long as I am open, you be open too. Why do you want to talk to Becker?"

The question caught me unprepared. "Why, I thought I'd like to see how a conservator works," I said lamely.

She looked at me oddly. "If that's all, you can watch Pistone. He's an N.Y.U. graduate and knows a good deal about conservation." I didn't know what to say. "You give me bullshit, Mrs. Gold, I give you bullshit. You still think I got this job on my looks? Or on my back?"

I shook my head. "I'm sorry; I can't."

She relaxed. "All right, I'll talk, just keep your face where I can watch it. Six weeks ago Becker stopped all work on a Hobbema I had assigned her. Bad as she was before that, these past weeks were like she was guarding the original Holy Grail. Wouldn't open the door even a crack for anyone. When I asked her, in the dining room, what she's doing, she tells me that it is important and it is for the museum, period. What do you think it is, Mrs. Gold?"

"Maybe she's doing private work on company time?"

"Becker? Are you joking? It is more likely that I should steal pennies from a blind newsboy than that she should do something against regulations. No, I know what it is; it happens several times a year. Mr. Belmont has decided to make another gift to the museum. His gift must be perfect, clean, beautiful. Becker is the only one he trusts. But he will let no one see it until he is satisfied with it. Am I correct?"

"I can't discuss anything about Mr. Belmont with you, with anyone. It's all privileged."

"Thank you. I'll go on. It is a Dutch or Flemish seventeenth-century painting, that is always the case, and it is less than eighteen inches square."

"What makes you say that, Larsen?"

"There is a security guard at the entrance to the conservators' area, with a registrar's list. Anything that goes in or comes out gets checked off and signed in.''

"People too?" I asked.

"Forget it. You are thinking that you could check the time Becker left the dining room and the time she got upstairs? You think she might be the killer?''

"Anything is possible," I said weakly.

"All right, wait until you meet her. But the book is useless. The guard doesn't check the exact time, why should he? You could sign in five minutes earlier, five minutes later, it makes no difference.''

"What made you say it was a small painting?''

"The guard would check if he saw a painting. When one of ours comes up, it is wrapped in glassine and comes with a slip from the curator, countersigned by the registrar. The guard checks the number and description against his daily register sheet. When something comes from Mr. Belmont, it comes wrapped in brown paper, no number, the guard marks down 'one package,' and we have no responsibility. When it is clean, Becker calls Mr. Belmont, he comes and looks. If he is happy he calls the curator and the director and me, champagne for everybody, the painting is registered and taken to the preparators area in the South Wing. There are big discussions on what kind of frame, where to display it, the lighting, the publicity, that sort of thing.''

"Evidently that didn't happen this time.''

"No. Yesterday Becker started working on the Hobbema again. She told me. Not to make me happy, she couldn't care less if I am happy or sad, but because she is a professional. So the painting has to be back in Mr. Belmont's house, which is just across the street. I checked the register, nothing marked in or out. So it had to be small enough to fit into Becker's tote bag.''

"Couldn't Becker, or anyone, steal a small painting that way?''

"We have other devices and techniques which prevent

an art work from leaving the area, or the floor, or the museum, without authorization. No, it could only happen with a work which is not ours. So tell me, you are working for Mr. Belmont. You come asking about the murder but you spend half your time talking about Becker. She is that interesting to you? I doubt it. Mr. Belmont did not come here to look when the restoration was finished. The painting is back at his house. Why?''

"I really can't discuss privileged information, Larsen.''

"So it is a very expensive painting, small, Lowlands, seventeenth-century, major artist. Why is it back at Mr. Belmont's house? Something is wrong? No, not wrong; doubtful. Only found when the cleaning was completed. A forgery? An incorrect attribution? A school of, rather than the master? What? You are trying very hard not to move your face, Mrs. Gold. All right, I know who it must be, and I will say nothing, although I think it must be impossible. Tell Mr. Belmont it is not real, not to waste his money. Since the scientific testing worked out— don't look so surprised, Mrs. Gold, why would Becker spend six weeks on a little painting otherwise? Unless the tests were positive and the painting very valuable? Since the tests are good, it must be of that period and that place. But there are none in existence as far as anyone knows. So it is a pupil copying the master; although we know of no such pupil, still there are so very few records that it just may be. Possible that there is even some work done by the master himself, that is why everyone is confused.''

"I'm not saying you're right, Larsen, but your logic is perfect.''

"People here all think I am slow. Not true. I am careful, as I must be in my position. It is my training and my experience. Tell Mr. Belmont that if he values my knowledge, I will give him my opinion. I would like to see this painting.''

I chose my words carefully. "I'll report to Mr. Belmont what you said.''

We both went to meet Alexander. Weren't there any *stupid* people on North Fifth?

# XIII

"**M**y god," I said, "I didn't realize it was so big." There must have been thirty people working in the huge room that ran the full length of the North Wing. The line of big picture windows had opaque shades that ran up from the bottom as well as down from the top. The exterior half of the room was under a pitched roof, like a greenhouse, made entirely of glass, again with light-control shades movable from two directions. Large portions of the flat part of the roof had domed skylights with draw shades. Screens were set so that each conservator's work area could be lighted to suit his requirements. There were movable fluorescent and incandescent lights hanging from the ceiling and bracketed out from the walls. "It's practically a factory," I told Alexander.

I looked at Larsen with new respect. Until I saw it in action, I couldn't have imagined the magnitude of her job; when she told me how important it was, I had put it down to vanity. Most of the conservators were women, most of them working at easels. One painting, at least ten feet long, had a dark bottom half; the difference between the cleaned upper portion and the untouched lower half was like night and day. I began to appreciate some of the things Larsen had described. A young man, sitting in a chair, was carefully cleaning this giant with a cotton swab; a lifetime job, minimum.

On the long inside wall was a set of big pegboard panels screwed to the wall, holding what looked like a hardware store sale: rubber, plastic, and wooden-headed mallets; hammers of varying sizes and shapes, some of which were like nothing I had ever seen; chisels, large and small, wide and narrow; gouges of different curvatures and shapes; screwdrivers by the dozen; nail-sets, picks, punches; saws in an amazing variety of sizes and types; rulers, straightedges, and T-squares; compasses, dividers, and gauges; squares, planes, rasps, pliers, pincers, spokeshaves; you name it, it was there.

On the tables in front of the pegboards were cans of brushes by size, mahlsticks, palette knifes and scrapers; surgical instruments, needles, clamps, tweezers, lancets, hemostats, and hypodermics, and tools and instruments I didn't know the names of. Boxes holding tubes of paint were stacked on every open area.

On a nearby table were electrical control boxes, extension cords, little electric stoves, things that looked like old-fashioned flatirons with oval bottoms, rollers, electric—were they spatulas?—and other things with wires sticking out. A rack held magnifying glasses and loupes. On the wall were hooks with portable lights: big, small, round, oval, long, shaded, oddly colored. Next to these were rolling tripods with microscopes on swinging arms.

Finally there were shelves of brown bottles in marked categories. I read the names into my cassette recorder, just in case: alcohols, esters, ethers, ketones, paraffin hydrocarbons, aromatic hydrocarbons, essential oils, chlorinated hydrocarbons, and alkaline reagents. Each section had several labeled bottles. There were small drums marked isopropyl alcohol, ethyl alcohol, acetone, turpentine, and clear varnish. Fire extinguishers were all around and there were sprinkler heads and Halon outlets on every flat surface. Big signs: IF YOU HAVE A MATCH OR A LIGHTER ON YOU—YOU'RE FIRED.

"I see you have sodium hydroxide," Alexander said to Larsen. "Isn't lye dangerous to have around paintings? And I don't see any acids."

"Everything here is dangerous to have around paintings. You think if someone spills a bottle of carbon tetrachloride on a painting, it is going to do the painting any good? We do have acids, but they are of very little use, and dangerous to use as well. I keep them in a locked cabinet and only allow a conservator to use one if I find nothing else that will work. In fact, I think I'm going to keep the lye, the ammonia, and the other alkaline reagents locked up too, they should only be used for removing the most stubborn repaintings." Suddenly she turned around and yelled, "Pistone!"

The young man working on the big painting got up and approached our little group. "Why does this place have to look like a pigsty, Pistone?" Larson asked. "You expect me to trust you with major works and you can't even keep the tools in their proper places?"

"It's Becker's fault," he said. "She never hangs anything up."

"Now you're blaming the old lady, Pistone? It's your responsibility; either get them to do it or do it yourself."

"You try to get her to do anything," he muttered and began hanging tools on the pegboard. "The big shots are worse; they take things and never return them."

We had moved a few steps away, so I asked her, "Why pick on the poor kid in front of everybody? If he's no good, can't you just fire him?"

"That poor kid is the one I'm training to be my assistant. You think I waste time criticizing hopeless cases?"

"Where are the scientific instruments?" Alexander asked.

"East Wing, at the other end of the building. We can't keep delicate instruments in this madhouse."

"Why does this area look more like a carpentry shop than an art gallery?" I asked.

"Old paintings are on wood. Canvas only came into general use in the seventeenth century. Lots of things can go wrong with wood: warping, splitting, raised grain, loose knots, fungus, rot, woodworm, you name it. It is harder, sometimes, to restore the support than the pigment layer. Clumsy workmanship or techniques used in the past often damaged the support, which makes it even harder to fix. You can't lift the paint layer off wood or metal support the way you can with canvas."

"Lift the paint?" I was shocked. "Does that mean what it sounds like?"

"We don't remove the paint from the canvas, we remove the canvas from the paint. It is not as bad as it sounds; there is always a ground between the canvas and the pigment layer. We only do it when the support is in very bad shape."

We came to the room at the west end of the conservators' area. The sign on the door said, simply, 'H. Becker'. Larsen knocked. "Go away," came the response in a high, thin tone. "I'm busy."

"Mr. and Mrs. Gold are here to see you," Larsen said. "Mr. Belmont sent them."

A limping-walk sound echoed on the bare wood floor and the door was unlocked. Hannelore Becker looked her age, her little round face covered with a network of tiny wrinkles. She was nowhere near as ugly as I had expected from Belmont's description, but she was no beauty either. Her gray hair, still very long, was pulled back in a big bun. In addition to her thick glasses, she wore a headband to which was fixed a pair of magnifying lenses on metal stalks, tilted up, so that she looked like a gnome with antennae. She was a little below average in height and slightly plump, holding herself stiffly upright; I remembered the fused vertebrae. Brown slacks showed below her spotless gray smock. As she walked back to her table, she limped a little on her stiff right leg, but it seemed to me that she took much smaller, apparently painful steps than her condition required.

"Still the sciatica, Becker?" Larsen asked.

152

"Two months already," she replied with a strong German accent, "and still it hasn't gone yet."

"Didn't you go to a doctor as I told you? It's free; we have major medical."

"Doctors, what do they know? What I need is rest and heat."

"Next week, Becker, then you can rest. How are you doing with the Hobbema?" Larsen motioned toward the painting on the table.

"I was just finishing the blisters, but all the interruption. . . ." She sat down at the table, snapped down her magnifying lenses, and with her left hand she turned on the infrared heat lamp hanging above the painting. With a pair of tongs she selected the smallest hypodermic from a batch sitting in a double-boiler full of hot water on the electric stove at the end of her table. The hypodermic was already filled with a pale yellow fluid. Carefully she wiped the needle dry. Guiding the tip with her left hand, she gently inserted the needle into a tiny blister in the paint and injected a bit of the yellow fluid. She repeated this on the rest of the blisters, then put the hypo back into the hot water. Becker then carefully spread a piece of tissue paper over the area she had just completed and with one of the little oval flatirons taken from another electric heater, she carefully ironed over the tissue paper. She then dampened the tissue paper and peeled it from the painting. "Pistone," she yelled, "come and clean these needles." She turned off the heaters and the infrared light and said to Larsen, with evident satisfaction, "That's how to do it."

"Becker," Larsen said, "that Hobbema took you twice as long as it should have. If you would just lance the blisters and spread on the glue size, you could produce twice as much work."

"Yah, and in your way, you know how much glue goes in each blister? Too much? Not enough? In fifty years, in a hundred years, you do it over again, no? My way, it is forever.''

Larsen looked at her suspiciously. "Forever? What glue did you use, Becker? Our regular glue?''

The old lady smiled triumphantly. "Polyurethane. Don't worry, I bought it myself.''

Larsen got red. "Are you crazy? What is some squeezed out of the blisters and got on the front? You know how to take off polyurethane? I don't.''

"Don't worry, I put the exact right amount in.''

"Becker, one of these days—''

"Yah? You fire me because I do the work too good? Go tell Mr. Belmont that.''

Larsen walked to the door, turned around and said, "Fortunately, it's just another few days. I have more important things to do than try to teach a stubborn old fool new tricks. Ask her anything you want.'' The door slammed. What I caught was that if we used rubber hoses and a thousand-watt bare bulb, that would be just fine with Larsen.

"I see you have windows facing the park too, Miss Becker,'' I said. "It's a lovely view from up here.''

"Who has time to look?'' she replied. "I took this room because I need the west light.''

"I thought artists like north light. It's uniform.''

"Jan Vermeer used west light.''

"Isn't very little known about Vermeer?'' I asked gently.

"There are maps to show where the Mechelen, his house, was. Right on the west side of the market square, near the church. In Holland, the houses are touching each other; his windows faced east and west. On the back side was a canal, the Vordersgracht, and more houses across the street. That's where he painted, on the west side, second floor.''

"Couldn't he have been on the east side?''

"No, the color of the light is west,'' she said with finality. "Go look at his work. Any fool can plainly see that.''

Alexander began at once. "About the Third Vermeer, Miss Becker. Four respected experts said it was genuine. Yet you disagree."

"Four *patzers*, but I don't disagree, Mr. Gold. When I first saw it, I thought, I was sure it was real too."

"You took one look and decided?" he asked.

"Mr. Gold, you put my Mitzi in a room with one hundred black cats, I pick her out in one minute. Mitzi I live with for twenty-one years. Vermeer was my life, all my life. You think I don't know Vermeer? After I cleaned it I saw— Vermeer did not do such things, I put my life on it. So I tell Mr. Belmont, ask Gröber-Eisenberg, he is not so stupid like the others. Tell him look at the details, the background, the patterns. Vermeer did skin so the light comes out. Ears are all skin, light goes *through* ears. Nobody can copy that, the way he made it."

"So if Gröber-Eisenberg says it is fake, then it is fake, agreed, Miss Becker? But what if he says it is real?"

"That he cannot do; I know. But if he does, then I keep my mouth shut and say nothing. Who will listen to a stupid old lady? I am not a Herr Doktor Professor like Maurice Gröber-Eisenberg."

Nothing to be gained there; we'd just have to wait two more days until G-E came. "You sit near the door of the dining room, don't you?" I asked.

"Closest door. Why should I walk more than I must?"

"When did you go in to eat the day of the murder?"

"About a quarter to one, like usual."

"And you left a little after one?"

"Like usual. I have work to do; I can't take one hour like the others. Larsen complains always I am too slow. I am not too slow, I am careful."

"You saw Mr. Pembrooke look into the dining room?"

"Sure, I always see him."

"And you left right afterwards?"

"As soon as I am ready, a few minutes."

"And you went right upstairs?"

"Not stairs, elevator. I don't like stairs."

"Did you have a long wait for the elevator?"

"A minute, I think."

"Think carefully, did you see anyone near Pembrooke's door. Or in the corridor? Either the corridor outside the dining room or the executive corridor?"

"Nobody."

I looked at Alexander. He had no more questions, so I went back to the painting. "Did you forge the Third Vermeer?" I asked suddenly.

Becker smiled sadly. "Mrs. Gold, I come from the wrong place and the wrong time. There, in my day, the law was respected absolutely, and a uniform, even a streetcar conductor's uniform, was holy. One did not break the law; one did what the uniform ordered. Even today, I cannot cross on red and I cannot take unearned coins from a telephone box."

"Will you please answer directly?" Alexander broke in. "Did you forge the Third Vermeer? The *Girl in a Blue Kimono*?"

"No," she said, mimicking his tone, "I did not forge the Third Vermeer, the *Girl in a Blue Kimono*. I have never forged any painting and I never will. I would die before I forged a Vermeer."

"Surely," I said, trying to soften the atmosphere, "surely you must have had some offers to . . . An artist with your skill . . . I have seen the copies you made for Mr. Belmont; they're perfect."

She relaxed noticeably. "Not perfect. Far from perfect. But not bad, either. Yes, Mrs. Gold, I had many offers, especially when I was younger. But it is illegal to forge a painting and I cannot do anything which is illegal."

"Can you do something which is immoral?" Alexander asked.

She looked at him in evident respect. "You are asking if I can lie. I understand. In the convent school the sisters told us that for this sin I burn in Hell for one thousand years, for that sin I burn ten thousand years. But sometimes, you are human, not an angel, sometimes you think this sin or that sin, it is worth to burn for. I have sinned in the past, and I may sin again, I do not know. But I am very . . . I feel very bad to sin and I would not do it easily. I would have a bad conscience.''

"What did you think of Mr. Pembrooke?" I asked.

"A terrible man, a monster. Always he tried to get me fired, but Mr. Belmont protected me. Larsen too, she would not fire me. She acts angry, but she knows I do good work. Just because I do not bow to Pembrooke he tries to fire me. I am happy he is dead. I know it is wrong, but I am happy. He deserved to die.''

"Deserved to die? Just because he wanted to fire you?"

"He did other bad things too. To everybody. All the time. I hated him.''

"Hate, yes," Alexander said. "But why did he deserve to die?"

"He killed Mitzi. He was a murderer!"

"Mitzi? Your cat?"

"My beautiful Mitzi. So good. So smart. She used to sit right here, on my table.''

"While you were working on an expensive painting?"

"She knew better than to swish her tail over a wet painting. I put a light over her to keep her warm. I had her ever since she was a baby. She understood everything that I said to her.''

"How did Pembrooke kill her?" I asked.

"He came into my room once, without permission. Mitzi knew him for what he was and properly scratched him. The next day he issued an order to the guards that no animals were allowed in the museum. I could have forced my way in, no guard would have dared to touch me, but then Pembrooke would have fired one as an example. They all had families, so what could I do? I had to leave her home; we had never been separated one minute in her whole life. Mitzi died a week later of loneliness, of a broken heart. Pembrooke killed her.''

"But Miss Becker," I said, "twenty-one in a cat is

equivalent to one hundred forty-seven in a human being. Could it not be that she died of old age?''

"She was almost human, you didn't know her. She would have lived as long as I did. Cats can live till over thirty. How many years you think I have left, hah? I took good care of Mitzi, liver and carp, cream, all her favorites. We would have been buried together. Pembrooke killed her deliberately.'' Tears filled her eyes.

To change the subject a bit, I asked, "How did you bring Mitzi to work, Miss Becker?"

"In my tote bag, with my purse and everything." She tried to reach under the table but her back was too rigid. She stood up and, holding the table with her right hand, her right foot sliding straight behind her, she leaned her whole body stiffly forward and with her left hand pulled out a large square canvas tote bag with leather edging and long leather handles. "She stayed in there very quiet. No one in the bus even knew she was in there. She never made any trouble.''

"Isn't it dangerous to keep your purse in a tote bag?" I asked. "A thief could pull it off your shoulder easily. Or reach in and take out your purse.''

"It has special long handles; I wear it over my left shoulder across my body with the bag on my left hip. Not on my right hip on account of my leg. I keep my left hand inside all the time to let Mitzi know I am there taking care of her. No thief could take anything out. Mitzi would scratch him.''

Enough of cats, time to change the subject. "Where is the painting now, Miss Becker?"

"I took it to Mr. Belmont's house yesterday, after work.''

"In the tote bag?''

"Sure, there is plenty room now, without Mitzi.''

"The security guard?''

"What is in my bag is not his business. He only knows from museum property. They have ways to know if you take out museum property. Electronic ways.''

"Miss Becker," I said, "let's get back to the Pembrooke murder. Who do you think did it?"

"How should I know?"

"All right, who *could* have done it?"

"Pistone. He's a nasty boy, always yelling at me. He shows no respect."

"Do you show respect for Larsen?" I asked.

"That's different," she said. "I'm older. She knows very well I respect her, even though she is all wrong on conservation."

Alexander and I left as gracefully as we could. I didn't even ask him his opinion, and it wasn't only because she was a cripple. If tomorrow's interviews were as fruitless as today's, and there was no reason they should not be, I'd have to buy a Ouija board. My only hope was that Pearl had dug up something. Or Warshafsky; that's how desperate I was.

# XIV

**P**earl's big contribution was the news that Pembrooke had worked three summers in an oyster bar on Cape Cod. "It's only been one day," was her excuse. I gave her the four cassettes of our interviews and we went upstairs. Alexander was already in the kitchen waiting to be revitalized; he suggested hot chocolate with whipped cream. He got cocoa made with skim milk, but I put in real vanilla plus a drop of almond extract to catalyze his thinking.

"Did you notice," I asked, "all the T-squares and straightedges lying around the conservators' area?"

"You're thinking of the smoothing out of the carpet around Pembrooke's chair?" he asked.

"Becker or Larsen could have picked one up easily; it would never be noticed. A twelve-inch ruler could have been kept in the breast pocket of Larsen's suit and an even longer one in Becker's tote bag."

"Can you see Becker bending down to sweep the floor with a ruler? It's a long way from the door to around Pembrooke's dining room table."

"Anyone in the museum could have a straightedge,"

Pearl said. "I'll bet, if you looked, there's a ruler in the desk of every executive on the floor, or in his secretary's desk."

"But it changes everything," I said. "Remember how we were talking about the killer doing everything in one minute, zip in to kill Pembrooke, zip to the door and peek out, zip across to the elevator or the stair? Well, there's no more zip. He had to bend down and smooth out the carpet first."

"There's something else," Pearl said. "How does he sweep the carpet near the door? If he's standing with his eye at the crack waiting for the coast to be clear so he can dash across to the elevator, first he has to step back, open the door, bend down and reach in with his ruler and straighten our the carpet pile, and then close the door. Ten seconds at least, and it's a very odd-looking position, bent over with his behind sticking out in the hall. Anyone who came past couldn't help remembering what he saw the killer doing at Pembrooke's door."

"That's good thinking, Pearl," I said. Then I had an idea. "Maybe the straightedge had a handle. I don't mean a brush necessarily, the wooden back of the brush, I mean a carpenter's folding rule. You can open a six-foot folding rule and fold it so you have a twelve-inch straight section in the middle, with two long arms turned up and brought together to make a long narrow triangle. It would fold up to fit in any pocket and you could use it to smooth the carpet without bending. Couldn't that have been used, Alexander?"

"I'm sure it could, but there's still the time it takes to fold and unfold, and to do the sweeping, and he would still have to stand in the corridor and reach in to smooth his last footprints. As long as we're on that subject, there's something else to consider. Burton said the carpet had been smoothed all around Pembrooke's chair. I'm sure he didn't mean that exactly since there was the footstool directly behind Pembrooke's chair. I'm assuming that the area around the chair and the footstool were smoothed—check that with Burton, Pearl, and if it's any different, let me know—all around the chair and footstool, which is a fairly large area to sweep across. It was not done on a whim. It had to be that the killer walked around Pembrooke to get from Pembrooke's left to Pembrooke's right. Now why would he do that?''

"Because he was left-handed?" I guessed.

"That's a good reason," Alexander said, "assuming he moved there after he decided to kill Pembrooke with the oyster knife.''

"But the oyster knife was on Pembrooke's left," Pearl said. "The killer would have to reach in front of Pembrooke to pick it up. Pembrooke could grab his arm, at least, if he tried that.''

"And if the killer first picked up the knife," I said, "and then went to the other side, why did Pembrooke just sit there like a dope. Was he drugged?''

"Positively not," Pearl said. "I asked Burton again last night. The medical examiner is wise to all the tricks, like an injection under the tongue.''

"The whole doping idea is silly," Alexander said. "If you can get your victim to open his mouth and lift up his tongue, why not inject poison instead of using a knife? No one was trying to hide the fact of murder.''

"A doctor could get you to open your mouth," Pearl said. "Or a dentist. Especially a dentist.''

"If it makes you happy," Alexander said, "check if Maxwell Korbin was treating Pembrooke for hoof-and-mouth disease. No, there has to be some reason why the killer stood on Pembrooke's right, the worst possible place.''

"Maybe it was a fake," I said, "to throw suspicion on Konrad Dorner because he's left-handed. How much extra time could it take to sweep the folded rule across that part of the carpet?''

"Or maybe it was a red herring," Pearl said. "Maybe sweeping the wrong side of the desk was done to hide the sweeping altogether, the fact that the sweeping was done to hide a distinctive shoe or an unusual walk.''

"Becker has the walk," I said, "and Larsen has high heels."

"And Dorner has big feet," Alexander added. "I'm sure every one of our suspects has something distinctive about his feet or shoes or walk. This isn't getting us anywhere, we just don't have enough data. Maybe tomorrow's interviews will give us more."

"Shouldn't we analyze the painting problem?" I asked. "If that one isn't solved, you don't even get a chance not to lose the hundred grand."

"All right, Norma," he waved his hand regally, "you have my permission to solve it."

"Don't get smart with me, Alexander. The brilliant way you set up the bet with Belmont, we're not even allowed to solve the painting problem unless Herr Doktor Professor Maurice G-E says the painting is authentic. All I want to talk about is what we learned today."

"We didn't learn anything today, although everyone else seemed to. You told me that Freya Larsen figured out what it was from what she already knew and your non-poker face. Konrad Dorner now has a good idea that such a painting exists and that he is being left out. You can be sure he'll do some digging. Harold Wechsler didn't volunteer anything about the painting, and why should he? With his brains he probably knows everything the others do and then some. If they're all telling the truth, and I wouldn't bet my life on that, they each are guessing pretty accurately, but they don't know anything. We know more about the painting than they do, and they're learning from us, not the other way around."

"Hannelore Becker knows more about the painting than we do," I told him.

"Sure," he said, "and she says she didn't forge it. But she as good as admitted that she tells lies, so where does that leave us? If she did forge it, why say now that it is a forgery, and how did she get it into the cellar of the Tretjakov Museum in Moscow?"

"There's something funny there," I said. "At first she said it was a Vermeer. Then it wasn't. Did she change her mind after Belmont told her that Pembrooke was the owner? She really hates Pembrooke and might take this means to get even."

"I'm sure, from what I've seen of Belmont, that he told her the whole story before he showed her the painting," Alexander said. "But that's a good point." He turned to Pearl. "Call Belmont later. Find out when he told Becker the painting was Pembrooke's. If she changed her mind after she found out about Pembrooke, it almost guarantees that the painting is a real Vermeer."

"But Alexander," I objected, "didn't you get the feeling that she loved Vermeer so much that she couldn't lie about him or his work?"

"Sure I did, but I also got the feeling that she would lie if the incentive were great enough and that there is nothing she wouldn't do to get even with Pembrooke. But this is premature; a waste of time. We'll find out about the painting after, not before but after, we find Pembrooke's killer. The two problems have to be connected."

"By the same logic," I said, "we'll find Pembrooke's killer when we figure out how the murder was committed."

"Isn't that obvious," Alexander asked. "Haven't I always said so?"

"Well, now that we know what to do," I said, "the problem is half-solved as of today. Tomorrow we talk to Zager, Rand, Gerson, and Korbin; the day after, Dr. Maurice examines the painting; the fourth day you unveil the dastardly killer; the fifty day you prove the painting is real or fake or whatever; the sixth day we get the check from Belmont; and on the seventh day we all go down to the seashore and rest."

Alexander squirmed. "It may not be exactly in that order," he said. "We should stay flexible. But if you think you can do better, Norma—"

Pearl tried to stop the fight. "Do you want me to keep on putting the Pembrooke report together, Alex?"

"It can't hurt, but I'd like you to spend a little time calling around your circle of gossips. See who's been sleeping with whom, or anything else that might be useful."

Pure fumbling; might as well drop the whole matter. "Did Art Kaplan bring you the applications for the pistol licenses the way I asked him to?"

"Yes," Pearl said. "Why three?"

"One for each of us; what did you think?"

"I don't want one," Pearl said. "The idea of having a gun in the house frightens me. I could never bring myself to shoot at another human being.

"Even if that human being is trying to kill you?"

"There are other ways to defend yourself."

"Such as?"

"Aikido. It's a form of Japanese unarmed self-defense—aikido means 'the way of harmonizing spiritual energy.'"

"Yeah? The Japanese are very good at poetic imagery. Can't shooting someone be called 'the application of gentle pressure to provide needed instruction in thermodynamic expansion'?"

"I don't care if you make fun of it, Norma, aikido is very graceful and beautiful. And spiritual. It's like Zen in motion."

"What good is graceful," I asked, "if someone is trying to kill you?"

"Yes, Pearl, why aikido?" Alexander asked. "Why not karate or judo?"

"They're too violent; aikido can only be used in self-defense. I took my first lesson today," she said defiantly.

"Without telling me?" I said. "I'm your partner."

"I knew you'd make fun of it, so I went by myself. Master Kori, he's my teacher, says I'm so flexible that I don't have to work on that and I was able to start on falling the first day."

"Falling? How about making the other guy fall down, Pearl?"

"You have to learn to fall yourself first, Norma, and to absorb the philosophy. The whole idea is to move circularly and to coordinate with your opponent's force so as to guide it around you harmlessly, like water flowing around a rock or a bamboo yielding to the wind. I'm going for an hour every day."

Hopeless. "All right," I said, "type out one application for me and one for Alexander. We'll sign them tomorrow."

"I don't want a gun either," he said.

"You?" I said. "*You* don't?" Two defections in one day? I'm proud to be a liberal, but when someone wants to kill me, political philosophy doesn't enter into the immediate problem. "But Alexander, they've tried to kill you twice already."

"A gun wouldn't have helped in either case."

"But the next time?"

"A gun changes the way you think," Alexander said, "and the way you think affects the way you act. My way is the way of logic, of rationality; if a confrontation comes to violence, I have already failed in some way. If I have a gun I may fail more easily, even possibly, want to fail, so that I can exercise the power of the gun. I am skilled in rational thinking, I am not skilled in gun use. The person I pull the gun on may be more skilled in its use than I am. I view a gun as a handicap."

"Alexander, you're depending on your strength to save your life. But what good is strength if your enemy is a thousand feet away?"

"What good is a pistol then?"

"All right, what if he's at the other end of the room, where your muscles can't reach him?"

"Anything is a weapon, Norma, it depends on the intent. A hammer can be used to drive a nail, it can also crush a skull. This hot cocoa can be drunk or flung at someone; the cup can be thrown, or broken and used to cut. This saucer—are these expensive saucers, Norma?"

"No, cheap stuff, earthenware. Why?"

"I want to show you something. Don't be frightened." His right hand went out—I'm used to his amazing speed of reaction, but this seemed faster than ever before—picked up the saucer by the rim and flipped it, like a Frisbee, across the kitchen, so fast it looked like a white ribbon. It smashed against the wall and broke through the heavy plaster. "I'll fix it myself later," he said, "but I thought it was important to show you, to give you the confidence that I can take care of myself. If a man with a gun had been standing there, this would have taken his head off. I feel bad knowing that you are worried about me."

"All right, Alexander, I won't press you. *You* can take care of yourself. Can you take care of *me*?"

"With my life, Norma, you know that. With my life. Pearl too."

What was there to say? That I didn't want him to take care of me with his life? That I wanted the *killer* to lose his life if he attacked me or Alexander? Or even Pearl, my partner? I would have to apply for a gun all by myself, take care of both of them all by myself. I just hoped that nothing would come up where I needed a gun for at least six more months from now, when I got my permit. Fat chance. Alexander had five more days to determine if the painting was real or fake. In order to do that, according to him, he had to find the killer first. I had better have plenty of saucers handy. Cheap ones.

# XV

**"I** started wearing a bow tie again," Rand said, "right after he was killed." Ken Rand looked more like a small-town banker than the stereotypical public relations man. Short, round, and gray haired, conservatively dressed in a navy business suit, Rand was wearing a red bow tie with yellow polka dots. Somehow it looked right. "That was the first thing he stole from me, and he wouldn't let me wear one again."

"You like bow ties that much?" I asked.

"Not particularly, but when you have no outstanding physical characteristics you have to leave behind something to remember, to focus attention. You, for instance, will always be The Tall One; Mr. Gold will be remembered because he has to go through a door sideways, but what is memorable about me?"

"Is it important that you be remembered? I thought that PR men gave their best lines to their clients."

"We are self-effacing," he said. "The day of the flamboyant Barnum type is long gone. But if I pick up the phone to call a network VP in Hollywood, I don't want to hear his secretary say, 'It's *a* Mr. Rand, sir'; I want her to say 'It's Ken Rand and you'd never believe the color of the tie he told me he's wearing today.'"

"Why did it bother you that Pembrooke took the bow tie symbol from you? Aren't you supposed to do things like that for your clients?"

"You never take another man's symbol. Never. Have you ever heard anyone but Joe Penner say, 'You wanna buy a duck?' or anyone but Jack Pearl say, 'Vas you dere, Sharlie?' Even today, after they've been dead for a long time? Have you ever noticed that no two circus clowns have the same clown face? You think that's accidental? In my business, symbols are valuable property and no one, not the worst, will stoop so low as to take another man's symbol."

"So you get another. Aren't you supposed to have fertile imaginations in your profession, Mr. Rand?"

"Once, when I was ten, I watched a pitchman in the street. He was selling magic decks of cards. Suddenly I understood the trick he was demonstrating, and without thinking blurted out, 'I know how to do that.' Without interrupting what he was doing the pitchman said, 'Don't talk, duplicate.' I learned a lot from those three words. I think I've never learned anything so well or so quickly, and I'm sure I became a PR man right then and there. I realized that it was an ordinary deck of cards he was selling, nothing magic or unusual about them at all. His smooth, seamless patter, his professional skill and his professional words, his professional presentation was the magic, the spell that transformed these ordinary cards into magic cards. So, Mrs. Gold, duplicate. Tell me what symbol I could have taken that would be firmly identified with me, that would be simple to maintain, that would be cheap, easy to use, go everywhere with me, not be too outrageous, not reflect badly on the institution I represent, not harm anyone, and yet be mine and mine alone."

I thought. And I thought. "A flashy regular tie?" He shook his head. "No ties; nothing close to what Pembrooke wore. No article of clothing, in fact, is permissible."

"Paint your nose purple?" I finally said in desperation.

"Not easy, is it? What I did was wear a small white

orchid in my lapel at all times. It cost me somewhat more than bow ties but there was one advantage. Whenever someone admired the flower, the next day she got a dozen white orchids in a beautiful box, presented to her in front of all her associates, with a nice note. Compliments of the museum. She never forgot me or the museum.''

"Then why did you go back to the bow tie?''

"It's mine. I feel more comfortable with it. You should only use symbols you're comfortable with.''

"Did you give Pembrooke the other symbols too? The shaven head, the oysters and champagne?''

"Who else? He had no imagination, just copied from others.''

"You seem to resent him,'' I said. "Wasn't publicizing him part of your job?''

"Not really. We clashed there; professionally, I mean. My job is public relations for the museum, and there is plenty of good stuff here to publicize. We have a great museum, great exhibits, the kind of newsworthy information that the media want and will take, if it's presented professionally in well-written releases with good, sharp, reproducible photographs. Couple that with well-prepared openings, good food and drink, interesting people—why there is no way *not* to get dignified, extensive publicity. Look at our attendance records, that's solid evidence.''

"I've seen pictures of gangsters and rock stars at your openings.''

His face darkened. "*That* was Pembrooke's idea. Maybe it brought us a few more lines in the sensational press, but how many of their readers go to museums at all? I'm sure it cost us sales of the promotional items; have you seen that picture of Miss Bigboobs wearing a Botticelli *Adoration of the Magi* T-shirt? Sickening.''

"So you objected to all his personal publicity?''

"It was overdone, but it wasn't the amount, it was the type. I could have placed one major article by him a year, maybe two, if he had taken the trouble to write them. I could have had them rewritten for the popular media, arranged symposia about them, gotten panel discussions on TV, no problem. Dignified, appropriate shows."

"What do you mean 'rewritten'? I thought Pembrooke was very literate, a scholar."

"That's the trouble; scholarly writing goes into scholarly journals. Very few scholars can write well for the mass media: Hoving and one or two others, that's all."

"Mr. Rand," Alexander said, "why am I getting the impression from you that you are the only person in the museum who didn't actively hate Pembrooke?"

"Normal protective reaction, I guess. I didn't want you to think I was a murderer."

"Are you, Mr. Rand?"

"No, certainly not. Let me put your mind at ease, Mr. Gold, I'm one of the great crowd. I didn't realize it would be suspicious for me *not* to hate Pembrooke."

"What did he do to you, Mr. Rand?"

He stopped for a while, then lectured. "PR is not like it was in the old days: a starlet dropping her bathing suit at Cannes, or a has-been singer walking a leopard down Fifth Avenue. That stuff is out. Modern journalists, especially in the arts, are a pretty sophisticated lot, and pretty cynical. They have their jobs, you have your job. My job is to make sure that all the *proper* information is available to *them* in a *clear* format which presents the information in a manner *I* think is right, in *time* to suit *their* needs and *their* deadlines. If the matter is newsworthy, they'll do the rest. If it is consistently *not* newsworthy, after a while they will kill you, or even worse, ignore you. So I make sure that everything is well prepared and that no one is slighted. Occasionally I give some information a little ahead of time or in a little more detail to someone who's been especially good to us, but I don't play favorites. Over a period of time everything is balanced out. I level with them too. If a press event only requires the second or third stringer, I tell them. They trust me, and I don't let them down."

"Pembrooke let them down?"

"And me, too. Deliberately. Out of general meanness and to keep me nervous, as if my job weren't ulcerous enough normally. I don't know why, I never did anything to him. If I had something important scheduled for 4:00 P.M., so the boys could get it on the six o'clock news, he'd sit in his office until 4:30, doing nothing. Meanwhile, the lights are hot, the TV people are wondering if they can make their next story or will their producer chew them out, the food is getting cold and the ice is melting. Then, just to vary things a bit, he'd come in a half-hour early, give the story to whoever was there, and disappear, leaving half the people, the ones who got there on schedule, sore at me. When I gave him a release to read, and I really sweated over some of them myself, making sure every word was perfect, he'd change my key words as he spoke, promising more than we were delivering, making the release sound like a miracle soap commercial."

"I've wondered about that sometimes," I said. "Sometimes, when I went to a special exhibit, I'd come out feeling a little disappointed, a bit cheated, and I never realized why before."

"Now you know, Mrs. Gold. But I could live with that. Every client has these stupid little tricks, only they do them accidentally. What really bothered me was the way he took credit for every idea that worked and blamed me publicly for every one he messed up. He attacked my professional competence in ways I could not fight. If I went public, the museum would suffer and I'd be marked a fink. I couldn't go around to disappointed donors and tell them it wasn't my fault. So I just took it and waited for his retirement."

"Or his murder?" Alexander asked.

"Believe it or not, Mr. Gold, I figured it for a real possibility, only I thought it would happen in the street somewhere, or in his apartment. He knew a lot of people I wouldn't like to be associated with."

"How are you going to publicize the murder?" I asked.

"I've already started. The general theme is to play up the museum as a rock of stability in the art world, that will go on playing its role no matter what, and to play down Pembrooke's part in it. I've already got a good guy doing an article about all of Pembrooke's mistakes, overpayments, lawsuits, sharp practices, things like that. Ostensibly it's about the poor judgments made by *all* museum directors, but believe me, Pembrooke will be the star. Naturally it will end with the idea that the murder was due to some personal problem and had nothing to do with the museum at all. Then I have another release on Wechsler, how competent he is, how different from Pembrooke, what his program for the museum is, how much the museum will benefit from this new quiet style."

"And if Wechsler appreciates, concretely, what you're doing for him. . . ?"

"Then there will be lots of goodies like this in his future."

"What if the killer is a top executive of the museum?" Alexander asked.

Rand looked Alexander straight in the eye. "It wasn't, Mr. Gold. Read my releases for the next few days. You'll see it was personal."

"But what if it really was one of the museum's executives?" Alexander persisted.

"Then you've got a real problem, Mr. Gold, because every one of them is smart enough to get away with it. And if there's any way to help him, whoever he is, I will do it."

Alexander clearly didn't like that. "When did you leave the lunchroom, Mr. Rand?"

"You think I did it?"

"I'll find out. Just answer the question. Or refuse to cooperate; I'll discover why."

"I left with Freya Larsen, Mr. Gold, as you already know. Do you think we don't talk to each other?"

"What was there to stop you, after Larsen went to the Ladies' Room, from going into Pembrooke's dining room? It's only a few steps from the Men's Room."

"Nothing stopped me, same as every other person on North Fifth."

I didn't understand why Alexander kept asking these questions. Did he expect a confession? Not very likely. I decided to try our other problem. "You would be informed of any new major acquisition, wouldn't you?" I asked.

"I'm supposed to be told as far in advance as possible, so I can make maximum use of it," Rand replied. "Pembrooke used to spring them on me at the last minute. Why?"

"Just wondering if you heard of anything like that, lately."

"Sure I have, but nobody told me. I figured it out. Larsen complains to me about the old lady taking so long on a new one, wondering what she'd do if Becker didn't finish before her retirement. Dorner's been on edge for weeks. Zager's been putting in very long hours the past month checking and rechecking his systems, especially the sixth floor. Pembrooke looked like hell three months ago, then a couple of weeks later he looked like he owned the world. Even Mr. Belmont, whose idea of public relations is that no one should know he even exists, twice looked like he wanted to talk to me. And now you ask me about a new acquisition. Then you tell me that Belmont hired you to investigate Pembrooke's murder? Come on, lady, Belmont hated Pembrooke more than I did. You were at Belmont's house—no one here has even *seen* the inside—*before* Pembrooke's murder. You're not here for the murder, you're here about a new painting. It was stolen, right?"

"That may be a possibility, Mr. Rand," I said.

"Now I know you're lying. If a Belmont donation had been stolen, Zager would have had half the staff, the lucky ones, lined up in the basement to get their truth serum shots.

The other half would have had cattle prods permanently inserted where it hurts. Nothing has ever been stolen from us and nothing ever will, as long as Zager and his gang are around. What you don't know, and you should have figured it out by now, is that I have more lines out than God, it comes with the job. So when Alan Davidoff, he's the best international exhibition man in the world, when Davidoff drops everything, including some very big clients, and flies off to Schiphol on an hour's notice, I begin checking. Right now, Alan is sitting in the best hotel in The Hague with instructions at the desk that any calls from New York are to be put through immediately. And guess who he has an audience with next Monday morning? Would you believe the Queen herself? What do you say to that, Mrs. Gold?''

"I find your information very interesting, Mr. Rand.''

"Mrs. Gold, I've been conned by experts; you're not one of them. The next thing I find out is that Maurice Gröber-Eisenberg is coming to New York tomorrow. All the way from Sydney. By private chartered jet. Somebody is spending an awful lot of money to get him here fast. Why fast? Could there be any connection with what Der Herr Doktor is coming here for and what Alan Davidoff is waiting to talk to the Queen about? Come on, Mrs. Gold, level with me. I could be a big help to you.''

"The only way you could help us," Alexander said, "is by confessing that you killed Pembrooke.''

"Okay, I confess," he said impatiently. "Now will you tell me the name of the painting, who the painter is, what it cost, who was the previous owner, when was it sold, everything I need to know to get a campaign ready. Can you imagine the shame if the Dutch papers get it first?''

Alexander got up, firmly said goodbye, and shook Rand's hand. Rand would not let go of Alexander's hand. "I can talk to the others, you know," Rand said. "If I put everything together I'll get the whole story anyway, you know I will. Do you want to tell me your side of it?''

In the hall I told Alexander that I didn't think we could keep the truth about the Third Vermeer secret much longer.

"Let him know. That way Belmont will think we're working on the painting problem instead of the murder."

"Aren't we working on the painting problem, Alexander?"

"Sure we are, Norma, by way of the murder. I told you they're connected."

I know what you told me, Alexander; what I don't know is if you're right. But what I do know, positively, is that if you find the killer and you're wrong on the painting, we're out one hundred thousand dollars.

# XVI

"You realize," Maxwell Korbin said with a false professional smile, "that, as attorney for the museum, everything I know is privileged." His voice was dry, his skin was dry and his desiccated little body looked as though it would puff apart if I so much as raised my voice. On the other hand, I had been around Burton Hanslik for twenty years, long enough to pick up a few bits of legal lore and I was tired of the half-truths I had been getting these past two days.

"As you wish, Korbin," I said, standing up, "I'm going to report to Mr. Belmont that you refused to cooperate. I hope you have a rich wife, because after Mr. Belmont gets through with you, you won't be able to get a job as a paralegal in Lower Slobbovia."

"Wait, wait," he said. "Don't be hasty. There may be certain questions I may be able to respond to to some extent."

"Bullshit, Korbin." I was still standing. I hate when professionals use their specialized techniques and jargon to bulldoze laymen. From watching Alexander I knew that the time to pin your opponent is while he is still staggering backwards. "The only thing that's privileged is what a client has told you as his attorney. Nobody here is your client; the museum is your employer, and Mr. Belmont is chairman of the board and he sent us to get information from you. Accurate and complete, is that understood?''

"Please sit down, Mrs. Gold." He was actually fluttering. "I'll do my best to . . . to satisfy your requirements."

I sat down but kept my scowl. "Okay, Korbin, why did you hate Pembrooke?"

"I didn't hate Mr. Pembrooke; I respected his ability."

"Korbin," I said, "you're a fool. Call Mr. Belmont right now and resign. It'll look better on your resume than being fired."

He shrank back and for a moment I felt pity for him. I was sure that no one had ever pressed him before in his safe harbor behind the breakwater of legal documents and boilerplate forms and equivocal answers for which only others could suffer. Then I thought of all the harm bad lawyers can cause, and I looked very pointedly at my watch.

He succumbed to this final, not-very-subtle pressure. "Mr. Pembrooke had characteristics which made it difficult to—" I glared at him. "All right," Korbin yelled, "everybody hated him."

"You too?" He hesitated. "Okay, Korbin," I said, "I'll put you down as the only one who didn't hate Pembrooke."

He was licked, I could tell, and he knew it. "I hated him too," he whispered.

It was time for Alexander to pound him. "How many lawsuits," Alexander asked, "are presently pending against the museum from donors and estates, Korbin? The bequests and donations that were illegally sold by the museum."

"It wasn't illegal; it's a matter of interpretation for the courts to decide."

"Evidently you haven't been told yet, Korbin. The Board of Trustees has decided to admit culpability and liability in all these suits. You know where that leaves you, Korbin."

"I didn't—"

"You didn't answer my question, Korbin. I'll let you know when to answer and what. I asked you how many lawsuits are pending."

"Fifteen," Korbin said sullenly.

"That's better, Korbin, keep it that way. The board is going to settle these suits and claim that the sales were made with your knowledge and approval."

"I'm an employee, an agent of the museum. I can't be sued directly by these people."

"You hold yourself forth as a professional. An agent who performs an illegal act which is not authorized by his employer, and the board is on record as not authorizing these sales, cannot claim he was in pursuit of his authorized functions. You want the museum to sue you or to file a complaint against you with the Bar Association?"

"It wasn't with my knowledge and approval. It wasn't."

"This is your last chance before the board makes its decision. Right now they think you did it because you were beholden to Pembrooke and were paid off as well. You want to give us your side of it?"

He looked from side to side; there was no way he could escape. I'm not usually a bully, and Alexander never is, but there was something unpleasant about this weaseling wretch. I hoped he was the murderer; sneaks are natural stabbers in the back.

"It's true Mr. Pembrooke hired me," Korbin said, "but I never gave bad legal advice merely because he wanted to use my opinion to sway a committee his way."

"What about those bequests and donations?" Alexander asked.

"He tricked me. Before coming here I had spent seven years with a big law firm that promised me the world and then passed me over twice for partnership. I had to leave, and I couldn't afford to open my own office, when Mr. Pembrooke hired me. After I had been here ten years—can you imagine how unsettling it is to be on an annual contract basis—he came to me one week before contract renewal time. He told me his idea of selling parts of the collections that had been given to us. I told him I didn't think he should. He ordered me to find a way to do it. I found only a few minor loopholes, nothing of substance, and I told him that.''

"Did you ever tell him outright that the sales were a breach of contract?"

"Not that explicitly. The day of the committee meeting he told me he hoped I would continue cooperating with him in the future as I had in the past. I knew what that meant. I asked him if he had signed the contract renewal I had prepared for him. He told me he might sign it the next day and was even considering a nice bonus. That afternoon, in the meeting, he brought up the deaccessions. He told the committee that he had checked the legal aspects with me and that I had told him I had no legal objections. He turned to me for confirmation, smiling. If I said I did have objections, he only needed to claim I had not been sufficiently clear, that he had had this trouble with me before, and therefore was not going to renew my contract. I would be out in the street, and at my age and in those times, no one would hire me, especially with a bad reference from him.''

"So you agreed?"

"Yes, as indirectly as I could. But he pressed me, and once I had agreed, however indirectly, I had to reinforce that opinion very firmly.''

"You knew it was wrong," Alexander said.

"Mr. Gold, nothing is that certain in law. Only when the court hands down its decision do we know.''

"I meant morally wrong, Korbin.''

"I could not have changed events. If I were fired, the next attorney Mr. Pembrooke hired would have said exactly what Mr. Pembrooke wanted, in writing, before he was hired, although the letter of opinion might very well have been post-dated. So what's the difference?''

"You were only doing your job, right?" I said.

"Exactly, Mrs. Gold. Then he made me give him a written opinion reinforcing what I had said. So every time he sold a donated painting, he made me give him another letter approving the sale. How could I refuse, having already given him the previous letters?"

"If he were alive," I said, "he'd deny it all, wouldn't he?"

"Of course. He was always blaming me for his actions if they went wrong."

"Is that why you killed him?" Alexander suddenly said.

"I didn't kill him," Korbin said. "Wechsler did. I left the dining room after Wechsler."

"Only a minute or two, Korbin."

"The dining room is very near Mr. Pembrooke's dining room. Wechsler's office is right next to it."

"Your office door is only a few steps farther away."

"Wechsler had more to gain than I did."

"Wechsler wasn't on his way to an ethics committee hearing. Or even jail. You are."

"When I explain it to Mr. Belmont, he'll see I was only doing my job."

"As part of your job," I asked, "did Pembrooke ask you to prepare papers for a donation recently?"

"Not recently, it was about two months ago."

"Anything unusual about these papers?"

"The name of the donor, and the description of the painting and its value, were left blank."

"That's all?"

"Mr. Pembrooke had me add a clause that the donor accepted all responsibility for authenticity and all other liabilities, costs, and expenses attached to the painting and its donation, and to hold the museum harmless in any actions arising out of the museum's ownership, possession, and exhibition of the painting. It was very unusual. Mr. Pembrooke read it over and over, made me change it several times before he was satisfied."

"Why do you think he wanted that done?"

"Possibly the provenance was not complete."

"Talk English, Korbin."

"The painting was stolen. But that can't be. Museums can't exhibit stolen paintings."

"Any other reason?"

"Not really. Unless Mr. Pembrooke knew the painting was a forgery. But if he knew it was a forgery, why would he accept it for the museum? It would make us, and him, a laughing stock in the field. Of course, he could blame Dorner, but it would still reflect on him."

Why indeed, I thought as we left. But if Pembrooke knew it was a forgery, who was the forger? Given what Belmont had told us, it was more likely that Pembrooke was in cahoots with the KGB than with Becker. Naturally the KGB had art forgers, but were they good enough to fool four experts? And even Becker for a while? Even so, they couldn't hope to fool Maurice G-E. Or could they? And if they had such experts, why Vermeer? They could turn out a hundred phony Rubens, Rembrandts, and Renoirs a lot easier than one Vermeer. And sell them, through tame KGB sources, to a thousand nouveau riche Arabs, Japanese, and Germans without a bit of trouble.

As we entered the staff dining room, Alexander turned back. He told me to stand in the middle of the corridor in front of Pembrooke's dining room door, facing the elevator, in such a way that I could look along the dining room corridor as well as down the executive corridor. He would go back into the staff dining room and then come out. As soon as I heard the doors squeak open, I was to step over to Pembrooke's door as though I were going to open it.

I stood ready. When I heard Alexander, I stepped to the door. For me, it was one long pace. Alexander came into view a full second later. I would easily have had time to zip into Pembrooke's room without Alexander seeing me.

"Did you hear the door squeak?" he asked.

"Yes, but I heard the increase of sound, the noise from inside the dining room, even more loudly."

"I tried to move in a normal way," he said, "and I didn't see you until I was a full step out into the hall."

"The suspects left the dining room at least one minute apart. Any one of them could have popped into Pembrooke's dining room unnoticed. Except maybe Rand and Larsen."

"Either of them could have done the same, the bathrooms are only a few steps away. You come out of the bathroom, if no one is in the executive corridor you turn left as though you forgot something in the staff dining room. When you reach the corner, if no one is in the dining room hall, take the position you were just in, in front of the elevator, even press the button as though you were going to go upstairs, or downstairs. Peek along the executive corridor and listen for the dining room noise. If it's all clear, jump into Pembrooke's dining room. Simple."

Alexander's analysis was correct. From this we learned a lot. One, that any one of the suspects could have committed the murder. And from Korbin, two, that even Pembrooke wasn't sure that the Third Vermeer was authentic. That's progress?

# XVII

"**Y**ou're amateurs, aren't you?" Sam Zager said to us with a tired smile. He was short and blocky, not as wide as Alexander, but solid enough. With his red face and his red hair turning gray, he looked more like an ex-butcher than an ex-cop. "When Lieutenant Warshafsky came here, he had every right to go and do anything in the book, but he came to me first and asked if I minded his looking around."

Like a good wife, I drew the lightning. "You're right, Mr. Zager, we acted like amateurs, and I apologize for it. We've only been licensed a few days, but that's not really an excuse. Next time we go into another man's backyard, we'll check with him first. So if you'll let me start fresh, do you mind if we look around?"

"No offense intended," he said formally, "so no offense taken. Hell no, I don't mind if you look around, some of the guys on this floor deserve to be shaken up. But it's professional, if you want to talk to any of my men, you ask me first. I don't want you messing up my security systems or giving any of my people troubles. You want to question a guard, don't bother him while he's on duty or talk to him in front of the other guards. I'll send around a substitute and you talk in here, privately."

"Don't you want to know if we find out anything from the security guards?" I asked.

"You want to tell me, you'll tell me; you don't, so don't. You think I'm interested in catching murderers? Solving crimes? Then you don't understand what my job is here."

"You're right," I said humbly. "I don't."

"Security, that's my job. It's more important to enforce No Smoking than to catch a pickpocket. Naturally my boys are trained to roust pickpockets; we have some plainclothes floaters—you wouldn't believe they were mine if I introduced you—who have the complete mugbook in their heads. But a fire—? You could pick a million pockets and it would cost less than one fire."

"What about theft? You have some very valuable paintings here."

"A very small worry. Not that we don't have everything here protected; there is no way anyone walks out of here with a painting. But a much bigger worry is vandalism. How do you stop some nut who hates the Pope from smashing the *Pieta*, to take an actual example? It's impossible to stop one hundred percent. We have psychological profiles of potential defacers, but it's not an exact science, it's an art. You want to see an expert? Maybe it'll help you." He pushed a button on his desk. "Montes? Get your ass in here."

"I'm on my break," the skinny little Hispanic man said as he came in. "You want me to tell the union on you?"

"This is Roberto Montes, my deputy," Zager introduced us. "Every once in a while he gets tired of wearing shoes and riding a desk, so he puts on his earrings and native rags and mingles with the lower classes. Like today. He used to have smarts, but he decided to go to college instead. You spot anything today, Bobby?"

"Two definites. Got rid of them."

"Tell Mr. Gold."

"The psychopath, I had Buster Brown follow him around, looking very fierce. The creep took it for twenty minutes, then practically ran out. The guy who was casing the customers, I had Lizzie snap a Polaroid in his face, with flash to make sure he noticed, then Little Joe and Timmy muscled him into a stairwell and put his hands on a shiny wallet. Little Joe told Timmy to go upstairs and check the prints on the Telex. As soon as Timmy left, the mug offered Joey a bill to let him go quietly and swore he'd never come back. Joey tapped him once and let him go. The bill is in the Fund."

"Only two, Bobby? And it's already two o'clock? You stay up late last night doing homework?" Then Zager got serious. "Mr. and Mrs. Gold are private eyes, don't blink, Bobby, Mr. Belmont sent them. Directly. They're not working for the museum, and we're going to cooperate. Tell them who killed Pembrooke."

"One of the top execs on North Fifth."

"Don't be funny, Bobby. Which one?"

"Who you gonna get to kiss your ass after I'm fired, Sam?"

"When I go, I take you with me, Bobby. We'll open a private eye business; I hear you meet lots of girls that way."

Bobby Montes looked us over for a full minute; most of the time was spent on Alexander. Finally he pointed to Alexander and said, "I want to hear him say something."

Alexander thought for a moment, then said, "I am everything you have just decided I am and I am reasonably honest. My wife carries a cassette recorder because she doesn't trust my memory. I reserve the right to use any information you give me as I see fit, to catch the killer. If I have to quote you, I will. When I catch the killer I will give him to Lieutenant Warshafsky. If in doing this I cannot avoid causing trouble for Mr. Belmont or the museum, I will cause that trouble. If you do not cooperate with me, I will not fight you, but I will find the killer without you. If you do cooperate, I will do nothing for you in return other than to take you with me when I catch the killer.''

Bobby looked at Sam Zager. Sam said, ''The sensible thing to do is to throw him out right now. He looks pretty powerful, you might have to use both hands.''

''Pembrooke was the bastard who was always trying to cut my budget,'' Bobby said.

''Yeah,'' Sam said, ''but one thing in his favor: he liked Jews a little better than he liked Nicaraguans.''

''We going to go equal partners on the private eye business after we're fired, Sam? Otherwise I don't talk.''

Sam sighed. ''You're always taking advantage of me, Bobby, but, okay, equal partners. It's Mr. Zager in front of the customers, though. And I'm only doing it so that bastard Pembrooke turns over in his grave when Buster Brown becomes Acting Director of Security.''

Bobby Montes sat down, his manner subtly changed. ''The killer was one of us,'' he said. ''No professional would bother with anything this complicated and risky. The killing was not an act of passion in spite of the use of the oyster knife. It was planned in every detail by a person who is accustomed to detailed, accurate planning and who has the creative imagination to figure out so complex a crime. It was not done out of hate—''

Alexander held up his hand to stop Montes. ''We are in perfect agreement so far, but I would like your reasons for saying it was not done out of hatred.''

''I'm not saying hate wasn't a factor,'' Bobby said, ''but it wasn't the *primary* motive. When someone hates, and decides to kill for hate, there is usually a lot of day-dreaming going on along with the planning. Visions of retribution, of torture, a full hour of having the victim chained to the wall while you tell him how bad he's been and what you're going to do to him; how long it will take and how much it will hurt. There has to be at least that much pleasure in it if you kill out of hatred only. No one who kills out of hate kills the way this one was done; quickly, silently, and painlessly. It doesn't figure.''

"Why do you say it was silent, Mr. Montes?"

"When do you tell Pembrooke off, Mr. Gold, before you ask him to bow his head and pray so you can stick the knife in the right place, or after you kill him? If you're going to ask me to justify everything you already know the answer to, just to prove to your wife that you're right, we could be here all day."

"Okay," Alexander said, "but I'm not overlooking hate."

"Neither am I, Mr. Gold. But this killing was for one of two reasons, maybe both together, which were more important to the killer than hate. Fear and money. Either Pembrooke was going to do something which would ruin the killer, or was standing in the killer's way, preventing him from getting a large amount of money; execs don't take risks for peanuts. I vote for both. I know who hated Pembrooke: everybody. I have a damn good idea who feared him: everybody. Pembrooke functioned by holding a knife at the throat of everyone he had anything to do with. What I don't know, and it really bugs me not to know what's going on in my own house, is what happened recently that involves Pembrooke and a lot of money."

"Recently?" Alexander's face was blank.

Bobby turned to Sam Zager. "Did you see that innocent look, Sam? How would you rate it? Two?"

"Not even a one, Bobby. Mr. Gold couldn't get a job as a store dick in a Burger King." Zager returned to Alexander. "Mr. Gold," he said patiently, "I just told you that Bobby is pretty good at reading people for a college boy. Don't you believe me, honest old Sam Zager?" He turned back to Bobby. "You took too long, kid. I could have done it in half the time."

"Sure you could, Sam, but I used finesse. When you learn to read, you'll find out they don't allow prisoners to fall down the precinct house stairs anymore." He turned back to Alexander. "So how much was the painting worth, Mr. Gold?

Five million? More, you say? Look at his shoulders, Sam, what would you say?"

"At least seven, Bobby; the last big one went for six. What with inflation since then, I'd say eight, at least. Make that nine."

"Alexander," I cried, "let's get out of here."

"Please let him stay with us, Mrs. Gold. I haven't had so much fun in years." Zager looked back to Alexander. "I know, Mr. Gold, that you can't tell us, but why don't you stick around and let us guess. It can't hurt you and Bobby may come up with something. Then I can take the suspect and beat his brains in until he confesses to anything I want. That's my specialty; I may be old and slow, but I don't have any problems with coddling criminals. And it's ten million even, Bobby, nobody stops at nine."

"Stop pulling, Norma," Alexander said. "I'm not leaving. I'm enjoying this as much as they are. I like watching pros work. So if this talk is as phony as everything else you've been trying to razzle-dazzle me with, you're the brains of the outfit, Sam, and skinny Bobby, here, is the brawn. Is that bulge a blackjack, Bobby?"

"I abhor violence, Mr. Gold, so I try to take them out quickly. And how could you possibly mistake Sam for any brains, much less *the* brains? Look at that face; is that the face of a brain? Okay, Sam, I concur; it's an even ten million. Now what painting could be worth ten million, Sam? You got your little handy pocket guide handy?"

"All right, boys," Alexander said, "I'm impressed. I'd be even more impressed if I didn't know you picked the lock on Becker's door. Thirty seconds?"

Zager looked hurt. "I'm a pro, Gold; less than ten. You think I like Bobby staying awake nights worrying there's something he doesn't know?"

"Do you have every secretary in the place on your payroll too?"

"Payroll? I just told you our budget is always being cut. We just act nice and friendly. Secretaries like to talk; what else they got to do all day for fun? Also the cleaning crew and the guards; you wouldn't believe what you can find out just by keeping your eyes open."

"You're telling me, Zager, that if I had come to you first, you could have told me everything I've been sweating to find out?"

"Practically, but not everything. But if I told you straight off, would you have believed me? What comes too easy is not valued. Besides, you got some talents I don't; you ask different questions from me. On the other hand, I got answers to questions you never even thought of. You want to trade? Give me your cassettes and your guesswork. You show me yours and I show you mine. Excuse me, Mrs. Gold."

"Sorry, Zager, but I can't. I'm being paid by Belmont; the information belongs to him. And you're not going to tell me anything you don't want me to know."

Sam Zager looked at Bobby Montes. "That's another buck you owe me, kid. And Zager and Montes, private eyes; that's going back to a sixty-forty split again."

"Now can I have your analysis, please?" Alexander asked. "Who killed Pembrooke?"

"The probabilities are," Bobby said, "forty percent Wechsler; twenty-five percent Gerson; twenty percent Rand; fifteen percent Larsen; Korbin and Dorner, ten percent each."

"That's over one hundred percent," I said.

Bobby shrugged. Zager asked, "What do you figure, Gold?"

"Why did you leave out Becker?" Alexander asked. "She was the first to leave the dining room after Pembrooke showed up."

"I don't doubt that she's involved, all right," Zager said, "if only through the painting. I think she might even know who the killer is, but you'd never get her to talk."

"You're hinting that Belmont was the killer?" I asked.

"Oh, no, Mrs. Gold," Zager said. "Belmonts never do the killing themselves. But he might have talked one of the other clowns into doing it, or set it up so the killer thought he had to."

"What do you think of the idea that they all cooperated in the murder?"

"You've been reading too much Agatha Christie, Mrs. Gold. People like that can't trust each other enough to make themselves so vulnerable to each other."

"There are two who do trust each other," Alexander said. "Tell me, Montes, you take over when Zager goes to lunch, don't you? And you don't always stay at your desk, do you? And you and Zager can talk to each other by walkie-talkie on a wavelength the others can't use, right?"

Zager sighed very heavily. "Sorry, Bobby, it's back to seventy-thirty again. I told you all that education would rot your brain." He looked at Alexander. "The way we figured it, I signal Bobby just before I leave the dining room. He starts walking down the executive hall towards the dining room. If either of us are seen, we try another day. Then we slip into Pembrooke's room and I put a gun on him, to keep him quiet. Bobby, who's a lot stronger than he looks, holds him in the right position. Then I slam the knife into his head from across the desk because I'm too stupid to know where the heart is. Then Bobby sweeps the carpet so no one can tell there was two of us. That's the way we had it figured. Perfect; only there are two problems left which dum-dum here couldn't figure out. How to get Pembrooke's fingerprints on the knife, and, even more important, how do we make any money out of it."

"If it was a big diamond," Montes said, "with my connections I could get it cut into a couple of medium-sized ones and still end up with a few bucks. But the painting is so small, who would buy a piece of a painting the size of a postage stamp?"

"Let's get out of here, Alexander," I said. "This is a big waste of time."

"Not really," Zager said. "I think you learned a lot."
He smiled broadly and his voice lost its mocking edge. "Give
my regards to your partner, Art Kaplan, he used to be a good
cop. And I'm glad I met you, Gold. I think you've got a real
shot at finding the killer. We can't and the cops can't, so I wish
you luck."

"Why can't you?" I asked. I really wanted to know,
even if it laid me open to more sarcasm.

"We don't think that way; I've been a cop too many
years. We put together evidence slowly and carefully, always
with an eye on what the DA can use. But more important, we
depend on our knowledge of the criminal world and on our network of people who tell us things. That's not only stool
pigeons; it's a matter of favor for favor, I close my eyes to some
things and open my ears up to others. Also, I know who
screwed whom lately and who wants to pay off a grudge. The
world of crime is a small world, and like any pro, I know the
world I work in. I know many of the people in that world and
each of them knows many more, so if you can get enough
bodies assigned, you can usually find out who did it. The problem is, can you prove it. So you talk to the participants some
more, find the weakest guy, or the most vulnerable guy, put a
little pressure on him, make a deal, and then you give it to the
DA."

"Which is something you can't do here," I said.

"Exactly. A murder like this, done by a guy who never
committed a crime before and who will probably never commit
a crime again, a guy with no sheet, who do I ask? What MO do
I look for in the book? Sure a lot of big ones have been solved
by the cops, but if you look close at them, you'll see the murderer left a lot of evidence and that the finger pointed straight at
the wife or the husband. So when you check back, you find that
they've been fighting for years, the wife's been screwing around
with the chauffeur, the chauffeur has a record, the missing jewels turn up with a fence. You dig enough, it all comes out. Not
here. Tell them, Bobby."

192

Bobby Montes took up the story. "Here you have six geniuses, tough, sharp, decisive, and they knew the territory. They're also very influential; no sweating any of those guys. The victim was very regular in his habits, so it took no fingering, only figuring out how to do the job. Any one of them could have, we checked the time table. Every one of them had a good reason; if you don't know that by now, you will soon. The only thing I haven't figured out is how the killer makes any money from the murder. I'm beginning to think that maybe money wasn't involved."

"Got to be money, Bobby," Zager said. "I *smell* it. What I was thinking, is it possible the picture isn't involved? Maybe there's other money in it somewhere that we don't know about? Shift gears, Bobby. Or do you know something we don't know, Gold?"

"I do, but I swear that the only money in this murder is involved, directly or indirectly, with the painting."

"Did you hear that 'indirectly,' Bobby? Stick to the money angle, Bobby, but look for how it comes in at the edges of the murder."

"I'm sure that the painting is tied to the murder," Alexander said. "Right now, I can't see how anyone can make any money out of killing Pembrooke."

"Okay, you go that way, Gold; for Bobby and me, that's a dead end. We'll see if we can find any other big money in this deal. And do us, and yourself, a favor. If you find Belmont is behind this, sit down with me and Warshafsky first, before you point the finger and blow the whole case. You have to be very careful when you deal with rich guys, especially if they're smart, and double especially if Burton Hanslik is his lawyer. You tell Mrs. Hanslik everything?"

I nodded. "She's my partner."

"She gets along good with her husband?"

"She would *never* do that," I said lamely. I *knew* she would. *I* would.

"Lots of luck," Zager said. "Come back soon."

We walked down the corridor, Alexander in deep thought. After a while I broke the silence. "Fun is fun, Alexander, but two killers working together makes a lot more sense than one."

"No one is crossed off the suspect list, Norma."

"They're smart enough and tough enough. They know everything that goes on in the museum. And I never believe anyone who keeps telling me how stupid he is."

"I never said Zager was stupid."

"Neither of them seemed to hate Pembrooke, though."

" 'The love of money is the root of all evil,' " he quoted.

"How do they make any money out of killing Pembrooke? How can anyone involved make any money out of it? Unless they hired out to Belmont."

"Please remember, Norma, if we hang Belmont, he may not feel like paying us. Besides, hired killers don't take that kind of chance. Nor would Belmont. And if he did, he would not involve the museum, his wife's memorial. No, there has to be a way to make money out of it. I haven't found it yet, but it has to be there."

"Maybe Gerson, the money man, can tell us," I said hopefully. Full of hope. Someone had better tell us; I sure couldn't think of a safe way for anyone to make one penny out of killing Pembrooke. Not even Belmont.

# XVIII

66 I've been waiting for you," Melville Gerson said. "Give
me the list of times when each Suspect left the staff dining room." He really spoke in capital letters. Gerson had his
shirt sleeves rolled up, a pencil in his right hand, and a computer terminal in front of him. He was surprisingly young, no
more than thirty-five, and not really fat, just sort of soft looking. And pale, like a *Talmud bocher*. "If we get everything
inputted accurately, we can cut the list down considerably."

"Which are the suspects?" I asked.

"The top people on North Fifth, naturally. It must be
one of them."

What could I lose humoring him? If Alexander got so
smart from reading whodunits, maybe Melville Gerson could
also get smart from reading timetable mysteries. "They left in
this order," I said. "Becker, Wechsler, Zager, Dorner, Korbin,
Gerson, and last, Larsen and Rand together. I don't know the
exact times, but Becker left about 1:05 P.M. more or less, and
the rest left at intervals of from one to three minutes."

"Becker?" He thought for a moment, then brightened.
"Very good. I hadn't considered her, but as The Least Likely

Suspect—yes, she can't be left out. But do you think she belongs on the List of Suspects at all? I mean, physically—?''

"She's involved in some way," Alexander said. "I'm sure of it."

"Then she stays on," Gerson said. "But right now we're looking for the actual killer, so we can cross her off, and of course, myself."

"Why you?" I asked.

"Because I know I didn't do it and I'm making the list. If you want to keep my name on *your* list, that's your privilege, but I'm not on mine."

"Why are you assuming only one killer?" I asked. "Couldn't there have been collusion?"

"Between any of these six? Never. Too individualistic, too competitive, and too uncertain of each other's loyalties."

"I was thinking more along the lines of Zager and Montes."

"Roberto and Sam? The two cops?" Gerson shook his head. "Agatha would love that. They're both quite bright, especially Zager, don't let his appearance fool you, but I don't see Sam letting Roberto have this kind of hold over him. No, it was an individual killer. Now, what was the exact time of death?"

"After 1:02 and before 1:30."

"Let's assume 1:15 plus or minus ten minutes," Gerson said. "That means any one of the six could have done it timewise. How about location? Did anyone see any of the Suspects anywhere in this time period?"

Alexander stopped it all. "Gerson, this camouflage is unnecessary and it just irritates me. Do you really want to irritate me? No? Then tell me who you picked."

Melville Gerson looked disappointed, as if I had told him that the butler did it before he finished the book. In mysteries, expecially whodunits, the slow unfolding of the analysis is more fun than knowing the name of the killer. "My calculations show it was Harold Wechsler, by any approach."

Alexander looked disgusted. "Do you really think that if they hang Wechsler, you're going to be the new director?"

Gerson looked defiant. "I'm the only one who understands the whole operation of the museum. The others are too specialized."

"What the Hell do you know about art?"

"Quite a bit," he said proudly. "Nobody knows it yet, but they will soon, when I'm ready. I've been studying, and I learn fast. It's old fashioned to think the director of a museum must be an art major. No one could possibly know more than one area or period well. The director must rely on his curators for expertise in other areas or periods. There is no reason why a director can't have one more curator to cover the area he would have been knowledgeable in, so that the director could concentrate on being the head of a big business. And we are a big business. Do you expect the head of General Motors to be able to design a car?"

"You ever mention this to anyone?" Alexander asked.

"You're the first, and you have my permission to go back to Mr. Belmont with it. I'll bet he'll see the sense in it."

"Wechsler won't like it."

"He's the murderer, so his likes or dislikes don't count. But if I'm wrong, if he's not the killer, he can have my resignation. I can go elsewhere a lot easier than he could replace me."

"No one in the museum was aware of your ambition before; why are you so forward all of a sudden?"

"I computed it was the proper time to make my move."

"Pembrooke's murder freed you?"

"His death made it necessary to present myself at this time. Harold Wechsler will be confirmed at the Board of Trustees meeting at the end of this month unless he is unmasked as the murderer. When he is, a new acting director must be available."

"And you're trying to put together evidence to prove Wechsler did it?"

"I was trying to give the correlations to you before. It's only circumstantial, but a killer rarely calls anyone in to witness the crime."

"I'm a bit puzzled about how Pembrooke's fingerprints were placed on the knife," Alexander said. "Have you figured it out yet?"

"That's not really my forte; I work by checking the timing and the movements of the Suspects. But since Pembrooke didn't stab himself, there has to be a way the fingerprints got on the knife and I'm confident that an intuitive type, such as you, will figure it out. More likely, when we prove by my calculations that Wechsler did it, he will explain the trick with the fingerprints."

Melville Gerson was so openly and confidently driving for the job as director, I thought I'd deflate him a little. "Isn't that trick," I asked, "more in the line of a man who reads mysteries?"

"Not necessarily, Mrs. Gold. We mystery fans know that the simplest ways are the best. The complicated ways leave too many clues and exclude too many people. This murder was committed by a brilliant man who does not read mysteries. Harold Wechsler is very clever; don't underestimate him."

"I'm not underestimating you either," Alexander said. "Did you also compute anything on Pembrooke?"

"Oh, yes, the computer turned up many interesting correlations concerning our late director."

"What kind of correlations?" I asked.

"Statistically, some events are more probably than others. That is, measurements of the height of one hundred thousand women selected at random, will show a large number clustered between five-foot three and five-foot five inches—I'm making these figures up—a smaller number between either five-foot one and five-foot three or between five-foot five and five-foot seven; a still smaller number who are between either four-foot eleven and five-foot one or between five-foot seven and five-foot nine inches, and so on, the numbers decreasing rapidly as we get farther away from the median. There might be one out of one hundred thousand who is your height, Mrs. Gold, or who is four-foot-seven-inches tall.''

"I'm aware of the properties of the bell-shaped curve,'' I said.

"Good. Now, suppose I were invited to a party and every woman there, all twenty of them, was six-foot-one-inch tall. I could reasonably assume, although it could have been pure coincidence, that my host had invited a group selected from the members of the Tall Girls Club. That is, the presence at that party of a group of people all of whom were so very far from the norm was not an accident. If I then noticed that all these women had red hair and were born on July 4, 1952, wore green nail polish and had on exactly the same blue dress, I would be certain that their presence at this party was not accidental. The negative entropy, the improbability of such a party, is so great, that this gathering, I would bet my life on it, was the result of deliberate action. The universe, Mrs. Gold, always works towards the most probable situation. Life, which is, in itself, highly improbable, works towards increasing improbability in the universe. Intelligence, the most improbable phenomenon in the universe, produces the greatest improbabilities of all. To put it simply, if it is very improbable, someone did it purposely. That is the essence of the mystery novel.''

"And of religions too,'' Alexander said, looking at Gerson respectfully. "I have thought along these lines myself, Gerson; you phrased it very well. So you found some interesting correlations involving Pembrooke?''

"A computer does this very easily. I pull all sorts of readings from my terminal about my colleagues, it's sort of a hobby, and I found that Pembrooke was a crook. From the time Pembrooke took charge, we bought practically every acquisition from one of only six sources. We paid above market for each of these acquisitions, although within six months to a year the market rose to meet these prices. We had no donors' lawsuits for breach of contract in all the years Ludwig was director, not one. We now have fifteen. Every one of Ludwig's appointees left our employ within one year after Pembrooke became director. Not one is left.''

"There's Becker," I said.

"I'm talking about executives and curators," he replied. "There are a few in low positions still hanging on, but that doesn't change the picture. The point I am making is that, when you put all this together, Pembrooke was the absolute dictator of the museum, and used his power for personal gain.''

"When did you discover this?" Alexander asked.

"About three months ago," Gerson said.

"What hold did Pembrooke have over you?"

"Hold? How could he have any hold over me? I've never done anything wrong.''

"Come on, Gerson, give me credit for a little sense," Alexander said impatiently. "You didn't suddenly decide you wanted to become the new director yesterday. You probably picked this field, this job, figuring that a smart business type could zoom right through all these artsy scholarly innocents. You've learned that there are very few innocents at the top anywhere, but that doesn't change things. Three months ago, you had Pembrooke cold. If you presented your readouts—where do you keep them Gerson, in a safe deposit box marked 'to be opened on my death'?—if you presented them to Mr. Belmont, Pembrooke would have his power broken, and might have been kicked out, opening the way for you. But you didn't give them to Belmont or anyone. So Pembrooke had a strong something to hold over you, right?''

"I repeat, I never did anything wrong.''

"You know, Gerson," Alexander said, "I believe you. Pembrooke must have framed you in some way. Put it on record now, what have you got to lose? If you don't—maybe Pembrooke also has a safe deposit box someplace in case of his death.''

Gerson idly punched his computer keyboard, not even

looking at the screen. He seemed to come to a decision. "A week after I told Pembrooke about my findings, he called me into his office. He told me he was not going to recommend me as his successor when he retired, and that I had better wipe all my work on him from the computer and burn the printouts. If he went down, I would go down with him. He told me that a few days ago, a short pudgy brown-haired man wearing rimless glasses rented a safe deposit box in Manhattan. In it he placed ten new hundred-dollar bills, bills which Pembrooke had drawn from his bank earlier that day. He told me that this procedure would be repeated every month. The box was not in my name, but in a name which would be easily recognized as close to my name. I understood that if I turned him in, he would claim that I had been blackmailing him. There was no way I could prove otherwise."

"Couldn't you hire a detective agency to shadow you for three consecutive months?" I asked. "That way, no one could say you have been to the bank during your lunch hour."

"I had no way of knowing which day or what time Pembrooke's friend went to the bank. It could even have been in the evening or a Saturday. And what good would that do? Anyone I hired would be automatically considered untrustworthy."

"You couldn't even be sure," Alexander said, "that Pembrooke had actually done what he said."

"I thought of that," Gerson said, "but the possible danger was not worth the risk. Besides, this cost Pembrooke very little, the loss of the return on an average of six thousand dollars for a year plus the cost of the box and the actor— If I were Pembrooke, I would have actually done it."

"I know where he learned that trick," Alexander said. "Pembrooke was really adept at taking other people's ideas and turning them to his own needs. It was good for you, Gerson, very good, that Pembrooke was killed."

"I wouldn't kill anyone," he said. "That's not the way I operate."

"I'm sure this was the first murder for whoever killed Pembrooke; I don't think it's Wechsler's style either. Or Larsen's or any of the others. Think about that, Gerson," Alexander said as we got up to leave, "and then give me a better reason why you are not a Prime Suspect." Capitals emphasized.

"But why would I take the risk of killing him when, by waiting until June, Pembrooke would be retired?"

I couldn't resist, so at the door I turned and said, "Because you thought you found a foolproof way to murder him."

Alexander didn't want to talk on the way home. I didn't blame him. Seven suspects, all prime. Eight, counting Becker, if Alexander was right about the connection with the painting. Nine, in fact, if Gerson was wrong about Bobby Montes. What we really needed was a setup where the suspects were all knocked off, one by one, until only the murderer was left. Oh, Saint Agatha, where art thou in this, our hour of need?

# XIX

"**W**hat did you find out, Pearl?" Alexander asked as we got home. Alexander was in his recliner before I finished putting the four new interview cassettes on Pearl's desk. Poor baby, he'd had a hard day, particularly when Batman and Robin ridiculed his lack of professionalism.

"If you shake hands with Pembrooke," Pearl said, "count your fingers afterwards. Who dines with the devil must use a long spoon."

"That we know already," he said. "Any sexual aberrations?"

"One. He's an admitted heterosexual. No long-term relationships."

"Married women?"

"None that anyone was aware of."

I stopped this line. "I don't want to talk about Pembrooke or the murder today. It's a dead end; rehashing what we already know won't help. If we don't solve the puzzle of the painting, we start our new agency with a hundred-thousand-dollar deficit, so let's concentrate on what's important for a while."

Alexander was agreeable to the suggestion. "All roads will lead to the killer. You'll see."

"One thing I don't understand," I said, "is why they're falling all over themselves to tell us how much they hated Pembrooke."

"They saw us in the first place because Belmont made them," Alexander said, "and there's a normal tendency to admit to a lesser sin when you're under suspicion of committing murder."

"Burton told me about this," Pearl said. "If you have a body in the trunk of your car, you admit the traffic violation openly and politely."

"The police use this in reverse, sometimes," Alexander pointed out. "If they want someone to confess to some minor crime, they accuse him of a major crime. Besides, it is no crime at all to admit hating Pembrooke, especially if everyone knew about it. Attempting to conceal the hatred would point the finger of suspicion at you." He turned to Pearl. "Did you type up the notes of our meeting with Belmont? The one where the tape was wiped out?"

"Yes, and Norma's and Burton's and mine, too."

"Any differences between them?"

"Only minor; there is perfect agreement on all important points. I put them on your desk."

"You never know what turns out to be important in an investigation. Even seemingly minor points may be clues."

"I've been thinking about something," I said. "Pearl, has the loudspeaker been installed on the phone yet? I want Alexander to hear this."

It was, so I called Freya Larsen with them both listening. "How long," I asked Larsen, "would it have taken you to clean off the varnish from the hypothetical painting we discussed yesterday?"

"The Vermeer?" she said sneakily.

"Call it anything you like. How long?"

"Less than half the time it took Becker."

"As carefully as Becker would have? And as well?"

"Molecule by molecule, and that includes repair of the wood support."

"What was she doing all the rest of the time?"

"What do you think?" Larsen barked a bitter laugh. "Making a forgery."

"Becker?"

"Even Becker. Normally sane people go crazy under the right conditions; Becker is not quite normal."

"How could she do that in the museum?"

"The museum is the best place. There is plenty of old Dutch junk in the cellar. You could get wood the right age and cut it to size. You could grind up three-hundred-year-old paint and incorporate it into your pigments. A skilled person could do it easily. Half my conservators could do it."

"You too?"

"Better than most."

"A Vermeer?"

"I would have difficulty with a Vermeer, but thanks for the confirmation."

"What about aging? Craquelure?"

"That's more difficult, if you want to do a right job, but with oxidizing agents, heat, and enough time you could produce something that would be hard to detect. Art forgers are always devising new techniques. You don't find out about them if they work."

"How much is enough time?"

"Normal oxidation of oil paint could be as much as four hundred years. If I were trying to forge a major painting, one which would be subject to the most exacting and complete battery of tests, I would use a very slow aging process for at least five years. Ten or twenty would be even better."

"Is there any way to do the same in one month?"

"Not that I know of."

I hung up. "See what this means, Alexander?"

"You're suggesting that the KGB general started this operation twenty years ago? The history too?"

"What else? Like putting money in the bank. He has to have art forgers at his disposal. Who could be disposed of later. It would be no trick to have the art student/janitor led to find the painting and led to the junior KGB officer and so forth."

Alexander thought for a moment, then said, "I don't think so, the pattern is wrong. Why a Vermeer?"

"Small size, rarity, high price," I replied.

"Small size is not important. A larger painting could have had a different story planted to justify its existence."

"Leonardo da Vinci is even rarer than Vermeer," Pearl said. "And there are others still rarer."

"If I were the general," Alexander said, "I would have chosen more recent painters: Renoir, Cézanne, Picasso, Gauguin, three or four paintings by each, so that if tastes changed in twenty years, I would have had a stock to choose from. I would not have staked everything on one very expensive work. I would have charged a relatively low price and sold them to private collectors, not charged a record-breaking price to a major museum with all the facilities and experts it has at its disposal. I would have used the twenty years to establish, at least, a recent provenance, with puppet owners. I would not have chosen a painting whose very appearance would set off a major controversy in the art world. No, Norma, it doesn't figure."

"It's still a possibility," I said. "I wouldn't close out the idea."

"I'll keep it open, but your talk with Larsen raises other questions." He dialed Sam Zager. Zager had left, but Roberto Montes was on duty.

"Did you check Becker's room once," Alexander asked, "or more than once?"

"You haven't been too cooperative with us," Bobby answered.

"You're right, Mr. Montes. Save me a dime. Call Mr.

Belmont, he's only across the street from you, and tell him that you won't cooperate with me about the painting and that you recommend Buster Brown as the new chief of security. Call Sam at home and tell him that you've just resigned his job for him."

"You're learning, Mr. Gold," Bobby laughed. "We checked her every night and took a Polaroid of the painting each time. It showed evidence of slow, careful change and repair, progressing daily."

"When was it finished?"

"Couple of weeks ago. Sixteen days, to be exact."

"Did she bring in a big view camera about that time? Big lights?"

"She didn't need to bring in big lights, there are plenty of movable lights in the conservators' area. If the camera could fit in her tote bag, she could have brought it in."

"It was a huge camera, Bobby, couldn't have fit in three tote bags."

"Then it didn't come in, Gold. Maybe the picture went out?"

"When did you first go into her room?"

"The day Larsen told us she had stopped working on her assigned painting, but it took Larsen at least one day, possibly two, to discover that."

"So she could have taken it home the first night?"

"Sure, Gold, but it doesn't figure. It had not yet been cleaned. And you'd have to be crazy to take ten million in a tote bag into that neighborhood."

"So where was she copying it, Bobby?"

"In the museum, and taking the copy home every night, just in case somebody had a key to her room."

"Which you did, Bobby. That lock-picking story was another of your jabs to put me off balance. Do you have keys to every room in the museum?"

"Sure, and every desk. Why sweat?"

"Discover anything important?"

"Little crap. These guys are too smart to leave any good stuff around."

"Suppose I told you, Bobby, that Becker works very slowly when she's copying a painting. How is she going to forge this one in the time she has?"

"She starts while the original is still dirty, preparing the wood and the paints. Even puts on the first layer or two. Spends one hour cleaning and seven hours copying. By the time the painting is clean, she's almost ready. She takes a bunch of Polaroid shots of the clean painting, and now she can work at home on the final details, finishing the painting."

"What about the drying of the paint, and the cracking?"

"I didn't say she'd be ready to sell it by Washington's Birthday."

"So you think the painting she gave to Mr. Belmont is the same one he gave her?"

"No doubt about it."

"Then why is she making the forgery, Bobby?"

"That's an interesting question, Mr. Gold. Maybe she figures on switching paintings a year from now, when she comes in as a visitor."

"Can that be done, Bobby?"

"The way Zager's got it set up, *I'd* have difficulty snatching a painting."

That's the way it is with hydras; cut off one head, two others spring up in its place.

The phone rang; the speaker was still on. It was Burton. "Maurice Gröber-Eisenberg will be at Mr. Belmont's house tomorrow morning at 10:30 to look at the painting."

"I want to be there," Alexander shouted.

"It's doubtful if he will make a decision right then and there."

"You never know, Burt. I have to be there. I want to see his reaction when he first sees the actual painting."

"I'll arrange it," Burton said wearily. "I'll be there too."

After Burton hung up, Alexander addressed Pearl. "Call Warshafsky, his crew ought to be good at this. Suggest that the police check all the studio-quality photo processing labs in New York. Find out if anyone brought in any eleven-by-fourteen-inch color transparencies of paintings for processing in the last three months. This isn't the kind of thing you can do properly in your kitchen darkroom."

"I'll ask him," Pearl said. "Do I tell him why?"

"If he has some information to trade, yes. Otherwise, no."

I sent Alexander upstairs to take a Valium nap, a name I invented for people like Alexander who take so few drugs that a five-milligram Valium is, for them, a sleeping pill. His heart attack wasn't all that long ago, and we had had a rough two days. I didn't want him thinking about crises of any kind for a while; even a subconscious deserves a rest now and then. I had a feeling that tomorrow the Herr Doktor Professor would give us as big a headache as all the rest of the Prime Suspects put together.

# XX

If you like Kewpie Dolls, the kind you win for breaking three balloons at the carnival, you'd love Doktor Maurice Gröber-Eisenberg, a king-size version of the doll, but cuter. Slightly taller than Pearl, in his Cuban heels, he had the little pot belly and the big round head down pat, with nineteen dyed hairs slicked forward over his baldness ending, I swear, in a spit curl. His chubby cheeks were rosy, his blue eyes sparkled, and his tiny little pouting mouth had deep red perfect Cupid's-bow lips. Today, for the formal occasion, he wore his work clothes: a cutaway and striped trousers, just like a real cookie-pushing diplomat. When we were introduced, I was sure he started to click his heels before he remembered I was not a duchess, although I have been told I have a regal bearing.

"I have studied all of the documents and photographs," he said, in a voice so sweet and high that I automatically thought—but no, these days *castrati* are born, not made. "All evidence points toward the authenticity of the work."

"But isn't scientific testing useful only for evidence of non-authenticity?" I asked. "It can't be proof of authenticity in and of itself." If you believe in Freud, marriage to a certain type of woman will result in castration, but that kind doesn't produce a soprano. Usually.

"Precisely," he sang, "but it adds to the weight of the evidence. The pose, the costume, the folds of clothing, the background, the angle of light, the palette of colors—a thousand factors. All are melded by the expert to produce an opinion, a professional opinion. I have studied the photographs and, based on them, I am inclined to favor a judgment of authenticity."

"But don't you have to see the actual painting to finalize your decision?" I asked. Maybe his mother started him on yodeling lessons too soon. No. Enough. This way lies madness. I'll think of something else. Good. I've conquered it. Sort of. I wonder what his wife is like?

"Obviously, Madame. That is why I am here. If I might sit in your chair, Mr. Belmont, with my back to the sun—?" Belmont graciously yielded his seat and went to get the painting.

"Would you especially check the minor details and the background," Alexander said. "According to Hannelore Becker—"

The Kewpie Doll face changed to baby rage, the sweet little mouth snarling. "I do not want to hear from that—that—cleaning lady. It is an insult to a person of stature to—" Then he calmed down. No wife, I was sure of that. Thank God. "I see your suggestion is made from lack of knowledge. For some reason, although he should know better, Mr. Belmont, too, has faith in her words. Let me put it in layman's terms. Suppose I showed you, you are a professional construction engineer I am told, a building which, it is claimed, was designed by Roger Allen Talbott. Some minor laborer tells you to be sure to check a screw on the tenth flor because it is not the kind of screw Roger Allen Talbott normally uses. What would you say, Sir? Would you not, if you were a gentleman, politely tell the laborer that you normally, as a professional should, check the screws, and the nails as well, and all the other, more important, evidence before making your decision?''

"I am pleased that you will check all these items, Professor," Alexander said. "But the analogy is not exact. The screws were not made by Talbott with his own hands; the brushwork of the pearls is either in Vermeer's style and technique or it is not.''

Maurice Gröber-Eisenberg was not pleased, but in the presence of Mr. Belmont, he could not get real waspish. "You may be assured, Sir, that I will check all the important details, not just these. The photographs, excellent as they were, were of an uncleaned painting and were useless for checking details. That is why no reliance can be placed on the opinions of the other experts Mr. Belmont retained due to my temporary unavailability." It was very clear what G-E thought of the other experts and their opinions. "That is the reason I must hold the actual cleaned painting in my own hands.''

Alexander seemed determined to provoke the Kewpie Doll. "You seem to know Hannelore Becker well. Did she speak with you before?''

"After my book on Vermeer was published, a definitive work, she sent me a twenty-page letter challenging some statements I had made, and going into tremendous detail concerning the mechanics of certain minor aspects of his brushwork and pigments and glazes, the sort of thing a conservator might be interested in but which did not really belong in a scholarly work.''

"I take it you followed her suggestion?" Alexander's face was bland.

Kewpie's face was purple. "I felt," he said in very stiff tones, "that if there was a possible interest in some quarters in mechanics, it might be helpful if, in the second edition, I added a few words giving the reader the benefit of my observations, observations I had previously made.''

Belmont placed the glassine-wrapped painting on the desk in front of the relieved G-E. "Do you want privacy, Professor?'' Belmont asked. "We'll leave you alone if you wish, just tell me how much time you need.''

"I have no objection,'' Maurice said, cute again, "if it gives you pleasure to watch me work. Actually, there is very little to see; the technical work was very professionally done, no need to repeat it. I was just telling Mr. Gold that I will check the mechanical details. For that, I have a small light,'' he drew an oddly shaped flashlight from his breast pocket, "especially made for me to provide tangential illumination so that I may check the brushwork. But most important for me is, of course, the feel, the rapport, the energy flow between a great work of art and a true lover of art. It sounds mystical, I know, but it works. Ask any major expert.''

"Does this happen right away?'' Alexander asked. "Or slowly, over a period of time?'' He was too far away for me to kick.

"Alec,'' Burton said, politely but firmly, "Doctor Gröber-Eisenberg is the acknowledged authority on seventeenth-century Lowlands art. His very presence here is an honor.''

"Thank you, Mr. Hanslik, for the compliment, but I will be happy to explain to Mr. Gold. It usually takes only a few minutes, sometimes only a few seconds, but if I am not disturbed, never more than an hour or two. That, of course, is for this phase only. Other phases of the examination, particularly the technical testing, can take months. Fortunately, all this has already been done.''

"Do you have to look at it''—Alexander was really trying to be nasty—"or will just touching it allow the energy to flow?''

Gröber-Eisenberg raised his hand to silence Burton. "Mr. Gold thinks he is being facetious, but I will answer. Yes, Mr. Gold, sometimes one touch or one look is sufficient. I am a scientific investigator, a historian, but I tell you, there is something that happens to me when I first see or touch a great work of art. I do not claim it is spiritual; it is a matter of expertise, I am sure, unconscious expertise. But it does happen, and I know it happens in other fields too.''

213

"You know of others who have had this experience?"

"I was directly involved, Mr. Gold. Six months ago—I beg Madame's forgiveness," he said to me, "the story is somewhat coarse—I had my regular medical examination. My doctor thought he felt a slight asymmetry in my prostate gland and sent me to Dr. Wohl, Europe's leading specialist. After checking my history, Dr. Wohl put me naked on a table, crouched on my knees, my bottom in the air. He put on a little rubber finger cot, applied lubricant, and thrust his finger into my rectum. He moved his finger around for a second or two, not more, pulled it out and said, '*Rein.*' Clean. That was all. I asked what he meant. 'No cancer,' he told me. 'So quick?' I asked. 'I know,' he said. 'You wish another opinion, get one. I, Dr. Wohl, say *rein.*'"

"Did you get another opinion?" I asked.

"Three," he said. "It was, after all, my life, in a field I was not familiar with. The others took hours, but they all agreed. I did not have cancer. Dr. Wohl, in two seconds, was right. In art, *I* am Dr. Wohl. You will see. I say this, not in boasting, but in confidence, based on my experiences."

Gröber-Eisenberg slowly and carefully removed the transparent wrapping from the little wooden painting. He held the painting in front of him, reverently, his eyes half closed. After a few seconds he murmured, "Beautiful. Beautiful."

"Does that mean it's an authentic Vermeer?" Burton asked.

"Well," G-E said with a sideways glance at Alexander, "there are a few nails and screws to examine first. But it is truly beautiful."

"He took a loupe out of his pocket and picked up his odd flashlight. "Will someone please close the draperie?" he asked. Mr. Belmont reached over and touched a button on the desk. The room became dark.

G-E switched on his light and held it parallel to the surface of the painting. He began examining the painting slowly and carefully through the loupe, holding it to his right eye with his hand, not fixing it like a monocle the way they do in the movies. I noticed he was paying special attention to the ears, the pearls, and the *pointillés*. I didn't blame him.

We were silent, all of us, watching the master work. Especially Alexander. One of his great pleasures is watching experts at their work. In spite of his deliberate provocation of G-E, I was sure he respected the man.

It was a full twenty minutes before G-E put down his loupe. In the reflected light from his flashlight his face looked grim, the little Cupid's-bow lips pushed far out. He stared straight ahead, not at the painting.

After a minute Burton spoke. "What is your opinion, Doctor? Is it authentic?"

Gröber-Eisenberg turned to face Burton. He spoke slowly, hesitantly, not with the confidence he had displayed before. "I am not certain. I will have to have more time."

"Is it fake, then?" Alexander asked.

Looking at Mr. Belmont, G-E answered carefully. "I am not prepared to say at this time."

"Can you say anything at all right now?" Mr. Belmont asked.

"This will not be in my letter," G-E said, "but as a courtesy, and because I respect your love of Vermeer, I will tell you, Mr. Belmont, what is troubling me. At first I believed it was a Vermeer, and I was happy. When I examined it closely, it could not have been painted by Vermeer. There are several possibilities, Mr. Belmont. One is that I am wrong, either in my first impression or in my more careful examination. I have never been wrong before, but that is not a guarantee that I am not wrong now. By this, I do not mean that I will give you an incorrect opinion; that I would never do. But at present, I have two mutually contradictory opinions; one of them must be wrong. Given time, I will make my decision; I am not a coward, I am only confused at present."

"What is your second possibility?" Belmont asked.

"That it is a forgery; one so technically perfect as to

overcome all the scientific tests and so artistically perfect that I felt, I actually felt, the thrill of holding a great work in my hands. I find it hard to believe in an organization which could bring together such skills, such talent, and such patience; the pigment is fully oxidized, hard as a rock, this does not happen in one day. I do not believe such an organization exists, or, that if it did, it would undertake this job instead of selecting one of several easier painters to forge. Surely they knew that I would be called in and that I would not miss the minor mechanical flaws that are always present in any forgery."

"If there another possibility?" Burton asked.

"The one I favor, at present, is this: the painting is of Vermeer's time; that's how it passed all the scientific tests. The little we know of its provenance is correct. But it was not painted by Vermeer, although there are some places where, I am sure, the hand of the master did its work. But it was not painted by a known painter of Vermeer's time. All of Vermeer's contemporaries had styles which I would recognize and name at once. Therefore this has to be a student of Vermeer, one to whom Vermeer taught all his secrets and showed how to use the *camera obscura*. A student whose style was an exact copy of his master's, whose model was Vermeer's model, whose hand was guided by Vermeer's hand, and who had the good fortune of having Vermeer paint some sections of his painting."

"Then why are you not ready to state that this is not an authentic Vermeer?" Alexander asked.

"Mr. Gold," Gröber-Eisenberg said, "I know you have contempt for me, the contempt of the physically strong for the weak; the contempt of the engineer for the artist. I cannot help the way I look any more than you can help how you look, but I am a man of honor and a professional in an extremely difficult field. People are willing to spend millions of dollars on my opinion. I do not give that opinion lightly, and I cannot give that opinion until I am sure. I am *not* sure, and until I am, I will not give my opinion. I must have more time."

Alexander looked touched. "Dr. Gröber-Eisenberg, I

admit trying to irritate you. It was for professional reasons and was clumsily done. I enjoyed watching you work, I learned much from you, and I respect you as a man and a professional. Please accept my apology."

The tension was broken. Mr. Belmont opened the draperies and the sun came in. It shed light on everything except my problem. What if Maurice G-E needed *three* more days to make a decision? Whatever that decision was, if he didn't make it in two days, we'd be out a hundred thousand without even a chance of letting Alexander solve any of the problems.

# XXI

"What will we do, Alexander," I asked when we got home, "when G-E announces that the painting is by a pupil of Vermeer?"

"That won't happen," he said. "I can't allow it."

"How can you stop it, Alexander? He's a brave little man."

"In his field I'm sure he's the epitome of honor, but every man has his weak points."

"Does that mean you think he's right? That our job is hopeless?"

"Either he's wrong or Becker is wrong, that I'm sure of."

"There's no hard evidence either way, and you're no expert in that field."

By that time we had finished hanging up our coats and gone into the office. Pearl had only one bit of news. "Warshafsky says that there have been no eleven-by-fourteen-inch transparencies of paintings processed in the entire metropolitan area in the last three months."

"It's not even twelve o'clock," I said. "How did he do it so quickly?"

218

"Phone. There aren't that many studio-quality processors around."

"Where are the transcripts of all the interviews?" Alexander asked Pearl. "I want to go over them again. Maybe a pattern will emerge."

"On your desk," she said. "Right in front of you."

"And the transcripts of the memos on the wiped-out meeting with Belmont?"

"All four of them are in a separate folder."

"Go shopping, the two of you. I need some quiet time."

When we got back he was lying on his recliner, eyes open and unfocussed. "Did you sleep?" I asked.

"I've been analyzing the transcripts."

"Anything come out, swami?"

He focussed on me. "There's something there," he said. "I sense it, but I can't put my finger on it. Before my attack, I would have had it already. I need a stimulant."

"I'll make lunch."

"Not food; something spiritual. A hot chocolate, a *real* hot chocolate."

"I don't have any chocolate in the house. Or any cream. How about cocoa with skim milk and sweetener? And real vanilla extract."

"Don't lie, Norma. You made a *Sachertorte* the other night."

"Cream and sugar is bad for you; you're still too heavy."

"Not solving this problem is worse for me. Start melting the chocolate. I'll go upstairs and take a nap after I get my fix; let my subconscious take over."

Sherlock Holmes used cocaine, so I figured one hot chocolate wouldn't hurt. But I did take the precaution of using half sugar and half sweetener. He never knew the difference.

I checked the bedroom two hours later. As I opened the

door I heard him on the telephone. ". . . exactly eight and one-half inches high and seven and one-quarter inches wide. Solid oak, not a veneer. . . . Stain it dark, what the British call fumed oak. . . . Okay, I'll be taking my walk in about an hour, I'll pick it up then."

"Wouldn't gold be better?" I said.

"Gold?" He looked astonished.

"I don't mean real gold, not for a photo, but gold leaf, even gold lacquer, would set off the picture better. The background of the painting is so dark that if you used a dark wood frame, you'd kill the effect."

"You want a gold frame?"

"A gilt frame, darling. It would be much nicer."

He thought for a moment, then agreed.

"Did you have a nice sleep, darling?" I asked as I kissed him. He talks big in public, but he likes smooching as much as I do.

"Very. Productive too."

"You have an approach to G-E?"

"I have the solution. My only problem is to—"

"You know if the painting is real or not?" Alexander's subconscious is very accurate, but it isn't always reliable.

"It's obvious; that's the easy part. I just have to figure out how to nail the killer.

"You know who the killer is?"

"I always told you the two puzzles were connected."

"Who is it, Alexander? Or would you rather eat Spam for a week?"

"I have a serious problem, Norma. There is no way I can prove who the killer is, no way at all. At the meeting tomorrow—"

"What meeting?"

"I'll tell you in a minute. At the meeting I want you to act perfectly natural, that's very important. Don't tell anyone, not even Pearl, that I know the killer. Let them think this meeting is for the painting only."

"Why bother about the killer then? Settle the painting business, collect the million, and give a hundred thousand of that to Belmont. Why knock yourself out?"

"You want to leave a puzzle unresolved? When I know the solution? Are you crazy?"

"Sorry, Alexander, I didn't mean to talk dirty. What do you want me to do?"

"We'll meet in Belmont's living room as early as possible tomorrow morning. Everyone must be there, no excuses, tell Belmont to arrange that. I want the draperies drawn completely, a big fire in the fireplace, and the only light is to be the one on Belmont's table, the one to the right of his chair, not the one where the brandy is."

"Any special seating arrangement?"

"That's very important. I wish you had made a sketch of that room. Tell me if your recollection is different from mine." He closed his eyes as he spoke. "Opposite the dining room door, across the hall, is the door into the living room. The door swings in to the left. Straight ahead is the street wall, with the fireplace in the middle of that wall, a little to the left of the door's location. To the right is the front wall, facing the park. In line with the door, a little to the right, is Belmont's wing chair flanked by a pair of small tables. The table on his right has a reading lamp and the controls for the draperies and the gallery lights; the table on his left holds the brandy decanter. Next to each table is a big chair. That's where Burton and I sat last time, Burton to Belmont's right, I to his left. That's where we'll sit again tomorrow. Am I right, so far?"

"Perfectly, but as I remember it, the chairs are a good three feet to the right of the doorway."

"Close enough. At the far left of the room is the art gallery, where all the Vermeer copies are hung. I want a set of chairs on the other side of the fireplace from Belmont and me, about fifteen feet away, or whatever is needed. Nearest the street wall, opposite Burton, you will sit. Next to you, on your right, Warshafsky, and at the end, G-E, opposite me. Don't let him take any other position, no matter what."

"It shall be as you say, Sire. Do you want the Prime Suspects there too, or have you decided that G-E is the killer?"

"G-E was in Australia at the time, and don't mention killer to Belmont. As far as he is concerned, this is for the painting only."

"Then how will you explain Warshafsky? He is in Homicide Central and he's been in the papers and he's questioned everybody."

"Make up a reason; to prevent violence when I announce my decision about the painting."

"He won't buy that."

"Don't bother me with details; let Pearl do it. She can charm Belmont." Meaning I can't. Well, if he wanted to marry a sexy blond he should have thought of that twenty-seven years ago. "The chairs for the suspects will be lined up parallel to the fireplace wall, making a big, rectangular U around the fireplace, with our sets of chairs. Make sure you leave open corners so people can get in and out of the U."

"In what order do you want the suspects, Sire?"

"Alphabetical order will do. Becker first, nearest the gallery, then Dorner, Gerson, uh, Korbin and Larsen, then Rand and Wechsler, with Zager on the end, near me."

"That puts Becker next to G-E. Is that wise? You know how he hates her."

"I suppose you're right, but it would have been helpful if they were next to each other; things tend to happen when sparks fly. Okay, leave it in alphabetical order but the other way around; Becker near me and Zager near G-E, towards the gallery end of the room."

"You've got G-E with Warshafsky on his left and Zager one space away on his right. What do you have in mind, Alexander? Is the little doll dangerous? Because if he is, there's only Warshafsky between G-E and your only wife. And I don't have a gun yet."

"Don't be silly, Norma, you'll be perfectly safe. I wouldn't let anyone hurt you." Where have I heard that before? Oh yes, I remember, just before I got shot.

"And a baby-faced killer is directly opposite you, less than twenty feet away. Is that guaranteed safe too?"

"Nothing is absolutely safe, Norma, but there is nothing to worry about. Really." That last 'really' worried me. Really.

"You left out Pearl. She deserves to be there."

"I forgot. Put her next to me, she'll be safe there." So why wasn't I next to him? "And don't forget the court stenographer. Put her in the far right corner of the room, behind Burt. And set up two TV cameras, one in each corner of the room against the street wall, so that all of us will always be either on one camera or the other."

"No bullhorn?"

"Don't be funny, Norma, I *needed* a bullhorn in the Boguslav case. Here we're all in one room. If Belmont objects to the videorecorders and the steno, remind him of the terms of our agreement."

"Alexander," I said severely, just to make sure it sank in, "will you please keep in mind that until G-E makes his decision, nothing you do has any financial value. I got a very strong impression that G-E is not going to make that decision very soon."

"Leave it to me," he said smugly, "I've thought of everything. It's all under control."

I went downstairs to the office. When I told Pearl what she had to do, she got all excited. She was positive that Alexander had really solved all the problems. Sometimes I wish I were a little less experienced. Or a little dumber. Or both. If I had my life to live over again, as the ads say, I'd like to live it as a blond.

# XXII

We sat in our assigned places in the half-darkness of Daniel Pereira Belmont's living room, waiting for Alexander and Mr. Belmont to come back. It might have been a winter's gathering, a group of friends sitting around the big fireplace, relaxed and easy, watching the flames. To me, it felt more like a group of distant relatives, mistrustful of each other, waiting for the lawyer to read the will.

Alexander and Mr. Belmont went right to their seats, Belmont to his big wing chair between the two little tables, Alexander to his left, next to Pearl. Alexander put his attaché case on the table to his right, gently pushing the little cut-crystal decanter of Napoleon brandy to the edge of the table to make room. He handled the case as though it contained ten million explosive dollars.

Mr. Belmont snapped on the small reading light on his right-hand table, and addressed the group. "Thank you all for coming on such short notice. Not all of you know each other, so allow me to introduce you. On my right is my attorney, Burton Hanslik. To my left is Alexander Gold, a consultant employed by AIK, Incorporated, whose purpose will become clear shortly. On his left is Mrs. Pearl Hanslik, who works with Mr.

Gold. Directly across the fireplace from Mr. Hanslik is Mrs. Norma Gold, who also works with Mr. Gold. To her right is Lieutenant Warshafsky of the New York Police Department. To his right is Doktor Maurice Gröber-Eisenberg, the eminent art expert. The people facing the fireplace are all employees of the Fine Arts Museum. Starting from Doktor Gröber-Eisenberg's right and coming down the line towards Mrs. Hanslik are: Sam Zager, security chief; Harold Wechsler, acting director; Ken Rand, public relations; Freya Larsen, chief conservator; Maxwell Korbin, counsel; Konrad Dorner, chief curator; and last, Hannelore Becker, conservator, who has been with the museum longer than anyone else here. Now Mr. Gold will take over.''

Alexander remained seated as he spoke. "Most of you, by now, have a good idea of why we are here. Mr. Belmont intends to donate a painting to the museum, a painting called *Girl in a Blue Kimono*, believed to be by Vermeer. Here it is.'' He opened the attaché case and carefully took out the little wooden square, protectively wrapped in transparent plastic. Holding it up by the sides, he slowly turned it so everyone could see, although I doubt, what with the dim light and the flickering flames reflecting off the plastic, that very much could be seen.

Konrad Dorner started up to get a closer look, but Alexander waved him back to his seat and put the painting, face up, on top of the attaché case. "Everyone will get a chance to see it closely," Alexander said, "as soon as Mr. Belmont is convinced of the authenticity of the work. That is why Doktor Gröber-Eisenberg is here. He has examined the painting but has not, as yet, made his decision.''

Alexander turned to Mr. Belmont and said, "Please turn on the gallery lights.'' Everyone blinked at the sudden brightness. Dorner got up again, and again Alexander waved him back. "Doktor Gröber-Eisenberg, would you like to examine those paintings?''

G-E sprang up and darted to the paintings, looking at each for a few seconds, then buzzing off to the next. Halfway around the display he turned and said, "I assume you know, Mr. Belmont, that these are all forgeries. Made within the past few years, I would think. The paint is still soft, and the craquelure is non-existent."

"Copies, Doktor, not forgeries. But very good ones, don't you think?"

"Excellent," G-E answered, "truly excellent. Can you turn off the lights please?" He was standing in front of *Girl With a Pearl Earring*, the one using the same model as *Girl in a Blue Kimono*. He shone his special flashlight parallel to the surface of the painting and held a loupe to his right eye. After several minutes he put the light away and returned to stand behind his chair. "A truly remarkable copy, absolutely perfect. It exhibits none of the flaws I found in the painting I examined yesterday. Who made it, Mr. Belmont?"

"Hannelore Becker was kind enough to give it to me."

Even in the orange glow of the fireplace I could see G-E's face grow redder. Finally his control snapped. "Hypocrite, liar," he pointed his finger accusingly at the old lady. "Thief, Murderer, FORGER!" he screamed. "You dared to criticize me for a few petty details, you FORGER? Now I understand. You are the one who FORGED *Girl in a Blue Kimono*. MONSTER! CRIMINAL!"

The old lady cringed. "No, no," she cried piteously. "I don't. Not Vermeer."

"You did, you miserable liar," he shouted, his baby face contorted with rage. "The one who did those," he said, pointing to the walls of paintings, "did that," and he pointed to the little square on Alexander's attaché case. "You think Maurice Gröber-Eisenberg cannot tell? You think I am the fool? I? It is you who are the fool to think you would not be caught. You should be guillotined." His eyes grew even wilder; his little red mouth twisted with rage. "But first I would cut off those evil hands, slowly, first one finger, then another finger," his voice jumped up in pitch, "then another finger and—"

"That will be enough, Maurice," Mr. Belmont said

sharply. "I am the only one here who has been injured, and I will decide what to do. Please sit down, Maurice. I know how you feel, but what we must do, we will do quietly."

"Perhaps I can help," Alexander said. Mr. Belmont nodded.

Alexander addressed Becker. "Where does your father's family live at present?"

"All gone," she said. "They were Jews."

"And your mother's family?"

"Berlin, still."

"Anywhere else?"

"Two aunts in Chemnitz."

"Which name has been changed to Karl Marx Stadt. In East Germany. I take it your mother's family lives in East Berlin?"

Becker said nothing, tears rolling down her wrinkled cheeks. Alexander turned to face G-E. "I believe I can explain some of the things which troubled you." He paused to gather his thoughts. "Imagine a young woman in New York, about thirty-five years ago, receiving a visitor. He is a young KGB officer, although she doesn't know it at the time. He shows her pictures of her relatives in East Germany. They are traitors to the State and will soon be executed. What can she do to save them? Easy. Just become a spy. But how can she be a spy? She can only work in a museum. She is easily identified because of her handicaps, and she has a strong Geman accent. For the KGB, she is useless. But maybe he can make something out of this for himself personally. He sees all the Vermeer copies in the loft where she lives and instantly devises a plan. If it works, it will provide for his retirement. The abilities which led to his becoming a general were evident even then. Forgery is against the law, and the young woman is very law abiding, but sometimes, as Miss Becker once told me, you think a sin is worth burning for. I am sure that any of us under similar circumstances would commit a worse crime in order to save the lives of several innocent people, or for any other overriding reason."

"You mean that Becker painted a Vermeer from scratch?" Dorner asked. "One good enough to fool several experts?"

"The KGB officer may have supplied the young woman with an aged piece of oak, probably planed down from another painting of that time, and ground up old pigments to mix in with the new so as to give proper dating readings, and all the other technical assistance she needed. And not all the experts were fooled. Dr. Gröber-Eisenberg was not fooled. The KGB officer took the little painting back with him. You may be sure he did not risk planting it in the cellar of the Tretjakov Museum, but had some of the KGB's art specialists work on it, aging it over the years, on some pretext."

"Yes, yes," G-E said excitedly, "that explains so many things. It is not possible in one minute, or even one year, as far as I know, to age a painting realistically. But in thirty-five years of slow, accelerated aging—that's a new concept, perhaps I will publish a monograph—heat, ultra-violet, infrared, desiccation, perhaps even hyperbaric oxidation, yes, there must be many ways to accomplish this. And the mistakes: the ears, the pearls, the *pointillés*, so minor, it is no wonder the others missed them; she was younger then, less experienced, less skilled." He stopped, deep in thought; in wonder, I did not doubt, at his own brilliance.

Alexander continued his story. "The history of the painting could have been typical KGB disinformation. I am sure that an innocent young art student working as a janitor at the Tretjakov, and a minor KGB officer, who deserved it for some other reason, were killed in Moscow on the same day in murders made to appear accidents but so deliberately clumsily done as to give the appearance of murder. This was in case anyone checked. I am equally sure that an Italian art expert was deliberately killed in the Rome airport massacre. But what else is there to check? What else is there to prove that the painting even existed forty years ago?"

G-E stood up. "Mr. Belmont," he said, "I am prepared

to give you my opinion now. I do not deny what I felt when I first saw the painting, but I assure you that, so perfect are these copies, had I lived in Delft in 1675, and had I presented any of these''—he pointed to the paintings on the walls—''to Jan Vermeer himself, he would have claimed it as his own. Yesterday, Mr. Belmont, I offered three possibilities: first, that either my first impression was wrong or that my more careful inspection was incorrect; second, that the painting was a forgery; and third, that the work was by a pupil of Vermeer. I freely admit I told you I favored the third version, but that was because I could not believe that a forgery could pass all the scientific tests and look so like a Vermeer as to give me the flash of recognition. But I had that same feeling when I looked at the forgeries in your gallery. It was then I knew that *Girl in a Blue Kimono* is a forgery, Mr. Belmont. That is my final judgment. You shall have my letter this very day.''

Mr. Belmont looked tired and very old. He put his face in his hands for several seconds. I was sure he was crying, but when he took his hands down his eyes were dry. ''I had hoped,'' he said, ''in memory of my wife. . . . But that was not to be. I cannot give a forgery to the museum nor will I let her name be linked to this.'' He took a deep breath and straightened up, erect in his chair. ''I am sorry, Mr. Gold, but in view of the circumstances, your services are no longer required.''

Alexander took a folded sheet of paper from his pocket and passed it across the little table to Mr. Belmont. ''Read the parts underlined in red,'' Alexander said.

Mr. Belmont glanced quickly at the paper, then went over it again carefully. He put the paper down on the table to his right and said, ''In that case, Mr. Gold, you may proceed with my full approval and cooperation.''

Alexander addressed G-E. ''What would you say this forged painting is worth?''

''Nothing,'' came the reply. ''Less than nothing. Its very existence is an abomination and a danger.''

''A good deal of work went into it.''

"Evil went into it. It has no value."

Alexander turned back to Mr. Belmont. "I'll give you a thousand dollars for it."

"I have no use for it and a thousand dollars means nothing to me in view of what I have lost." I was sure he was not thinking of the ten million. "Give the thousand to the museum and take that thing out of my house."

"I'll give two thousand for it," Hannelore Becker said loudly. All eyes turned to her. "In expiation of my sins."

"You're not a rich woman, Miss Becker," Alexander said. "I'll take it and give three thousand to the church in your name."

"Four thousand," she said quickly. "This is something I must do myself."

"Five thousand," Alexander said firmly.

"Six thousand," from Becker.

"Ten thousand." Alexander was no longer smiling.

"Fourteen thousand six hundred." It was clear to me that this was every penny she had.

"Fifteen thousand." Alexander picked up the painting.

"What are you going to do with it?" she asked, her hands clasped in front of her, almost as in prayer.

"I was thinking of having you make a copy of it," he said, "but without the imperfections Doktor Gröber-Eisenberg found. It is a very beautiful painting, forgery or not. But Mr. Belmont and the good doctor are right. Four people have died because of this painting. I must make sure that no more harm will come to anyone because of this." With a quick snap of his wrist, he scaled the little wooden painting into the fire.

# XXIII

With a scream, Becker launched herself across the room, her limp almost unnoticeable. Fast as Alexander was, she had her hand in the flames before he could get his right arm around her waist. He lifted her bodily back into her chair and brushed the sparks off her sleeve with his hands. The flames rose from the little wooden painting, giving a momentary brightness to the scene.

"You fool!" she screamed. "You don't know what you've done. You monster! You devil! You've destroyed the most—the best—the greatest painting on earth. Oh God," she held her head, "God forgive me. What have I done?"

Alexander calmly went back to his seat. "I don't understand," he said. "Why all this fuss about a forged painting? I didn't realize you wanted it so badly. Look, Miss Becker," he was trying to be conciliatory, "paint another one. I'll even pay for your time and the materials."

She kept cursing him and crying and cursing him again.

Alexander's voice hardened. "That was a real Vermeer, wasn't it, Becker? You made me destroy a real Vermeer. You did it, not I. That is the punishment for your sins."

"You destroyed it, you devil," she screamed. "I committed no sin."

"You committed a crime, Becker. Forgery is against the law."

"I did not forge. I never forged. Never!" she cried. "Forgery is to paint in another artist's style and say it is his work."

"You are right, Becker, you did not forge. All you did was take an authentic work and paint some of your own work on it, just a subtle touch here and there. And you deliberately did it in a way which was not that of the original artist."

"That was what Larsen always wanted us to do, so that the new work, the restoration, could be identified."

"Yes, but you lied to Mr. Belmont. You told him the painting was a forgery."

"No, I did not lie, devil, I told the truth. I said that there was work on the painting that was not by Vermeer."

"Again I stand corrected, Becker. You did not lie, you committed murder. You killed Pembrooke. You broke the law."

"I did not break the law. It was a citizen's execution. He deserved to die. *He* committed murder. *He* killed Mitzi."

"There is no 'citizen's execution' in America, Becker, as you well know. There is only citizen's arrest. You should have told the police, not killed him."

"The police would have done nothing. What's the difference? Mitzi is gone, the painting is gone, my life is over."

"You're lying, Becker, lying to yourself as well as to me. You killed Pembrooke because you wanted the painting for yourself. You've always wanted a Vermeer, a real Vermeer, not a copy, and Pembrooke stood in your way. You knew he would never have accepted your hints and insinuations and Doktor Gröber-Eisenberg's doubts; that with ten million dollars riding on the outcome Pembrooke would have insisted on another set of technical examinations that would immediately have revealed your subtle little changes. You may have deluded yourself that you were acting as an instrument of a higher morality, but I know that it was your obsession to make the *Girl in a Blue Kimono* your own.''

Becker stared at him sullenly, silent.

''Your sciatica seems to be gone,'' Alexander went on. ''You moved very quickly before. A miracle cure, heaven's reward for ridding the world of an evil cat murderer? No. Two months ago, that was when your sciatica started; when you decided to steal the painting. The sciatica, plus your stiff spine and rigid right leg would convince anyone that you were physically incapable of killing a man or even moving fast enough to slip in and out of his room. But the timing made me suspicious. I was sure that the painting and the murder were connected. Your retirement, the Doktor's arrival, and Pembrooke's murder, all in one week; too great a coincidence. Then you got sciatica just after the painting was given to you. I began checking what you told me and what you told Mr. Belmont. You never actually said the painting was a forgery. You could kill, but you could not bring yourself to lie; that's what was in the transcript I gave Mr. Belmont before.''

I couldn't stand it any longer. ''How did she kill Pembrooke, Alexander?''

''I'll give you a scenario, though it may not be exact in every detail. Becker makes a habit of leaving the staff dining room a minute after Pembrooke pokes his head in. As soon as she is past the door, she leaps across the hall to the elevator and presses the button. When the elevator comes, if anyone is around, she goes upstairs; another day will come. One day, no one is around. She goes into the elevator, presses the sixth floor button and, if no one is coming out of the dining room, hops out again. Remember, she can move a lot faster than anyone thinks she can, as we've just seen. She stands at the intersection of the executive corridor and the dining room corridor. If anyone comes along, it looks as though she's waiting for the elevator. Remember where you stood the other day when we were checking the noise from the dining room?''

I nodded, recalling the test.

"She goes into Pembrooke's dining room. He looks up and says 'You're fired.' She says, 'Don't be silly, Director, I've just found something wrong with the Vermeer.' The one thing that's bound to attract his full attention. She limps over to the footstood behind his chair and says, 'Turn around, the light must hit it in exactly the right way.' He puts down his oyster knife, takes the glove off his right hand, and turns around. She takes the painting out of her tote bag, removes the glassine wrapper, puts the painting on the footstool, and adjusts the position until it is exactly right. She is, by now, on Pembrooke's left in his turned-around position. She hands him a loupe, again from her tote bag, and points to a pearl with her left hand. 'Look at that, Director.' He puts the loupe to his left eye with his left hand—he was left-handed, remember—and bends over the painting. He cannot now see anything on his left, especially if it is happening behind him. With her right hand, which is behind Pembrooke's back, she takes a rubber mallet from her tote bag—remember the one we saw upstairs? You could straighten a car door with one of them—and hits him with the *edge* of the head of the mallet, right at the base of the skull. With his shaven head it was easy to see the little bump at the bottom of the occiput that indicates where the head bone stops and the neck bone starts. He slumps down as she grabs the loupe and the painting and stuffs them back into the tote bag."

"The oyster knife is on the table on the other side of Pembrooke, Alexander," I said. "It was his fingerprints on it. How does she pick it up and stab him without smearing the fingerprints?"

"It's obvious. She places the rubber mallet on Pembrooke's back for a moment, reaches behind the back of Pembrooke's turned-around chair and picks up the knife with her right hand, by the blade. With her left hand, she feels for the right spot and places the tip of the knife exactly there with her right hand. Any artist knows enough anatomy to know where that is. She transfers the grip on the blade to her left hand, picks up the mallet with her right hand, and hammers home the knife, like a nail, into Pembrooke's medulla. Her fingerprints on the blade are wiped off by the passage through bone and ligament. If the angle is slightly off, the power of the blows will cut through small bones, even large ones. The knife is hit on the big, round, flat end of the handle; Pembrooke's fingerprints are not disturbed.''

"What about the blow with the mallet?'' I asked. "Couldn't the medical examiner tell?''

"The handle of the oyster knife was hammered home in exactly the same spot three seconds later, no way to tell the trauma was caused by anything but the violent knife blow. Same with the slight brain concussion.''

"But Pembrooke wasn't found in that position,'' I objected. "He was facing the desk, his head in a plate.''

"As soon as she finished banging home the knife, she turned him around in his swivel chair and put his head on the plate. That way it would look as though he had been killed in that position. It did make my life harder.''

"I suppose,'' I said, "she had the ruler to wipe out her footprints from the carpet in her handy tote bag?''

"No,'' he said. "It was difficult for her to bend down; she has a problem with her balance because of her leg. All she did was drag the full tote bag with its stiff leather edges along the carpet behind her as she walked. This also made it unnecessary for her to reach in as she was leaving Pembrooke's office to wipe out her last prints at the door. It made it possible for her to move quickly when the coast was clear. She just peeked out through the slightly opened door, and at the right time, zipped out, pressed the elevator button, and was safe. The whole operation took about one minute, less time than it takes to tell.''

"What do you have to say to that, Becker?'' Mr. Belmont asked.

"I wasn't going to keep the painting, Mr. Belmont. I only wanted to have it for a while.''

"Until you died?'' Alexander asked.

"How much longer do I have to live?" she asked bitterly.

"What would you have done if you won the bidding?" Pearl asked. "With all your money gone?"

"I would have disappeared," she said. "I would have been like all the others. There are many old ladies without money. They live."

"With a ten-million-dollar Vermeer in your shopping bag?" I asked.

"I would have guarded it with my life. I wrote a will giving it to the museum, and a confession, begging forgiveness. But that is all over now. That devil burned it."

"Yes, Mr. Gold," Mr. Belmont said, "you have given me the solution to both problems as you always wanted to do, even over my objections, but couldn't you have done it another way? I do not cry over what has been done, it is not my way, but this was to be in my wife's memory. I cannot forget that."

"I wouldn't burn the Third Vermeer," Alexander said, reaching into the attaché case. "What I burned was the full-size color photo you gave me, glued to a piece of stained oak, and covered in plastic. In the dim flickering light of the fireplace, looking at the bright spot of your table lamp, you couldn't tell what it was from ten inches, much less ten feet, even if you weren't as nearsighted as Becker."

"Let me see it once more, Mr. Gold," Becker said, reaching into her tote bag, "and I'll give you my will with the confession." She got up and walked behind Pearl's chair towards the table with the attaché case. As she passed behind Pearl she reached out and placed the point of a big hypodermic syringe at the side of Pearl's neck and grabbed Pearl's long golden hair in her left hand, twisting her fingers in the hair so Pearl could not pull away. "Sodium hydroxide, Mr. Gold," Becker said viciously. "Thirty cc's of a concentrated solution of lye. Even if I miss the carotid artery and the jugular vein, anything I hit will kill her in terrible agony. Once it's in there's no way to get it out."

God! I knew something like this was bound to happen. I just knew. But why Pearl? Sweet innocent beautiful Pearl? I knew why. Because I had reminded Alexander that he had left Pearl out; because Pearl was small and weak and had long hair. Maybe even because Hannelore Becker once was beautiful and had long golden hair. I don't know. If I had a gun . . . but I didn't. I reached slowly into my bag and grabbed my little oyster knife. Futile, I was too far away, and even if I weren't I didn't want to kill Becker in such a way that she fell forward and pushed the— It was too horrible to think about.

"Hand the real Vermeer to Mrs. Hanslik, Gold. Slowly. No tricks." Alexander slowly handed the Vermeer to Pearl. Out of the corner of my eye I noticed that Warshafsky had his gun out, in his lap, casually covered with his left hand. Zager, I saw, had his right hand behind him, under his jacket. Neither man moved, just watched with patient professional eyes. I wanted to scream, to tell them not to take any chances with my Pearl, but my throat was dry.

"Reach back slowly, Mrs. Hanslik. Don't turn around. With your left hand place the painting in my tote bag. It's on my left hip. I can't bend down, so if you drop it, you die." Pearl tried carefully to put the little painting into the tote bag, but the bag was hanging closed, the edges of the opening tight against each other. I gasped, we all gasped, as the painting slipped from her hand, but she caught it just in time with her hip against Becker's, and was able to change her grip. Finally the painting slipped into Becker's bag. We all breathed again.

"Walk slowly to the door," Becker said. "Take short steps."

"Where are you taking her?" I asked.

"Don't try to follow me," Becker said. "If I even think you're trying to stop me, I'll kill her instantly. I have nothing to lose."

"You can have the painting," Mr. Belmont said. "This is my word and a formal contract, an exchange of values, if you let her go. A witnessed agreement. Mr. Hanslik will draw up a valid receipt.''

"I'm sorry, Mr. Belmont, but she is my insurance. You cannot speak for the police. I will take a taxi, and when I am sure no one is following me, then I will free her.''

I knew what that meant. As soon as she was in the taxi, she would kill Pearl. She could not afford to let anyone know where she was. A careful planner, a watcher of tiny details, as she was by training, she would leave no loose ends. I was sure she had another hypo or two in her murderous tote bag. And if we found a dead cabby near Penn Station or Grand Central or any subway, that wouldn't mean that Becker was necessarily hiding in that place. And if she were, how could you find her? Don't all bag ladies look alike to us? And even if we did find her, would that bring Pearl back?

I looked helplessly at Alexander. He was sitting quietly, relaxed, bent slightly forward, his arm resting lightly on his attaché case, his right hand wrapped around the globe of the decanter. Around the decanter? Yes, like a softball, ready to throw. If anyone could, Alexander could. But could he? You don't throw six or seven pounds like a softball. And if he hit? How could he be sure Becker wouldn't fall forward, plunging the needle into Pearl's soft white neck? And could he throw at Becker at all? Alexander cannot hurt a woman physically. Just cannot. And Becker is a little old lady, a *crippled* little old lady. Could he take *her* head off? Throwing a saucer at a wall is not quite the same thing as taking the head off a little crippled old lady. But if Alexander didn't, or if he missed, Pearl would die. Even if he hit, if Becker pushed or fell the wrong way, Pearl would die.

Still holding her fingers twisted in Pearl's hair, still holding the big needle at Pearl's neck, Becker reached the living room door. Once they went through, Pearl was dead. Once the door was closed behind them, no one would dare open it for at least five minutes, in case Becker was waiting in the hall.

"Open the door slowly,'' Becker ordered Pearl. "Very

slowly. No sudden movements." Pearl reached for the door with her left hand, turned the knob, and slowly, very slowly, pulled the door toward herself. She and Becker stepped back to let the door pass. For a tiny fraction of a second the edge of the door was in line between Becker and Pearl, and Becker's weight was on her good left leg.

In that tiny fraction of a second Alexander struck, as fast and as powerful as he had ever been. He snapped the heavy decanter forward as if it weighed nothing, catching Becker behind her left knee at exactly the right instant. As he threw he yelled, "Fall, Pearl!" The heavy crystal decanter slammed Becker's left knee forward, towards the hall, snapping her body backward as her knee bent, her left forearm cracking into the edge of the door, her right hand, with the deadly hypodermic, pulled away from Pearl's neck instantly. Pearl fell forward to the right, in a half roll, pulling Becker's left hand, still twisted in Pearl's hair, with her, completing the twisting of Becker's body. Becker fell heavily on her belly, her left arm outstretched, locked by Pearl's hair; right arm, still holding the hypo, straightened out in the other direction.

Heavy as he was, Zager was at the fallen pair of women a second later and calmly planted his left foot on the hand holding the hypo. Warshafsky, a second behind him, snapped a handcuff on Becker's left wrist, disentangled her hand from Pearl's hair, twisted it behind her back to her right hand, and cuffed both hands together as Zager removed his foot.

# XXIV

Zager and Warshafsky had taken all the others out to make statements. Belmont was complaining. "That was the last of that wonderful brandy, Gold. Very careless of you to snap the neck of the decanter." He sounded like my mother had, the last time Alexander broke a decanter.

Pearl was unexpectedly calm, hugging Alexander, enfolded by Burton, with me holding everybody from the outside. "I told you, Norma," she said, "that Aikido is beautiful. Isn't it great that I learned falling first?"

It wasn't really the time to point out how much more useful a gun would have been; that I would do tomorrow.

Belmont decided to kiss Pearl too, and I'm not sure it was entirely congratulatory. Well, with the brandy gone, lesser pleasures would have to do.

"If you knew Becker was guilty," I said, "why did you bring all the other suspects in, Alexander?"

"I had to get G-E to say the painting was a forgery first, so I could shock Becker into confessing. If I had just accused her in privacy, she would have said nothing. After G-E's violent accusation, she was full of guilt. A convent school, especially European, instills a strong desire to avoid sinning, and to purge yourself of sin by confession. Burning the Vermeer was the final, to her, sacrilegious act that shocked her into the need to cleanse her soul. I needed something dramatic, and it worked.''

And it's more fun, I thought, to show off to your girl in front of a large audience than a small one. Boys will be boys and Alexander, in some ways, was a *very* little boy.

But Alexander wasn't finished showing off yet; I could tell. I could use his owing me a big one, and to be honest I was curious myself, so I played the good wife and asked, "How did you figure it all out, Alexander?"

"It was obvious," he said. Meaning 'coax me.'

"What was obvious, Alexander?"

"Once I decided that the knife could not have been picked up by the handle without smudging Pembrooke's prints, the only other way it could have been picked up was by the blade. This needed two things: one, something to drive the knife in with, and two, something to make Pembrooke put his head down. This led to my remembering the rubber mallet that hung on the wall of the conservators' room, which led to Becker. And of course, the only thing Pembrooke would stop eating for and bend over to look at had to be the Third Vermeer, which again led to Becker. When I checked the transcripts of the interviews I noted that she never said the painting was not a Vermeer, only that there were things on it which had not been painted by Vermeer. Then everything fell into place.''

"Why did she pick this complicated way to kill him?" Pearl asked.

"She was a little crippled old lady," Alexander answered. "She didn't have too many choices. I am sure, too, that she didn't want anyone to be punished for Pembrooke's death and was sure that the police would never solve this case.''

"How did you find out about the young KGB officer approaching her thirty-five years ago?" Burton asked.

"I made that up," he said smugly. "It *could* have happened that way, it fit what we knew, and there was no way Becker could deny it. In fact, if you remember, it shocked her speechless; she didn't know what to say. After all, she had to convince Belmont that the painting was a forgery. That was the whole point of the murder; to own a real Vermeer herself, not a copy. That Pembrooke was a monster and a cat-killer helped her convince herself that she was carrying out God's will rather than committing a crime.''

"I'd like you to represent Becker," Mr. Belmont said to Burton. "It should be easy to show that she is not fit to stand trial. I'd prefer a minimum of publicity, too.''

"Any public defender could do it, Mr. Belmont," Burton said, "and much more economically.''

"I'm relying on you to make sure she is sent to a nearby institution with good art therapy facilities.''

"You want a copy of *Girl in a Blue Kimono* that badly?" Alexander asked.

"A portrait of my wife in the style of Vermeer.''

"You had better take, uh, possession of her camera and projector, the contents of her loft, Mr. Belmont.''

"I have already thought of that, Gold. As soon as everyone leaves, I'll arrange it.''

"I don't think I want to hear any more along those lines," Burton said.

"Quite right, Hanslik. Thank you, Gold. I'll send you a check for nine hundred thousand dollars tomorrow.''

"Our deal was for a million, Belmont.''

"But we had a wager, Gold, don't you remember? I didn't beg you to clear me of suspicion.''

"It wasn't that specific, just that you would beg me to do something for you that you would pay me a million to do. However, I don't mind that you're in a hurry. After I cash your *certified* check, I'll charge you double the next day for what I'm ready to give you now. And you'll pay. In fact, even now, when you're on guard, I'll double the bet. What do you say?''

Belmont eyed him suspiciously. "I think I'll stay with the original bet. What is it that you want me to give you a million-dollar fee to do and that you are betting me I will beg you to accept?''

"I'm not twisting your arm, but I can tell you how to get the ten million dollars in Pembrooke's Liechtenstein account.''

"The code is in a sealed envelope, Gold. Even the Liechtenstein attorney doesn't know what it is. Once it is opened to check a claim and the code is wrong, the money is gone forever.''

"You do agree, given the fact that Pembrooke met the lawyer only once, and in a dim light at that, that your Swiss actor friend, the one who helped you in Basel, could get the money for you? That if he gives the correct code to the bank in the presence of the attorney, the money will be transferred to any account he wishes? Yours?''

"I had thought of using him, but without the code—"

"Beg me for the code, Belmont.'' Alexander was triumphant.

"What if you're wrong, Gold? You could be bluffing.''

"I'm not. But if I am, you're out the million for the bet only. I don't get the million for giving you the right information.''

Belmont studied Alexander. "You never cheat, do you, Gold.''

"I don't have to.''

"You do lie. I heard you lie today.''

"I misled Becker and Gröber-Eisenberg deliberately; it was the only way, but I did not lie. I'll have Pearl send you a transcript of today's tape.''

"Gold, do you believe that you have the correct code?''

"I do.''

"Very well then, I'll gamble on you. Please tell me the correct code to Pembrooke's ten-million-dollar hoard.''

"Say the magic word.''

Belmont stiffened, then laughed. "All right, Gold. I beg you.''

Alexander grinned. "Ten million in Europe that no one knows exists. Tax free. You're getting a bargain, Belmont. What took you so long to decide?"

"You're not reneging, are you, Gold? I thought better of you than that. We had a deal."

"I don't renege, Belmont. Though even if I did, you'd owe me a million right now. What I wanted to do was to offer you another really terrific deal."

"Before the first one is consumated? You're building a castle in the air on top of a sand castle."

"Don't you even want to know what it is? Costs nothing to ask."

"All right, Gold. What *really* terrific deal do you have to offer me?"

"For twenty percent, I'll give you the new sealed code to Pembrooke's old personal account in Basel."

"Sit down, Gold," Belmont said. "Everybody sit down. I don't accept that offer and I don't accept your offer for the ten million. I owe you a million now, and I'll give it to you if you want, but you don't want it, do you?"

"No," Alexander said. "If you don't try to collect the ten million, I don't want you to think I might have been wrong."

"It's more than that, Gold, isn't it? You don't care for money, do you? Or the power that money brings?"

"It hasn't brought you much happiness, Mr. Belmont. I gather there have been times when you would gladly have turned everything over to your brother. You mentioned that you would have given it all up for your wife, I remember. Your money couldn't even buy you the right decision on the Third Vermeer."

"It bought me your services, Gold."

"I offered to solve both problems for nothing. It wasn't the money, it was the pleasure of solving the problems."

"What do you intend to do with the two million dollars, Gold, if I give it to you? Plus the twenty percent of

Pembrooke's personal account?" Belmont held up his hand. "Don't answer, let me tell you."

"You've had me investigated, haven't you, Belmont?"

"Of course. Do you mind?"

"I'd be happier if you hadn't, but it's not important."

"You have enough money now so you could live on the interest for the rest of your lives."

"Since you know that, why bother telling me?"

"A prelude, Gold. A prelude to my offer. You were going to give all the additional money over your fee for solving the murder/painting problem to charity, weren't you?"

"Norma would have agreed."

"The same charities you usually give to? HIAS, UJA, Tay-Sachs, Wiesenthal, and the rest?"

"You've done your homework, Mr. Belmont."

"I always do before I offer a deal. Your earnings aren't enough to make proper use of about two-point-five million in charitable tax deductions."

"All right, Mr. Belmont," Alexander's face broke into a smile. "It's a deal."

"Good. I knew we would understand each other. Hanslik, spell it out to make sure there is no misunderstanding. I see Mrs. Gold is looking puzzled."

Burton cleared his throat. "The fee for solving the painting problem will be paid as agreed. There are three other payments Alec should get: the million for the 'begging' wager; the million for the code to get the ten million in Liechtenstein; and approximately six hundred thousand for the code to Pembrooke's personal account in Basel of about three million. Total: two-point-six million."

"My god, Alexander," I was overwhelmed. "What would we do with all that money?"

"Don't worry, Norma," he said. "By the time Burt is finished talking, we'll end up with only about three hundred thousand; the after-tax money for proving the painting was real. Unless I find a good tax-shelter in a hurry."

"Good," I said. "That kind of money I can conceive of."

"Exactly," Burton said. "Instead of Mr. Belmont giving Alec two-point-six million, which would not be tax deductible for Mr. Belmont, and which Alec was going to give to charity anyway, Mr. Belmont is going to give thirty percent of Pembrooke's thirteen million in Europe to the same charities directly."

I didn't believe this, knowing how millionaires operated, but I spoke politely. "Why should Mr. Belmont give more than he agreed to?"

"As an inducement to Mr. Gold to acccept my proposal," Mr. Belmont said. "That way, the charities get fifty percent more than if you had given them the money directly, and I make a profit."

"How do you profit?" I still didn't see it, although I ran the checkbook in our house.

"If I gave Mr. Gold the two-point-six million I owe him, he would be able to keep only about thirty percent of it, at most, since it is ordinary income for him and rather late in the year to find a sound tax shelter. I could not deduct any of it as a business expense; can you imagine me telling the IRS about the money in Europe? So it is better that I *give* away three-point-nine million which *is* tax deductible; my income is big enough to support that kind of charitable deduction. It costs me less to give the charity directly, in *your* honor, than it would be to pay you a fee."

"Okay, I see that," I said. "But it's still not a profit."

"You're forgetting," Burton said, "that there's thirteen million in Europe in cash and gold, unrecorded, which Mr. Belmont can make very good business use of. I am sure that Mr. Belmont is quite satisfied with the arrangement."

"But some of that money was sort of stolen from the museum by Pembrooke," Pearl said.

"Not directly from the museum," Burton answered. "But knowing Mr. Belmont, I am sure that he will take that into account when he makes his donations to the museum. And don't forget, Mr. Belmont is donating the Third Vermeer to the museum, a ten-million-dollar painting, as well as arranging the Vermeer Retrospective.''

"For which he gets another tax deduction," I said. "I approve, Alexander. A brilliant deal, Mr. Belmont. For a while there, I thought Alexander was going to take advantage of you, but I guess that can't be done."

"I told you before, I lose many battles, but I never lose a war."

"And the only one hurt," I said with great pleasure, "is the IRS, which makes everything even sweeter. Now enough of the high finance. I'm dying to know. What is the code? The codes?"

"Wait, Gold," Belmont said. "Part of the deal is that you explain how you figured out the codes."

"I would have done that anyway, Mr. Belmont. Part of the fun is in the explaining. Do you remember, Mr. Belmont, when I asked you if you were an *accurate* reporter? You said you were. The identification for the bank account, you said, was a ten-*number* code. Not ten *digits*; ten numbers. Then I asked you if Pembrooke had atherosclerosis. You said he had suffered a slight stroke and didn't even know it until later when the doctor caught it."

"You knew the codes when you bet me, you rascal?"

"Right then and there. But I knew you wouldn't believe me until I solved the murder and the painting problem. So I had to wait. There was no way you would have said 'I beg you' four days ago."

"You're right, I wouldn't. So from these two clues you figured out the codes? I don't see it. Ah, Gold, it's bad to get old; the brain doesn't work well anymore."

"So I've noticed, Mr. Belmont," Alexander said sarcastically. "There was one more clue; *you* told it to me. Look, suppose you had a big bank account that could only be entered, even by you, with a code. You wouldn't want one you had to *write* down, there's a guy named Belmont who has it in for you, who can find out anything. So you need a code you can *memorize*. But you've suffered a stroke, and didn't even know it; you're likely to suffer another, you're not getting any younger, and when you get the next stroke, your memory may go, or be partially lost, so the code must be related to something *very important* to you, something you *see every day*, yet it must be something *not obvious* to others. And it must be *simple*. The old code for Pembrooke's account in Basel was T-D-N-A- and so on; REMBRANDT, spelled backwards. A nine-*letter* code. But the code for the ten million dollars is a ten-*number* code, not ten-*digit*. In order to keep things simple, uniform, and easily remembered, the new code for the Basel account is also a ten-*number* code, and it must be *related* to the Liechtenstein ten-number code.''

"I would have used a simple number-for-letter transposition code," I said. "One for A; two for B; three for C, and so forth."

"Exactly," Alexander said. "Now all you need is a ten-letter word that fits all the requirements. Turn it backwards, substitute the numbers, and there you are."

"Jan Vermeer," Belmont said. "JAN VERMEER!"

"Right," Alexander said. "Now what's the second code?" He looked around expectantly. "The one that's related to the first code?" Blank faces. He sighed disappointedly and quietly said, "Ten letters?" He waited some more, than said, "BLUE KIMONO. It's obvious."

Belmont smiled widely. He seemed, for the first time since I met him, almost happy. "Mrs. Gold," he said to me warmly, "I've had a wonderful time today: excitement, sadness, joy, life, death, puzzles, solutions, and battles of wits. I spent a lot of money and made a lot more, and some very good charities will get some very big donations. Evil was defeated and justice triumphed. I've lived more these past few days than since . . . than in the past twenty years. Please let Alexander come and play with me again. Soon.''

Just like little boys, all of them, no matter what the age. I promised I would, next rainy day, when Alexander got underfoot too much.